"I HAVE ALL KINTHOUGHTS. A

His voice had deepened. It set off alarm bells in her head. "Indeed?"

"Like right now, when you get that snippy tone in your voice. It makes me want to kiss you."

"I don't get a…" then her voice trailed off as she realized what he had just said. "Kiss me?"

He nodded as he stopped in front of her. "Yeah, I do. All the time. Have you noticed that I don't run the meetings anymore? I can't. All I can think is that I really, really want to kiss you."

Her brain went numb as heat spiraled through her.

"You don't want to kiss me."

He nodded again, his mouth kicking up on the right side. Damn him, and damn that crooked little smile. Every time she saw it, her bones seemed to liquefy. He cupped her face and bent down to brush his mouth over hers. And just like that, her world exploded around her. He deepened the kiss, thrusting his tongue into her mouth, as she slipped her hands up over his shoulders and around his neck. Pressing against her, she could feel the long length of his erection, and her body lit up like the Aloha Friday fireworks.

MELISSA SCHROEDER

Seductive Reasoning

MELISSA SCHROEDER

This book is a work of fiction. The names, characters, places, and incidents are products of the writer's imagination or have been used fictitiously and are not to be construed as real. Any resemblance to persons, living or dead, actual events, locale or organizations is entirely coincidental.
Edited by Noel Varner and Fedora Chen
Cover by Scott Carpenter
Copyright © 2015 Melissa Schroeder

All rights reserved.

ISBN-13:
978-1517290580

ISBN-10:
1517290589

DEDICATION

To Peter Lenkov

He will probably never know about it and will probably never read it. But thank you for bringing Hawaii 5-0 back. And to all my fellow Friday night tweeters!

ACKNOWLEDGMENTS

No book is every done without the help of many people. From my first ideas about the book that I shared with Joy Harris and Brandy Walker, to Betas Gina Dewitt and Sheri Vidal, to the Addicts who have been dying to read it. Thank you all for your help. I would have never made it without you.

MELISSA SCHROEDER

HAWAIIAN TERMS

Aloha - Hello, goodbye, love
Bra-Bro
Bruddah- brother, term of endearment
Haole-Newcomer to the islands
Howzit - How is it going?

Kamaʻāina-Local to the islands

Mahalo-Thank you

Malasadas- A Portuguese donut without a hole which started out as a tradition for Shrove (Fat) Tuesday. They are deep fried, dipped in sugar or cinnamon and sugar. In other words, it is a decadent treat every person must try when they go to Hawaii. If you do not try it, you fail. Do yourself a favor. Go to Leonard's and buy one. You are welcome.

Slippahs - slippers, AKA sandals

MELISSA SCHROEDER

CHAPTER ONE

Martin Delano stepped out of his pickup and shut the door, as a light trade wind danced over his skin. He slipped his shoulder holster on, then looked up and down the street. Finding no traffic, he jogged over to the other side, following the lights set up by the Honolulu Police Department.

Being former military, he should be used to the early morning wakeup calls, but it didn't mean he had to be happy about it—especially this morning. The lights burned his eyes. Damn, he was getting old when he couldn't seem to make it up and to work without a cup of coffee. He should have grabbed one before he left his house in Hawaii Kai.

Police tape marked off the spot, and a very serious looking young officer in uniform stood by the entrance. His militant expression told Del this was his first big assignment. The kid raised his hand as if to stop him...or die trying. God save him. He wasn't in the mood.

"HPD only, sir," he said, his voice stern.

Del sighed and pulled out his Task Force badge. He'd been there a year and people in the department still didn't know who he was. Of course, the officer looked like he was straight out of the academy, so that was probably the reason. However, the department was small, and Del had been on TV enough that he thought everyone knew his face. And, as the local members of his team kept telling him, everyone knows everyone else on the island.

The officer's face reddened. "Sorry, sir."

Del nodded and attached the badge back onto his belt. "I'm looking for Rome Carino."

"Of course, sir." He turned and motioned with his hand. "He's right over there, by the medical examiner."

Del glanced over and saw where he was talking about. There was a barrier set up along the opposite side of the bridge. That would have been done probably before the ME had shown up.

"Mahalo," Del said, as he walked past the officer towards the ME. He passed a few familiar faces. Some smiled, some frowned, and others barely acknowledged his existence.

The air was muggy from the recent rain, and the sun would start rising soon. Traffic in Honolulu was always a bitch. The influx of tourists added to the locals' aggravation, but figure in the water main breaks and the rail construction, it could be a real pain in the ass. Being Monday made it worse, and the McCully Bridge over the Ala Wai Canal was always busy.

As he approached the group, he noticed a handful of detectives he knew. He still felt like an outsider. Being a haole didn't make for easy detective work in Hawaii. Not to mention, a few of them thought he shouldn't have been given the job. Carino had been offered the job at one time, but he'd declined. Now, Del was starting to understand why.

Del knew it was a bad sign when Carino called him. Del's team only handled the major crimes, the ones that would require more than a little diplomacy working with various law enforcements. Not that he was always good with diplomacy, but in other words, Carino didn't want the headache.

He noticed Drew Franklin, the ME assistant. Nice kid, local, tall and skinny, with a world class mind and an irritating habit of trying too hard. But he was good on the job, even if he did have an odd sense of humor, and an odd choice in clothing. He was wearing a pair of jeans today, his regular sneakers, and a T-shirt that said 'I like big books and I cannot lie.'

"Howzit, Del, I just got here too."

Del nodded. "Did you get the call?"

He pushed his horn-rimmed glasses back up the bridge of his nose. "Dr. Middleton called. She said I didn't need to be here, but I thought maybe Cat would be called out."

"Nope, I was on call last night, so I took the call."

"Makes sense."

"I'm glad you think so," he said, his voice dripping with sarcasm, but it went over Drew's head. He just smiled as they walked together. The closer they got to the scene, Del's worry grew. He knew it was a dead woman, but for him to be called out, it had to be huge. Maybe a celebrity or dignitary. That meant it would hit the news services soon. Damn, he hated dealing with the press.

Carino noticed him and turned to greet him. Lean and tall, with feral eyes, he'd moved to Hawaii from Seattle several years earlier. The homicide detective had been one of the most welcoming in the HPD. His wife had insisted on inviting him over for dinner several times. A lot of folks weren't happy when they hired an outsider like him, but Carino had been a transplant also, and Del had an idea he had wanted to make everyone know that he accepted him.

"Sorry about calling you out, Del, but Dr. Middleton thought it was important. Usually, I go with her gut, and when she showed me, I was sure of it."

He nodded. "No problem."

Carino looked at Drew. "Dr. Middleton could use some help."

"Of course," Drew said and hurried off, almost tripping over his larger than average feet in the process.

Carino and he watched Drew greet the doctor with as much enthusiasm as he had Del. Del shook his head. Was he ever that young and eager? He couldn't remember, but he was sure that he had been when he entered the military. When he turned back to Del, he offered him a grim smile.

"Man, to be that young again," he said, voicing Del's thoughts.

Del nodded. "Makes me tired just listening to him sometimes."

Carino's smile faded. "I didn't want to say anything in front of him, not yet, but I have a bad feeling this might be a serial."

Del knew Carino wasn't jumping to conclusions. When there had been a serial killer terrorizing Honolulu, and especially the BDSM club members at Rough 'n Ready, he had been at the head of the case. He had caught the killer no one else had expected—with the help of an FBI agent, who had later become his wife. Carino did not make assumptions.

A heavy lead weight started to tighten in his stomach. This was going to be a fucking nightmare. He just knew it. And, it would put his team to the test again. He didn't have a background in investigative work. Being an Army Ranger did give you a skill set that helped out in some things, but investigating a serial killer was different. Thank God he had a team with more experience in that department. Both Cat and Adam had been in the department during Carino's investigation. And he knew his ME had experience with that kind of thing.

"What makes you think that? Does it resemble any other killings?"

The detective shook his head. "No, but she was posed, grotesquely. There's just something about the way she was left…" He sighed and rubbed his temples.

"Long night?"

Carino nodded. "Yeah, and I was just thinking I was getting too old for this."

"Nothing going on with Maria?"

He knew the detective's wife was pregnant and entering the final few months.

Flashing Del a smile, Carino shook his head. "No, just horrible insomnia for her, which means I have it because she wanders through the house constantly." His smile faded. "It's going to be a bitch of a day today, considering who I think is down there."

His head was already pounding from the lack of caffeine, and this was just ramping it up to a whole other level of pain.

"Who?"

Carino looked toward the scene, then back at Del. "We have to wait for official word, but I think it's Grace Singh."

The name hit him like a ton of bricks.

"Well, fuck."

Del knew the story. Hell, everyone in Hawaii knew the story. Two weeks earlier, a pretty schoolteacher had disappeared. Right off the street in a good part of town. There was no sign of her anywhere, which was definitely odd. From all accounts, she was sweet and unassuming, a bit of a homebody who lived with her parents—not an uncommon occurrence considering the housing situation on the island at the moment. When the news had hit, everyone had shown up to help. Honolulu might be a big city to some, but Hawaii still operated like a small town. When one of their own went missing, especially a cherished teacher, they called out the reserves. Citizens, law enforcement, everyone. They all had looked for her and could not find one bit of evidence as to her whereabouts.

"Exactly. I wouldn't normally jump to conclusions, but she's fresh, and I know her face, of course. That means she has been alive the last two weeks. And, it's bad. There is no doubt in my mind someone tortured her."

Fuck. Nightmare did not cover it. They would get attention from the mainland on this one, and this always sent the local press into a frenzy.

"Okay."

They walked side-by-side down to the scene. With each step they took, he felt the weight of the oncoming investigation. This was going to be a bitch—and more than anything, he wanted to do right by the woman. Her poor family had been so sure they would find her alive, and now they would forever be without one part of the whole. No one deserved to die like this.

"Hey, Elle, how's it going?" Del asked.

Dr. Elle Middleton was an English transplant, and one of the best in her field. He knew he was damned lucky she had been assigned to his team when she had arrived in Hawaii.

"Hullo, Del. Not good, especially for this young woman."

She stood up and wiped her forehead with the back of her wrist. Since she'd cut her light blond hair, the fringe of it appeared just above her blue-green eyes. He read the horror in her gaze. This was not going to be pleasant for anyone.

"You got a time of death?"

"Within the last six hours from the liver temp. I would say less than three when she was actually found. She was left here after the rain stopped."

"Yeah?" Carino asked.

Elle nodded. "The impressions of shoes are there and there," she said pointing to the ground. "Drew is going to take a cast of them, but I am not sure we will find anything particularly important in that. They look pretty common. So, I'm assuming he waited on purpose until the rain was done. That ended about half past eleven last night here in Honolulu."

Del sighed and shook his head. "Poor woman."

"Indeed. I can tell you more when I get her on the table, but this woman went through hell."

"Show me what you have right now."

"Hey, I have a meeting with the brass at the top of the hour. They wanted an update. Call me if you need anything."

"Sure. Give my love to Maria," Del said as Carino slapped him on the shoulder and walked away.

He turned back around just as Elle moved and he finally saw the body. The memory of the smiling picture did not even seem like the same woman. Her eyes were closed, but he knew they were dark, always twinkling in all the photos. She was short in stature, five three if he remembered correctly, with short hair, and probably weighed no more than one hundred pounds. At least she had. If she had been posed, she had been moved, probably by Elle.

"We have pictures of her body before she was moved?"

"Yes," she said, irritated.

He looked up and offered her a smile. "Sorry about that. Just thinking things through, and I didn't know who was here first. You know I am still new at all of this."

Elle sighed. "Sorry. Knowing just how bad it was…it hurts."

He heard the memory in her voice. "I understand." And he did. Elle would comprehend what Grace Singh had endured more than most others.

She straightened her shoulders, then squatted down. "If you look here, she was tied up."

She held up the hand of the woman and pointed to her wrist. He saw the burns on her wrists. Some light, some dark, and with different patterns pressed into her flesh. It was done with some kind of rope, and probably impossible to narrow down.

"Her ankles are in the same condition."

"And the different shades of the bruising?"

"Repeated injuries. And with different ropes from the burns. So, he kept her like this for some time. Probably the entire time she was there. I'm pretty sure of sexual assault, but I will verify that in the lab. There are also burns on her body."

He squatted down beside her and looked over the body. There were small cylindrical burns over her flesh. Scabs had formed over some of them, while others were fresh.

Jesus.

"Looks like a cigarette lighter from a car."

"Yes. Bastard really hurt her. This isn't just about power. This is more about pain, and getting off on it. He should not be allowed in public."

Her voice wavered at the end, and he knew what it cost her.

"We'll get him, Elle."

She nodded, but said nothing else as he stood and looked over the crowd. It was early, but there was always some kind of hum in the early morning there—especially on a Monday. Hell, that's probably why the sick fuck had left her there on that particular day. More coverage, with a frenzy that would last for the entire week.

He saw one of the detectives taking pictures, and he wandered over to him.

"Did you get the crowd?"

"Yeah," he said. "But I was going to take a few more because it is really gaining attention."

He pulled out his card and gave it to him. "Could you make sure you get those to me as soon as possible?"

"With pleasure," he said, grim determination filling his voice.

Del paused, then the detective said, "I knew her. We went to the same school, a few years apart. A real sweetheart. Always had a smile for everyone."

Del nodded. That was the thing about Hawaii. Everyone had about six degrees of separation, or fewer. Either they knew Grace, or they knew someone who knew her. Her disappearance had been the focal point of the Hawaiian news shows since she had disappeared. And now, their focus would be on a killer.

The crowd was growing by the second, and he knew it

would only be minutes before the news crews showed up. As if on queue, they appeared, screaming to a halt. He saw Jin Phillips, one very irritating newswoman, jump out of the van. Damn, the woman got on his nerves. She stood by, waiting for her crew before she attacked. And it would be an attack. The woman didn't know how to deal with news any other way.

Del looked away from her and up the canal toward Diamond Head. The scent of plumeria hit him, and he realized he was standing by a bush filled with them. It was usually something he liked to smell, but now, he knew he would always associate it with Grace Singh and her last night on earth.

The sun was just starting to peek over the crater. The brilliant streaks of orange and yellow lightened the sky. Even after a year, the beauty of it still stunned him. Del didn't think he would ever get used to the sight.

He looked back at the scene as Drew helped Elle put Grace Singh in a body bag, then lift her up onto the gurney. The buzz of the crowd was growing, and he could already hear Jin asking annoying questions.

Just another day in paradise.

CHAPTER TWO

Charity Edwards rushed into her lab, irritation pulsing through her. She wasn't late if it had been a normal day, but they had a killing dropped in their laps. Since no one had called her, she had to rush to get in. The team was still getting accustomed to working with their own forensics tech, but it was starting to make her feel unwanted. Before she had been hired three months earlier, they had to wait in line with everyone else. The governor had scraped up the funds to give her a position just for the team. She'd hit the ground running, taking on a case even before she'd unpacked her household goods when they'd arrived from Atlanta.

She was hot, sweaty, and frazzled. She had a bare amount of makeup on and, because she hadn't had time to do anything with her hair, she had to pull it up into a knot on top of her head. A cursory glance down her body told her that she should never be in a hurry when she dressed for work. The hot pink shirt and black Capri pants with pink strips were cute together, but not with her red shoes. What the hell had she been thinking? Oh, that's right. She hadn't had time to think. She'd heard the news and had to rush into work, because she was the red-headed stepchild of the team.

On top of it, she'd forgotten to finish up her laundry, and she was going commando at the moment—which she did not like to do without a reason. Not the way she wanted to start out the week. On top of it, she had forgone coffee to rush to the office. Definitely not the way to handle a Monday. People ended up bloody when she was low on her favorite drug.

"Hey," Drew said, walking into her lab. "Got some samples for you."

She nodded but didn't look around. She had so much to do and little time to get it accomplished. "Thanks."

"Brought you a coffee too."

She stopped and turned. Sure enough, he had a cup of Kona for her. He truly was the sweetest man.

"You are a god."

He chuckled. "No problem, my ebony queen."

The first time he had called her that, she had thought he was hitting on her. She soon found out that was just Drew's way, and that another team member had his interest. Tall and lanky, he looked much younger than his thirty years. Dorky, but in a sweet way, he had been a good confidant, and helped her as the *haole* who needed help navigating Honolulu.

Being the smart man he was, he handed her the coffee first. She grabbed it and smelled the aroma of it. Charity had a love affair with Kona coffee. If it was legal, she would marry it in a ceremony on the beach.

"So, tell me about this one," she said, as she took another big whiff of her coffee.

His smile faded. "Grace Singh."

"Oh, *damn*. I was hoping she had just run away."

"I think everyone was. But then, we have a body, so someone was going to be dead."

She chugged the coffee, ignoring the burn as it slid down her throat. All she cared about was the caffeine.

"I know, but it felt like I knew Grace. We kept seeing her picture. I went out weekend before last to help with a search. I even met a few of her students. They are going to be devastated."

Drew nodded. "Yeah. And, it is one of the things you will learn about this island. We're close knit and always have someone we can call on. But, that usually means if someone is hurt, you know them."

She grew up in a tiny town in Southern Georgia, so she understood.

"They found her at McCully?" she asked, as she set down her coffee and took the evidence bags. "How did they miss her all this time?"

"They didn't. She was posed, and from her liver temps, dead less than a day."

She looked up from her work. The implications sunk in. Two weeks. "Oh, *damn*."

"Yeah. So, Dr. Middleton took swabs. I also sent you some pictures of the markings around her wrists and ankles and her throat."

"Damn," she said again. The thought of being kept for two weeks, tied up...the implications were bad. Really bad. She pushed through that, and moved on. She had to for now. It was her job, and Grace deserved the best.

"She was left at McCully, so there might be video of the bastard. I'll start looking through the feeds, see if I can find something. Of course, at night, it isn't the best resolution, but I might find something. Anything."

He nodded. "I'll let Del know."

She smiled. Charity knew the real reason he was going up to the squad room. "Just ask her out already. Quit coming up with excuses to go see her."

They really didn't have to say Cat's name. He'd been mooning over the woman for months.

He shook his head. "Not time yet."

"You can't keep waiting. I did that once and ended up regretting it."

"It's all about the timing, Charity. I need to take my time and do it right."

"Just don't wait too long."

He smiled and left her alone. With a sigh she looked

over her evidence before grabbing her lab coat. There wasn't much for her to work with, but she hoped to find something for Grace Singh. After taking another healthy sip of her coffee, she rolled up her sleeves and got to work.

* * *

By the time Del started on his fourth cup of coffee, he was ready to head home and go back to sleep. There was a lead hammer banging against his brain, and his eyes were burning. It wasn't even past ten in the morning, and things had gone completely to shit. Thanks to someone leaking the possibility that Grace Singh had been found, the press had become relentless. Add in the mayor and governor calling him for updates almost every twenty minutes, and Del just wanted to pretend today had never started.

Adam Lee, his second-in-command, popped his head into Del's office. He was dressed in his customary Hawaiian shirt, jeans, and hiking boots. The Hawaiian had been regular HPD when he had applied for the job working for Del. He had deep roots in the community, and that went a long way in Hawaii. He was always damned good at his job, and had a more refined sense of diplomacy—which meant he had one. Del was much better at barking orders.

"Hey, Dr. Middleton just called. She's got some info for us. You wanna go down there, or do you want to have her come up here?"

"Let's get the hell out of here," he said, grabbing his cell phone and slipping it into his pocket. "I can't deal with the damned office phone."

As if the gods had aligned against him, it rang again. He read the number and shook his head. He was *not* talking to Jin Phillips. The woman was too eager to make a name for herself. She had been calling him on the half hour since he'd arrived. If they didn't get a handle on this situation, she was going to make his life a living hell until they did.

Adam shook his head. "You know better, Boss. Or,

you should by now. This island is just one big town. By the time I came in, I had four texts from friends, two of them who have nothing to do with law enforcement."

Adam was born and raised on Oahu, a former star quarterback of Kamehameha schools and the University of Hawaii. The little bit of Polynesian in his blood had give him his massive build. His bald head gleamed beneath the office lights, as he smiled at Del. Del was convinced Adam polished it to a high shine before coming in, even though his second-in-command always denied it.

They walked out into the squad room. The governor had spared no expense for the team—and he was glad of it. With more and more people coming to Hawaii each year, not to mention, the arrival of a president every now and then so he could visit family, the number of high profile cases had risen. HPD was good, but they were being overwhelmed with press issues. TFH filled that role better, allowing HPD to keep up with the regular crime.

The room had various screens hanging on the walls, covering current events on TV, one showing the many alerts around the island, a weather advisory screen that also sent alerts for hurricanes, tsunamis, and earthquakes, and one they used for their meetings. The first few months he had worked there, Del had to fight the feeling of vertigo. A long table was situated in the center where they all sat during the team meetings.

"Hey, what's up?" Graeme McGregor asked as they passed his office. He popped up out of his chair and came to the doorway. Three inches taller than both he and Adam, McGregor was another transplant in his office, but from Scotland. He always reminded Del of an invading Highlander, from thick Scottish accent to the long blond hair. He was only missing a broadsword, although he had one tattooed on his back.

"We're going to see your favorite person," Adam said.

"Have fun with her," he said, his irritation easy to see.

He turned back into his office. Graeme had taken an

instant dislike to Elle the moment she'd been hired. The feeling was reciprocated from the good doctor. Their bickering was getting to the point that Del might have to stage an intervention. McGregor did not accompany them, of course.

"Why do you think he hates Elle?" Adam asked as he punched the elevator button.

"I don't know. Not like I have a lot of time to think about my team's love lives."

Hell, Del barely had one right now himself. With his long hours, it had been hard to find the time, but there was another aspect to it too. At the ripe age of thirty-five, he didn't really like the club scene.

"You think there's something there?" Adam asked, bringing him out of his morbid thoughts. It took Del a second to remember what they had been talking about. The man was worse than any woman he had ever dealt with. He seemed to think it was his duty to always meddle in people's lives.

"I don't know, and I don't care."

The elevator dinged and the doors slid open, revealing Elle and Drew. She stepped out, her head down, and ran right into them.

"Oh, pardon," she said, then realized who she had just run into. Her eyes widened. "Are you going somewhere?"

"Coming to see you," he said.

"And I was coming to see you. I thought you might want me to go over this with everyone," she said as Drew stepped up behind her. "I have some preliminary findings. I thought it would be easier to do this up here."

He nodded, and they headed back into the squad room of the Task Force offices.

"From what I understand, there was little to go on, evidence-wise," Del said.

"Indeed, but I did get a few things, especially one alarming one that I think we need to have researched."

Dammit, when she said that, he knew who she meant,

and he didn't want to deal with *her*. He had kept his distance for the sake of his sanity. His attraction to Emma was still causing him issues, even though he had not seen her in about a month.

"McGregor," he yelled out, then looked around. "Where are Floyd and Cat?"

McGregor stepped out of his office. "They are on their way in with Grace Singh's parents." When he saw who was with them, he frowned. "I see the Queen of the Dead is here."

She sniffed in his direction, but did not comment. Del rolled his eyes. He was not a principal of a high school, but there were times his team made him think he was—especially these two. There was a part of him, the one who hated to deal with their behavior, that really wished they would just give in and sleep together. Unfortunately, it would lead to more problems for him to deal with. He was screwed either way.

"Come on, she has some findings," Del said.

Graeme grumbled, but he did as Del ordered. Once a Marine—even if it was a Royal Marine—always a Marine.

"So," she said slipping her flash drive into the computer, "I am still waiting on the DNA results. Charity said it will take a little while. I'm pretty sure this is Grace Singh." She sighed. "And she did not have a pleasant time when she was missing."

Del nodded. "Did you get anything off the body?"

Elle shook her head. "No."

"Nothing?" Adam asked.

"Let me start at the beginning of my findings. When her body was found, she had only been dead for three hours. Maybe less. She was definitely alive yesterday."

Damn, he knew she had said it before, but hearing it again left his blood cold. The idea that she had lived for two weeks in the hands of a sadistic bastard had his stomach roiling.

"Then where the bloody hell was she?" Graeme asked.

"I wish I could tell you that. What I do know is that this woman was tortured, raped repeatedly. I took swabs from beneath her fingernails. If she didn't nick the bastard, I thought there might be some fibers. I found next to nothing, but Charity is still running those. If we can find anything, including pollen, *something*, we might be able to pinpoint where on the island she was kept."

"And he kept her somewhere for two weeks," Adam said.

Elle nodded. "If we go by when she first disappeared, it was fifteen days. I have a feeling he spent his last hours cleaning her off. He wanted to remove any trace of him, or where he had kept her."

"And to keep a person hidden on this island would be hard, Boss," Adam said. "Everyone was looking for her. Her face was plastered in the newspaper, on TV, and all of social media. I don't know how many times her picture was shared on Facebook. Last count I saw was over one million."

"Indeed," Elle said. "And to do what he did to her…you are right. He needed something secluded, or at least soundproof."

The explanation sent a chill through the room. The woman had been through hell, and her pain…well, that would have been loud. The bastard needed to be hurt…and a lot.

"Could be that she was kept at one of those fancy new condos. Some of them have been specially built according to the individual's requests," Drew said.

Del shook his head. "No. Most of those buildings have a good security system. That would risk being caught on tape. They might be soundproof, but the chance he would be caught on tape, or run into someone…that is just too much. He wouldn't even want to be associated with Grace, seeing that the search for her killer exploded the way it did."

"And, Charity is looking at the traffic cameras to see if

she can find anything," Elle said. "If we can catch someone on tape, especially that time of morning, we might be able to follow him back to whatever rock he crawled out from under."

"No other reports here on the island for something like this?" Del asked.

Adam shook his head. "I haven't found anything. Even went on to search the mainland. Nothing."

He sighed. "So, this is his first, and that means there will be more. Make sure to expand the search internationally. We need to cover all our bases here. There is no way he is going to stop at just one. Although, make sure there are no suicides in the next twenty-four hours."

"You think he would kill himself after this?' Graeme asked.

Del shrugged. "You never know. Sometimes, they just pop off, you know? They know the woman, they do this thing they have been dreaming about for months…years. Then, they accomplish it, and just lose it. Most of the time, they go on to kill again, but we just need to make sure that we check out each suspected suicide."

"We need to get ahead of this, Boss," Adam said.

"You're not telling me anything I don't know. We are fifteen days into the investigation, if you look at it from the time she disappeared. Means we will be working a lot of overtime to find this bastard."

"Fine by me. We need to find him and string him up by his bollocks."

Elle cleared her throat.

"You have something to add?" Del said.

"Other than I agree with the bollocks part, I truly think this isn't his first time. Maybe on this island, but he did something like this before, even if he left the woman alive."

"Why do you say that?" Del asked.

"The fact that he grabbed her off the street, kept her hidden, then posed her the way he did. He did all of this undetected. Even if he knew her, it would take someone very skilled to do what he did. Planned it out, and he made sure there were no witnesses. We might find him, but it makes me think that he has done this elsewhere."

A sinking feeling filled his stomach again. He rubbed his hand over his belly, but it did nothing to help with the rising irritation.

Graeme chuckled. "And we all know which lass can help with it, but she told Del she wouldn't work with him again."

Del tossed a glare in the direction of the irritating Scot. He hadn't spoken to her since their last fight, and Emma had been very clear about her feelings. He regretted the fight, but he hadn't come up with a way to approach her yet. There was a good chance she would hit him with a two-by-four. Again.

"She isn't the only person who could help with this. We're all experienced." Well, *they* were all experienced. They could even call in a profiler from the FBI.

"Don't even think about it," Adam warned.

"What?"

"We are not calling the FBI any sooner than we have to. You just need to man up and go talk to Emma. She'll help if you ask."

"I would say get her in here as soon as possible."

Elle's solemn statement made the hairs on the back of his neck stand up. He glanced at his ME. She wasn't an alarmist.

"Why is that?"

"First, she is the best at making the connections we need here. You know that. You all are very good at your jobs, but she is good at giving all of us direction. Which normally, isn't that important. But, this is…" she sighed.

"Spit it out, Sassenach," Graeme said.

The usually cool-headed Elle narrowed her eyes. "I've told you not to use that term with me."

Before they could develop a full-blown fight, Del

stepped in. "What's up?"

It took her a few seconds to gather her control before she looked at him. "She has a tattoo. On the small of her back. It's a picture of Hina."

"Hina?" Adam asked. "The Hawaiian Goddess of the moon?"

Elle nodded. "It is just a face, and I would not have known, but it is inscribed beneath her face. What do you know about her? I found a few sites online, but I wanted to do some deeper research."

"There are a few stories about her. She left Earth to live in the Moon, because she could not stand the crowds of people. And, then there was one that is close to her being the queen of the underworld, but, of course, in Hawaiian culture, she would be beneath the sea. But I don't see where it is that important." He shrugged. "So, she had a tramp stamp. Not that uncommon around here."

"Or anywhere for that matter," Graeme said. "They are pretty accepted in today's world, Dr. Middleton."

His tone was condescending, and Del wouldn't really blame Elle if she smacked him. Maybe that was what the giant Scot needed. But, Elle just straightened her spine and ignored him. Instead, she concentrated on Adam.

"Be that as it may, Grace did not have any tattoos. Not when she disappeared. They would have been noted in the missing person's report. And, she did not get one the night she disappeared—at least that we know of. I believe this work was done over a couple of days."

"Wait, are you saying she got the tattoo in the last couple of weeks?" Del asked.

She nodded, her gaze revealing the horror of what she had discovered. "I'm telling you this monster tattooed her and kept her while it healed. I believe it might be his calling card."

A hush swept through the room. The morning had given them enough chills to last a lifetime, but this was depraved.

"And that means we need Emma, Boss. Seriously. She will dig to find connections all over the world for this," Adam said. "If Elle is right, and I'm pretty damned sure she is, you need to hire Emma for this. We can be running down the leads, but you know how her mind works."

Dammit, he wasn't telling him anything Del didn't already know. *Fuck*.

"I'll call her."

Fifteen minutes later, he realized that was easier said than done. Apparently, Emma had not forgiven him for their fight. He'd called a couple times, then it went straight to voicemail.

"Did you get hold of her?" Adam said walking into his office.

Del shook his head. "I need you to ping her. She didn't answer any texts or calls. She might still be pissed at me, but she would at least tell me to bugger off."

Adam nodded. "You know she won't be happy about it, bra."

He shrugged. "When has the woman *ever* been happy with me? I don't have the luxury to see if she will come off her high horse and help us."

Adam nodded. "I got that feeling too."

He left Del alone. Yeah, the feeling. It was a ticking time clock linked up to a massive bomb. Hell, he would rather deal with a bomb than deal with this nutjob.

And, he would definitely rather defuse a bomb than face Emma, but if there was one thing he learned while in the military, you can't always get what you want.

CHAPTER THREE

Emma Taylor raised her leg, then pivoted to deliver a roundhouse kick to the foam shield that her brother Sean held up for her. He barely acknowledged the kick, the wanker. She was sweaty—something she hated—and every muscle ached. She was trying to remember just why she was there in the first place.

Sean nodded. "Good, you landed it right in the middle that time."

She drew in a deep breath. "Yeah, and it wouldn't have taken anyone down. You didn't even show any sign that I hit you."

He shook his head. "You have more power in your legs. You know I keep telling you that. A little bit more training, and you will be ready. Besides, I'm ready for the kick and I'm holding a shield. On top of it, you're small and people will think they have you at a disadvantage. Then, you'll kick their ass."

She nodded and grabbed her water. She had been working out for the last two hours, and she was ready to go back to her condo. Sean was doing what he thought big brothers were supposed to do. Since they had only known about each other for the past year, he had been trying to make up for what he called 'lost time'. And, because she wanted to make him happy, she went along with it.

Expecting her to work out in the sun without breakfast...that was just mean.

"Something else is bothering you," he said, as he set down the shield and studied her. "You're distracted. More than usual."

She shrugged. It was hard to put her finger on it, but she felt...restless. More than usual. As someone who suffered from ADHD, it wasn't that unusual, but this time, she felt off. It was as if she was missing something. It had affected her appetite and her sleep. She was used to dealing with insomnia, but skipping meals was just something she did not do, unless she was deep in a project.

"You know, Jaime, Randy, and I have a trip next month to Japan. You should come with us. Change of scenery would do you good."

She glanced back up at the house that her brother shared with his two lovers. Emma didn't have a problem with their lifestyle, and they were a lot of fun on trips. All three of them had been all over the world, so no matter where they went, she ended up seeing the real parts of the city, which she preferred over the tourist traps. Best yet, they always had wonderful stories about their time spent in other countries. When she went, she always was part of the whole.

At the moment, she just wasn't in the mood to travel. Not right now. She had been moving around most of the last eleven years—really most of her life. It was nice now when someone asked her where she was from, she could say Honolulu.

"Emma?"

She shook her head. "No, I have some things I'm working on."

He opened his mouth, but there was a shout from the lanai on the second floor.

"Hey, Del's here," Randy said.

"What's he here for?" Sean asked, but Emma knew—*just* knew—why Del was there.

Randy chuckled. "The answer is who. I think he's looking for Emma."

She rolled her eyes. Since she had walked out of his office last month, she had not talked to Del. Elle had called her a couple of times, and she and Drew had lunch last week. Charity and Emma texted on a daily basis and that had not changed. She had avoided Task Force Headquarters.

Their fight last month had been brewing for months. He routinely ignored her advice right off the bat. She knew his job was to be diplomatic, but she felt he was hindering her abilities. When he ignored her suggestion on who the insider at the bank was, she had lost what little temper she had held onto. She had been right, of course, but he had said that it was just one of the possibilities. In the end, they still got the people responsible, but she couldn't deal with working for him. She could handle people being assholes, but she would *not* deal with someone denying her intelligence.

"I take it you two haven't talked," Sean said, watching her.

"No."

Sean sighed. "You knew he was going to hunt you down."

"No, I didn't. He actually said he was sick of working with me."

Which had hurt. Granted, the man wasn't the easiest to work with, but she had felt a connection to him early on. Other than Sean, he had been the only other person she trusted for the longest time. When they had their fight, they both said some horrible things. Of course, she had done her best not to show how much it hurt her, which wasn't difficult. She hid her emotions easily—years of living on the street helped with that. It didn't take away the pain, though.

She watched as Del came striding through Sean's house. Tall, muscled, and with a gun. He wore it in a shoulder holster, and she had seen more than once he knew how to use it. But, she had the idea that he would rather use his fists. He was one of those types of guys who hit first and asked questions later. That was okay, because she was the same way.

As he stepped out onto the lanai, she tried not to sigh. It was difficult though. The man was built, and he had these milk chocolate eyes that she knew people called bedroom eyes. Dark, short hair, those eyes, and skin that just seemed to stay bronze naturally, and he was one delicious treat for the eyes.

Bloody hell, he was gorgeous. The green T-shirt with the pocket TFH logo stretched across his massive chest was tucked neatly into a pair of khaki cargo pants. She'd had more than a few thoughts about what he would look like without those pants…even though they gave everyone a good view of his ass. That had been part of her problem. The ongoing fantasies she had been having about him had made her grumpy. Especially since he treated her like he was her older brother.

"Taylor, I've been trying to get a hold of you."

And people said *her* manners were rude. She didn't know why he insisted on using her last name. Like she was some kind of recruit. Del seemed to have forgotten he wasn't in the Army anymore.

"When?"

"When, what?"

Sean rolled his eyes. "Emma is confused by you saying you have been trying to get hold of her. She would like to know when you were trying to get hold of her. Damn, now I feel like a translator."

"This morning. We caught a case I'd like to hire you for."

She didn't directly work for Del. She was contracted out, mainly because they didn't need her on staff, and because they couldn't afford to hire her full time. She also had made sure that her contract had her attached to the governor. He seemed to forget that…all the time.

"I'll let you two talk this out, because I'm sure there are things I don't need to hear about the case," Sean said. He kissed her on the cheek. "I think Randy said something about going to Leonard's to pick up some treats."

She nodded, but barely spared him a glance when he walked away.

"I told you I wasn't working with you again."

He sighed. "*For* me, Taylor. You work for me."

She sniffed. "That's not what the contract says, boy-o."

He settled his hands on his waist. "While I would like to have a rehash of our argument from last month, this is more important. We found Grace Singh."

The name gave her pause. She had been working on some software development the last couple of weeks, so she had missed a lot. Still, she had taken note of the schoolteacher's disappearance. It was hard to miss since the entire island seemed to be looking for her. There were regular updates on the telly and online. Every hour during the day, the local radio stations were reporting the newest developments.

"I take it not alive."

He shook his head and sighed again. In that moment, she saw it in his gaze. There was a horror there that could not be denied.

"She was murdered, and not in the usual way," she said.

He nodded, once. "Did you see the news this morning?"

"No. I got up and came over here. Sean thinks I need to learn to protect myself."

Del snorted, and she couldn't fight the smile. Seeing that she had smacked Del with a two-by-four the first time they'd met, he probably thought she didn't need lessons.

"Exactly. But, he insisted." Then she realized she hadn't told anyone but Sean where she was going to be. "How did you know I was here?"

"I called you several times. When I couldn't find you, I had Adam run you down."

She opened her mouth, then snapped it shut. The implications of the casual statement he had just lobbed at her sunk in. "You tracked my mobile?"

"Yes."

He didn't even deny it. "That's creepy, Del."

"Answer your phone and I wouldn't have to do it."

Of course, that's what the wanker was thinking. He had a right to track her down.

"Don't do it again."

He hesitated, then nodded. Oh, he wasn't happy about it, but he agreed.

"Just so you know, I am not the kind of woman…"

She let her voice trail off when she realized what she was about to say. Good lord, he didn't need to know that she was attracted to him. He'd be mortified.

"What?"

"Nothing. Just don't do it again."

She started to walk toward the house. "So, what do you actually need me for? I know that several of your team has handled a case like this."

Elle had handled several back in England before she had left to move to Hawaii. Adam had been around for the last serial killer to hit Hawaii, so he would know more than she would.

"Yes, but I think we need your expertise. The woman was tattooed and with Hina, a Hawaiian goddess. I'm sure it was symbolic. We're good at connecting the dots, but developing those dots…you might help. If we can get a lead, maybe we can beat him before he hurts someone else."

She nodded as she stepped into Sean's house. "If he hasn't already disappeared from here."

"There is that. But, if he shows up elsewhere, whatever we develop can be put to use. We're going to have a late afternoon meeting with everyone. Four…this afternoon."

She nodded.

"Taylor?"

"I nodded." He crossed his arms. Stubborn man. "Yes, I'll be there."

"Okay."

Then he hesitated again.

"What?" she asked, not even bothering to hide her irritation.

"This isn't going to be a fun case."

"Are any of them?"

"True. This one though…already have a bad feeling about it."

"And you thought to include me," she said with chuckle. She turned and was surprised at the stunned look on his face.

"What?"

"You used sarcasm right."

Embarrassment flooded her as her face heated. She did have issues with social cues, and sarcasm was one of the ones she could never seem to get right. The team had been merciless in making fun of her because of it.

"I've picked up a few things." Thanks mainly to Jaime Alexander, one of her brother's lovers. Jaime had a smart mouth, and after a period of mutual distrust, Jaime had taken Emma under her wing. Sean had said it was a sign of the coming apocalypse; she now understood the humor behind the comment.

"Good."

Then he did nothing but stare at her. She always had issues when he looked at her like that. She knew he was just trying to assess the situation or her mood, but for her, the attention made her go all hot inside. It made her want to do silly things like jump on top of him and demand a good hard shag.

"What now?" she asked.

He shook himself. "Nothing. Sorry. Four, and don't be late," he said heading out the door.

She watched him walk away, admiring the way the faded material cupped that marvelous ass.

"He is an amazing piece of man," Jaime said from beside Emma. She jumped at the sound of her voice.

"Bloody hell, Jaime, I said don't do that."

She smiled. "My time with Randy is finally paying off."

Randy Young filled out the trio of lovers. The former SEAL was well known for his ability to sneak up on anyone. Sean was good, but Randy was better.

"I think you got some other payoff from him and my brother."

She winked. "True. Now, tell me why you haven't munched on that man yet."

"Randy?" she asked walking away, trying to avoid the conversation. Jaime had taken too much interest in Emma's sex life, or lack thereof. "That's gross."

"You find Randy gross?"

"Well, I see him like I see Sean, like a brother. Just, eww."

Jaime chuckled. "I wasn't talking about him. I was talking about Delano."

She shrugged. "Not my type."

"Honey, that man is every straight woman's type. If he went that way, I know both Sean and Randy would have had a go at him at least once. You know he has to be a tiger in bed. Hmm, those sexy eyes make me want to do all kinds of terrible things. They should make you think of those things too."

"Okay, he's hot, and yes, I have thought about those things." She sighed. "I have never really been into those alpha males with guns, but when he comes striding into the office wearing his...he makes my head spin."

"So, why not try him on for size?"

She laughed. "You have the oddest terms for sex. I wouldn't mind a go at him, but he sees me as a sister."

Jaime looked at her for a long moment. "Uh, no he doesn't."

"I know what you are trying to do here, but Jaime, I do not inspire lust in men. Not like you do."

"I am not doing anything but telling you the truth. He watches you."

Emma shook her head as Jaime nodded hers.

"He does. When he thinks no one is looking, he watches you."

She snorted and started gathering up her stuff. "I am sure he does. More than likely he's wondering if I'll hit him over the head with another board."

Jaime chuckled. "I have a feeling it's for a whole other reason."

"Why do you say that?"

"Because when he looks at you sometimes, he looks like he wants to take a big bite of *you*."

"Living with two men has made you daft."

"Bollocks, but I will let it go for now."

That was a good thing since Randy and Sean were walking down the stairs. Both men had gotten a little too interested in what was going on with her love life. It was weird having that many people worrying about what she was doing.

"What are you two talking about?" Randy asked.

Jaime opened her mouth, but Emma stopped her with a shake of her head. She did not need both Randy and Sean thinking there was something there with Del, especially since there wasn't.

"I'm going to have to take a rain check. I need to get back to my place and clean up."

"The case?" Sean asked.

She nodded as she brushed a kiss over his cheek. "Maybe we could all do dinner tomorrow night?"

Sean agreed, then Randy frowned.

Good lord, he was worse than a five-year-old. If he didn't get attention, he sulked. She leaned over and gave him a kiss.

He was smiling when she pulled back. Since they had

settled in Hawaii, Randy and Jaime really had become like another brother and an older sister she had never had. Most people would find it weird, but for someone who had lost her entire family in one blinding moment on Boxing Day, she loved it. Over ten years without a real connection, and now she had three.

"I'll call you later."

"Be careful," Sean said.

"Always, brother dear."

"Hey, watch it," he said with a laugh.

She waved behind her as she stepped out onto the driveway. She needed a shower, and she needed to talk to Elle about the case. After slipping on her helmet, she started the short drive from her brother's Kailua mansion to her condo in Honolulu. As the sweet Hawaiian air whipped by her, Emma tried her best not to worry about why she felt so happy now. She would just assume it was the job. Being infatuated with a man like Martin Delano was just going to lead to trouble.

* * *

Adam stepped up to the coffee stand when he felt someone beside him. He didn't have to look to know who it was. He could smell her perfume. Worse, he could smell *her*. Lilies with a dash of spice. He remembered getting drunk on it, as he licked his way over every inch of her body.

"Howzit, Lt. Lee," Jin said with a smile. Her flirtatious tone told Adam she wanted more than just a simple conversation.

"No," he said. Then he looked at the clerk. "Mahalo."

The cute woman smiled, and he wanted to curse himself. She had been dropping hints for weeks that she wanted a date, and he had thought about it. But, now that Jin was there, he couldn't think of a reason why he would even want to talk to another woman.

He was a schmuck.

Stepping away from the coffee cart and Jin, he started

walking back to headquarters. He had come outside after dealing with Grace Singh's parents, needing some fresh air. Their grief had almost been too much for him. They had known, definitely, but seeing their daughter laid out on a slab eked away any remaining hope they had.

Unfortunately, Jin didn't give up easily. Her heels clattered on the sidewalk behind him.

"Adam," she called out. "Wait up."

He stopped and faced her. Half African American and half Japanese, she was a unique beauty. It was what drew him to her to begin with. She'd cut her hair short recently, allowing the natural curl to take over. Today, she was dressed in a white top with splashes of red flowers all over it. The short little red skirt and heels to match completed the outfit.

She pulled off the designer sunglasses. Damn, those eyes. Dark brown with little flecks of gold in them. They mesmerized him every time he saw her.

"I'm not about to comment on an ongoing investigation."

For a second, something close to hurt came and went in her gaze. She didn't truly have feelings though. He had learned that a long time ago.

"I'm not here for a comment."

He snorted and turned around to start back to the office. With the situation they were in right now, he did not need to get tangled up with the woman again.

"Well, either way, no comment."

"Adam."

He stopped and looked over his shoulder.

She walked around and stood in front of him. "I just knew you were probably the one who had to handle her parents."

He sighed. "I did, and it wasn't pleasant. So, I'm not in the mood to deal with you right now."

"I just wanted to say hello. I know you never liked this part of the job."

"Who would?"

She shrugged. "Delano makes you do the notification a lot of times."

"I didn't do the notification. I just accompanied them. But I volunteer. You know how locals are. They would rather deal with *Kamaʻāina*."

She nodded. "Why don't we get a drink after work tonight?"

He wanted to. He wanted nothing more than to have that drink, then talk her back into bed. The memory of their weekend together was still seared on his brain. But, in the end, she'd disappeared sometime on Monday morning and refused his calls for weeks. And he *had* called for weeks.

Schmuck.

He shook his head.

"Oh, come on, Adam, you're still not mad at me, are you?"

He hated when she put that tone in her voice. He knew she dated a lot of policemen, and if she hadn't been a reporter, Jin would definitely get the label of badge bunny.

But she always had a motive, just like now. It hurt just to look at her.

"No, thanks. I like to date women who are after me for my body. Not what I know about a case."

Again there was a flash of hurt in her dark brown eyes, but it disappeared so fast, he knew he had been wrong. She didn't have feelings or morals when it came to the job. She always wanted a story and damn anyone who got in the way.

"Nice try, Phillips," he said, then walked away.

The sooner he got away, the better chance he had of resisting her. Even now, he wanted to turn around and take her up on her offer. He didn't understand, never would. Adam knew he always wanted the damaged ones. Somewhere inside of him, he felt a need to fix them, to kiss all their hurts away. Meanwhile, they were figuring out

ways to stomp on his heart.
   Schmuck..

CHAPTER FOUR

"Are you going to eat that malasada?" Charity asked, as Emma looked over the information. She shook her head and absent-mindedly handed the last one over to her friend.

"I can't believe you found nothing."

Charity bit into the treat and hummed. "I owe you. I was in such a rush to get here this morning, I've had nothing to eat."

"That's not a good idea. You need to keep your energy up."

She sighed. "They forgot to call me again."

Emma sighed. "I can't believe the swabs brought back nothing."

Charity nodded. As the resident geeks of Task Force Hawaii, Emma and Charity had hit it off right away when she'd arrived. Being geeks were about the only thing they had in common. Their love of anything dealing with Doctor Who had sealed the friendship. But that was where the similarities had ended.

While Emma could be quiet, Charity was loud and Southern. She'd explained that it was a whole other level of noise if you were from the south. Emma rarely worried about what her hair looked like—or if she was in fashion. Charity changed her fashion with the days. Today, Charity was wearing hot pink and black...although, Emma had no idea why she had worn red shoes with it. Maybe she had been overwhelmed. Emma would have a meltdown on a daily basis if she had to choose from Charity's wardrobe. Emma was convinced the woman had more pairs of shoes than Emma had ever had in her entire lifetime.

"Nothing. Even the scrapings under the fingernails. Elle told me she thought the bastard cleaned them. And now, seeing what I have, I would say she's right. It takes a particularly dedicated person to get every fiber or bit of dust cleaned out. You have to be one sick fuck to do that."

"You have to be sick to do *any* of this. Leaving her like that was bad enough, but just reading some of this makes my head hurt."

Needing to collect her thoughts, Emma closed her eyes and leaned her head back.

"Praying to the gods?" Elle said.

Emma opened her eyes and smiled at the doctor. "No. Trying to get my brain clear. It seems to be all bungled about at the moment. I can't think straight."

"Why is that?" Elle said.

Emma shrugged. "Probably overwhelmed by all the information. Plus, Sean made me go work out this morning. I was sweating."

Charity snorted.

Emma frowned at her friend. "What?"

"I have a feeling it has to do with the very delicious Delano," Charity said.

"It does not."

Which was a big fib. Of course it was. Just thinking about being in the same room with him had her pulse pounding. She thought by now she would have learned to control herself around him.

"He's been grumpy since you left," Charity said. "In the last few weeks, he's been all fire and brimstone. No one could get him out of the funk he was in."

"Del is grumpy all the time," Emma said, ignoring the way her heart danced at the sound of his name. Bloody hell, this wasn't good. She was going to embarrass herself.

But she didn't want to rain on Charity's parade. She knew that part of the gossiping nature of the team served to relieve the stress they were all under.

"I have to agree with Charity," Elle said. "Del has been a real bugger to deal with since you haven't been in. He even yelled at Adam one day, and you know how those two are. Like brothers. He's just been in a right funk."

"Well, let's hope it doesn't get worse." Emma looked at the clock and noticed it was almost four. "We need to get upstairs. Are you coming?" she asked Charity.

Charity shook her head. "I have some more video to watch. I need to see if I can catch this bastard. Say hi to Del for me."

Emma didn't respond to that. She picked up her messenger bag and followed Elle out of the room. The sooner the meeting was over, the sooner she could get to work.

And the sooner she was far away from the man who made her think stupid things.

* * *

Del hung up on another reporter as he grabbed up his cell and headed into the squad room again. He was sick to fucking death of the calls. Vultures, every single one of them. To make matters worse, it was five minutes to four and Emma still hadn't arrived.

From the time she started working for him, Emma had tested his control. She had questioned his authority and refused to admit she worked for him.

"You told her four, right, Boss?" Cat Kalakaua asked, smiling at him.

A sharp shooter, and world-class black belt champion, she didn't seem to be worried about giving him hell. They all did since he'd first brought Emma on board. Even before that. Being her keeper, when a terrorist had targeted her brother, had given them a glimpse at his attraction. Thankfully, the woman in question didn't realize it. The team, though, they liked to mess with him. And Cat was one of the worst. It probably came from having four older brothers.

"Yes, I did."

And he couldn't check her cell again. Emma would definitely lose her temper if he did that. It *had* been creepy, but then, it was just the way it was with Emma. She disappeared for days…weeks. He'd have to start using her brother to keep tabs on her. Being the owner of some of the most valuable electronics patents in the world made her a target. She was worth several million at least, but after years of living on the street, making her way in the world by herself, Emma still didn't understand.

The doors swung open and Emma, Elle, and Drew walked in. She had changed into cargo pants and a T-shirt. She had also pulled her long straight black hair back into a braid that hung down her back. He always liked her hair, the feel of it. During the mess with her brother earlier that year, he had taken her to his place for safekeeping. He'd had to carry her because she had passed out. He could still remember the feel of her fine, silky tresses sliding over his skin.

All of the sudden, Emma came to an abrupt halt, and Drew walked into the back of her.

"Oh, sorry, Emma," he said.

"No worries, Drew." She looked at him. "What?"

"Nothing. You were almost late," Del said.

He thought he heard Cat snicker, but the warning glance he gave her was enough to shut her up. When he turned back to Emma, she was staring at him as if he had lost his mind. Which he had. It made sense, since all the blood had headed south, and every one of his brain cells seemed to go on permanent vacation around her.

"Almost late?" Emma shook her head. "No. I showed up early to talk to Charity about some of her findings. I didn't think everyone wanted to hear it all over again."

And now she made him look like an ass. It made sense, because she would have interrupted the meeting over and over asking questions. She was starting to learn how to work with a bigger team, and he should happy for it, but, for some reason, that wasn't the case. If she already knew what they knew, the meeting would be short, and she would be on her way.

Adam came in on their heels. "Seems like I'm late to the party."

The light comment didn't hide the darkness in his gaze. He'd been with the Singhs for the identification. That was never easy, especially when they had been hoping for days that she would be found alive.

"Everything okay?" Del asked.

"Yeah. They took it better than I thought they would, but I think they were expecting it, thanks to Jin."

Del nodded and marked off another complaint to lay at the feet of the reporter. Jin was pushing herself further and further into the story, and that meant she was going to be more and more trouble for them. There was a good chance that he would have to do something about the situation.

Sighing inwardly, Del took his seat to let Adam take over. His second-in-command was much better at electronics than he was. And truthfully, there was a very good chance that he would lose his train of thought with Emma in the room. That would not only be bad, but also embarrassing.

"So, we all know the story." Adam punched a few buttons on the massive tabletop screen. A picture of Grace Singh appeared. "Fifteen days ago, Grace Singh went missing. She was at Ala Moana, just doing a little shopping, then she disappeared. All recorded traffic cams and security cameras yielded us nothing. Friends couldn't understand her disappearing, since she was from a good family and adored her work with the students. Next week is the annual Science Fair, and it was her baby. Her colleagues all said she would never have missed that. From what Elle said, the tattoo was new—I confirmed that with her parents. They both said she didn't approve of them."

"The suspect did it himself," Emma said. "What is that a picture of? Do you know that background?"

"Hina. In Hawaiian culture she is the goddess of the moon, but in several other Asian and Polynesian cultures, she is identified as the matriarch and/or linked to healing."

Emma nodded as she continued to look at the picture of the smiling Grace. Adam punched a few more buttons, and it brought up the picture of the way Grace was posed. It was vulgar, her legs spread, naked...degrading.

It was totally irrational, but Del didn't want Emma looking at this. Yes, he'd brought her onto the case, but there was a tiny piece of him that wanted to keep her from this, to shield her from the horror of the case. And that was why he needed Adam handling this. The woman made him do stupid things.

"He hates women, that's for sure," Emma said. "I think we need to do some research on that goddess. More than likely, it has to do with her, or whatever the guy is trying to say. Can you send me this picture and the picture of the tattoo?"

Adam glanced at Del for approval. Del nodded. Emma missed the byplay, because she was focused on the picture of Grace Singh.

"Sure thing," Adam said.

"We need to find him to make sure he doesn't get another woman," Graeme said.

"Too late," Emma said.

Everyone looked at her as she walked toward the screen. He knew better than to question her, or her assumptions. She didn't just make outlandish statements without something to back them up.

"What?" Del asked.

Emma jolted as if she'd forgotten all of them were there. "Oh, sorry, I was thinking out loud."

"Why do you think it's too late?" Adam asked.

She sighed. "This level of obsession...it's unhealthy.

He needs something to replace the rush he got this time around. It will grow each time he kills...that need. If he doesn't have one already, he's at least zeroed in on a victim."

"And you think he has someone already," Elle said nodding. "It actually makes sense."

"What the bloody hell does that mean?" Graeme asked.

Elle opened her mouth to respond, but Emma stepped in and saved them from a drawn out argument.

"You have to think of it like he's an addict. As a cop, I'm sure you have had your run in with an addict or two. Think about them. At first, they are just having a good time. Sure, they are spending too much money on their drug of choice, but it isn't like it controls their lives. Then, before anyone knows it, they are selling anything to get that next fix. They'll steal from family, sell their bodies, anything. Because nothing is as important as that next high they can get.

"Each fix is a woman he obsesses about. Sure, he might have had a high yesterday when he killed her, but now the low is setting in. He's going to need another one. Since it appears Grace didn't like tattoos, we know he gave it to her. He knew how long to keep her, and he knew their time was running out. He would have already been looking for a new woman. One to abduct. Or...he left this morning on a flight."

Adam nodded. "I could check all out bound flights from this morning."

Marcus stirred then. A veteran cop with fifteen years with the DC Metro, he had the most experience of his entire team. Tall, commanding, with a baritone voice and knowing dark cop eyes, he always gained attention from walking into the room.

"Waste of time. We have no description. Unless he's wearing a big shirt that says *I killed a woman this morning*, I doubt we could find anything."

Emma nodded in agreement. "Marcus is definitely

right."

"A waste of our resources," Marcus continued. "What we should look for is someone who arrived in the last two to four months. Someone rich. And any rentals of houses off the beaten path. That would give you more direction. It can't be too hard to find out long-term rentals or new purchases like that. Not that common around here, right?"

Adam nodded. "Yeah, and you would have to plunk down a large sum of money on this island to get some land around your house and find seclusion."

Emma was still staring at the screen of the body of Grace, and Del gave Adam a look. He took it down. She blinked and turned her attention back to the team.

"Elle, you want to tell us everything?" Del asked.

Elle nodded. "As you saw from the previous picture, she was dumped nude, no remnants of what she wore that night. All of her jewelry was gone."

"That was in the original report," Adam said. "No word from any of the pawn shops about that, though."

"You wouldn't find it. This man has money, and he probably kept them as souvenirs," Cat said. "I can go back around, see if we can find anyone who has tried to pawn anything in the last few days."

Del nodded for to Elle to continue.

"So, as documented, she was bound for a lengthy bit of time. The bruising around her wrists and ankles tells me that. The impression tells me that it is a rope of some sort. I sent it up to Charity to analyze, and I hope she can find something with that."

"Cause of death?" Del asked.

"As I suspected, manual asphyxiation, and from the bruising, it was probably his hands this last time."

"What do you mean?" Cat asked.

"I think he used other devices throughout her incarceration to torture her."

"So he strangled her with different implements until the end," Emma murmured. He could see her working the issue out in her head. "The other times he was just toying with her. The last—that was personal. You have to get right up in her face to do that. It's almost intimate."

"Indeed. A true sociopath more than likely. Of course, I noted the burn marks earlier. She was definitely raped and sodomized. The contents of her stomach didn't give me anything either. Nothing."

"Does that mean you think he didn't feed her?" Marcus asked.

"I am sure he fed her something, but not in the last seventy-two hours."

"He knew his time was ending," Cat said. "No reason to keep feeding her.

Emma nodded. "Okay, is there anything else you need me for?"

He blinked as his mind went completely blank. For a second, he couldn't come up with a word. She was leaving already? He hadn't talked to her in close to four weeks, and now she was popping off just like that.

"Not really. Do you have another job?"

Emma had a wealth of contracted work she handled. Most of it was done over the Internet, but he knew that every now and then she would get a local job.

"No. I want to start on this. I have an idea."

Which meant she was going to run with it, and he needed to let her go.

"Answer when I call."

She grabbed up her messenger bag and started toward the door.

"I'm not your dog, Delano."

The door shut just as the snickers started.

"That woman definitely knows how to handle you," Marcus said.

"You want to work graveyard tonight?" Del asked.

Marcus shook his head, but he didn't stop smiling. Del missed the days of being in the Army and just looking at one of his lieutenants would cause them to pass out. This team was seasoned and tended to know just how to handle him. Dammit.

"So, McGregor, you and Cat go do another canvassing of the site. I assume that traffic cams picked up nothing?"

"I haven't talked to Charity, but I know she was going through them. I'm sure we'll hear from her if she gets a hit," Adam said

"Nothing yet, when I was down there," Elle said. "She was still going through all the footage."

Del nodded. "Marcus, see if you can call her friends again. We'll leave the family alone for now, but make sure there was nothing different in her life. We need to start looking for patterns, so we can put the word out."

As everyone left, Adam approached him. He kept looking at Del, as if he wanted to offer him some advice. Adam always had advice.

"What?"

"The best thing you could do is take her to bed. It would relieve some of that tension."

Del didn't respond. He didn't want to. Bringing her in had been smart for the case, but not for his peace of mind. She tested him on so many levels, but she had no idea. Or pretended not to. Just being in the same room with her drove him to distraction. He headed to his office and tried to look busy. Which he should be, but he had to get his head unscrambled. Spending time with Emma always left him like this.

"Boss?"

He glanced up at Adam standing in his doorway. He saw the expression and knew exactly what it meant.

"I don't want to talk about it."

Adam sighed. "But you should. Otherwise, you might end up shooting someone."

"Namely you," he growled.

Adam spread his arms out with his palms up. "Listen, I'm just trying to help here."

"Then maybe you can go make the announcement

about the identification of the body."

"No, thanks. I handled the family, and that was enough."

He sighed and stepped into his office. "They already knew. It was hard not to."

Adam pursed his lips. "How did they find her to begin with? Was there a witness?"

He shook his head. "A call. So there was a witness, we are not sure who, though. Or, it could have been the bastard himself. They have the tape and are supposed to be sending it to Charity."

"What kind of call?"

"An anonymous one from a payphone down the street."

Adam folded his arms as he leaned against the doorjamb. "That sounds too convenient."

Del nodded. "Check with Charity and see if they sent it. If not, check with dispatch and get it to her ASAP. Maybe she can line up any traffic cams with the phone too. Carino was in charge until we took over. But I doubt he has anything more than we do. Plus, he's still considered a *haole*, so you might get further than either one of us."

Adam nodded. "Got it."

He turned to leave, but paused to look at Del. "You know, Emma really has no idea of your attraction."

Del said nothing but stared at him unblinkingly. Adam was the brother he never had, especially since neither of them had a brother. He'd been welcoming and eased Del's first year. He knew without a doubt he would have not made it through the first year with him.

"No comment?"

"What do you want me to say?" Del asked, trying to keep his voice level.

"I thought you might want to share a little. Talk it out."

Del rolled his eyes. He had a good family, but they were Italian. There was a lot of yelling, lots of eating, and lots of love. When it came to his love life, there wasn't much discussion—other than his mother pointing out that he hadn't given her any grandbabies. His father had been gone most of the time, serving overseas in places that he now knew about all too well. But, even so, Joe Delano did not discuss things like feelings.

Adam had been raised differently. His father had died in the line of duty with HPD, and he had been raised in a houseful of women and girls. He always wanted to share things that were just…wrong. Or maybe it was just Hawaiians. Lord knows his landlord always wanted to talk to him about Del's lack of a love life.

He realized Adam wasn't going to leave until he answered him. "No, I don't want to share. I don't want to talk about it, because there is nothing to talk about."

Adam just shook his head as he walked away with a smile on his face. Maybe if Del said it out loud enough times, he could force himself to stop thinking about her all the time.

Fat chance, Delano.

* * *

The wail of a woman crying pierced his thoughts. Dammit, he was trying to concentrate and she would not shut up. They never did. He could hear it seeping from the room he had built. He didn't feel any kind of remorse. Why should he? Women deserved nothing more than what he offered—an escape. They would no longer be tied to the convention of this world. They would be free of their baser needs.

The sobs grew louder. Bloody hell, this one was louder than usual. She just would not shut up. It was time for another injection, so he could work on his art again. They were always so much better after he gave them something to calm their nerves. He went to the cabinet and pulled out the syringe. It was so much easier to keep the women quiet when he worked on them.

Working in silence was a must.

CHAPTER FIVE

In the seventy-two hours following the discovery of Grace Singh's body, Del had been put through the wringer. The press had hounded him, and all of the elected officials felt the need to tell him how important this was. It wasn't like he was smart enough to understand anything.

Del tossed a few aspirin back and took a swig of his cold, stale coffee. The bitter taste was so strong it almost made his eyes water.

"Living the life, Delano," he said, to nobody in particular.

His head had been pounding for two days. He'd only gone home to take a shower and get a change of clothes. He needed sleep…a lot of sleep. Unfortunately, Jin had found out where he lived and had hounded him there until he threatened her and her station with a lawsuit. At least there he could claim it was private property. But, she was always waiting for him when he showed up at the office.

On top of all of that, he hadn't heard from Emma. He had made sure not to bother her, because he knew what she was like when she got in the *zone*. He really did worry about his safety when he interrupted her. Still, he wanted to know what she was working out, and he wanted to make sure she wasn't zoning in too much. She had a tendency to forget about everything else while she worked.

"Hey, Boss," Adam said when he stuck his head in his office.

The last few days had been tough on all of them—especially Adam. He'd been in law enforcement in Hawaii longer than any of them, and locals often went to him with their problems. HPD had been relentless, and Adam had done his best to shield Del. He had a better temperament than Del. The constant second-guessing from HPD was starting to get on Del's nerves. It wasn't that it was a slight at him. It was, but he was more pissed off that they were attacking his team. His team had not been in charge of the search and rescue. But for some reason now, they were supposed to solve a case with almost no evidence or leads in less than four days.

"Yeah?" he asked, as he took another swig of coffee, quickly remembering it was stale. Fuck, that was nasty.

"Have you talked to Emma?"

Del shook his head and moved the coffee cup farther away. "Not yet."

Adam sighed and walked into his office uninvited. It had been like that since Del had hired him. While it had annoyed him at first, Del had realized it was just part of the way Adam operated. He didn't bug Del unless there was something important to discuss. Now Del knew to pay attention.

"Do you think she's still working on this?"

He grunted as he started going through his emails. Fuck, Satan had to be behind the idea of email. He'd just checked it half an hour ago, and there were one hundred new ones. If one more politician emailed him, Del was going to hunt down the bastard and punch him in the throat.

"Boss?"

He looked up and realized Adam was waiting for an answer. "Of course she is."

Adam looked out into the squad room, then shut the door to Del's office. *Dammit*, he would never get any peace, even from his own team. If Adam closed the door, he felt they needed to share again.

"Why do you say it like that?"

He shrugged. "Emma always finishes what she starts. It's an illness almost."

"Hmm."

He did not like the sound of that hum. When Adam had time to think, it usually ended badly for Del. "What?"

"You seem to know her well."

"I told you. I dealt with her when her brother had that business before. You were the one in charge of her that night."

"Yeah, but she has never connected with me like she has with you."

Del thought it best to ignore Adam's needling. "You've worked with her for the last few months. You've seen her obsession. She latches onto something and doesn't let go. It's why she makes so much money testing games. They know she will go in and test every angle there is and then some. When they get the report back from her, they know how to make it more difficult, or easy, depending on what they want to do with it. It is just the way her brain works."

"Man, that's a lot of words about a woman you claim not to have the hots for."

"Listen, I know that you like to talk about feelings, but I don't have the time. We have the mayor and the governor breathing down our necks, and that damned Jin Phillips is stalking me. She wants a fucking interview. I don't have the time or energy to even think about a love life."

"Ah, so you *do* think about her that way."

Fuck. He needed some sleep. How did Emma operate on no sleep? He had been trained in the Army to go without sleep, but right now, even after drinking a ton of coffee, he couldn't seem to concentrate. He was too old for this kind of sleep deprivation. Of course, just thinking that pissed him off. Seriously, he wasn't even forty yet. He'd just hit mid-thirties this year, but he was already thinking like he was middle aged.

This case had been driving him mental—as Emma would say.

He didn't address Adam's assertions, but he did say, "We should probably check on her."

"Did you call her brother?"

He nodded. "He said he talked to her yesterday morning when I called him last night. He assured me they were all keeping tabs on her."

All of them understood her interest could often turn to obsession. He was sure a shrink would say it had to do with her losing her family at the age of fifteen. Add in that she survived the natural disaster that had destroyed her family, Emma was a prime candidate for having issues. The fact that she had this one quirk was easy enough to deal with. Tag teaming with her family seemed to help.

"But you haven't talked to her?" Adam asked.

He shook his head. It was the end of the workday, and while he had called her several times, she had not answered.

"You might want to check on her. You know how she can get," Adam said.

"What?"

"Just like you said. I have seen her like that. Remember that first case we were on with her, the dog fighting ring?"

Emma had been devastated that people were abusing dogs that way. They had caught the case thanks to a fight between two of the operators, which had left one of them dead. The investigation had uncovered a multitude of activities, including prostitution and drug selling. Emma had obsessed about the dogs so much so that she hadn't slept for a week.

"I'm sure her brother will keep an eye on her."

But he knew better. Sean did overprotect her to a

point. At the time of their blow up, he had noticed that her older brother was giving her more space. It had made Del even more nervous about her well being. The woman needed a keeper.

"Go on and check."

Del looked up from his email. "Why don't you come with me?"

"I have a love life, and to prove it, I have a date tonight."

"Jeanine, the coffee girl?"

He nodded. "So go check on Beautiful Mind."

Damn, he forgot about that nickname the team had given her. All of them were very careful not to use it around her, but it didn't mean one of them wouldn't slip up. They didn't mean anything by it and, in fact, it made her part of the team. Del was just worried she wouldn't understand it because things like that often didn't make sense to her.

"Hell, you could walk over there, Boss."

Del knew too well where she lived. He had avoided it as if the plague had been detected there. It was almost too much temptation, but he went out of his way to go down a couple blocks so he didn't stop by. It would be too damned easy to come up with a work excuse to stop by there and say hi.

"I always thought it an odd choice," Adam said.

"What? Where she lives?"

He nodded. "She survived a tsunami. Why would she live right there in Ala Moana, with the ocean just out her window?"

"I don't know."

But now, he wanted to know. He wanted to know why she would choose a condo right next to the ocean. Was she crazy, or did she have the need to prove something?

Dammit. His infatuation with her was getting stupid. It was definitely making him stupid. When he got stupid, people got hurt. Del had promised Sean he would do everything in his power to keep her safe. Obsessing about her, or just how she would sound when she moaned his name...

Fuck.

"You just need to go by and check on her. She's bound to have found something by now."

He hesitated, not wanting Adam to think he was going because he told him to go. But Adam smiled.

"If anything, just get out of here for awhile. You need a break."

"That's definitely true. I can't think in here."

Adam remained silent as Del picked up his gun and shoulder holster. After slipping it on, he grabbed his cell.

"Call if anything breaks."

"Always, Boss."

He didn't pay attention to the looks he got as he strode to the back of the building. He would walk it out, get his mind back into the game and return.

He was not going to show up at Emma's condo.

* * *

"Where's he going?" Marcus asked as they watched Del walk down the hall to the back door.

Adam smiled. "Beautiful Mind."

"Okay, who has today's date?" Cat asked as she and McGregor joined them. "I know I have Tuesday next week."

Adam knew that if Del had any idea they were all betting on when he and Emma would end up in bed, there was a good chance they would all get written up, or shot. Probably shot. But it was their way, and there had been running bets since she had first joined the team. Hell, what could he say? They were detectives, and it didn't take much to detect the heat between those two. Emma and Del both were attracted, and they were completely oblivious about it. That made it even more fun for the team.

"Not sure, and we agreed we needed verification," Floyd said.

"How the bloody hell are we going to get that?" McGregor bellowed. The damned Scot was loud, and that was saying a lot considering Adam's family. All the women in his family were damned loud. But the man always seemed to shout every comment or question.

"I don't know, but we all agreed to it," Adam said just as Elle joined them.

"What's up?" she asked.

"Beautiful Mind," Cat said as she wiggled her eyebrows.

"Oh." She said nothing for the moment. "I have today."

McGregor looked at her. "You bet on it?"

She shrugged, but said nothing as her cheeks burned. Adam blinked. It was hard to remember that Elle was often times shy around all of them if she wasn't talking a case.

"There is no verification. Who has the sheet?" Cat asked.

"I think Drew is keeping it," Elle said. She pulled out her phone to text him.

"And I didn't say it was going to happen, but he's on his way over there now," Adam said.

As usual, they ignored him. If there was a chance someone was going to cash in, they paid attention to nothing else.

"Yes, Drew has it," Elle said.

"Hey, who has tomorrow?" Cat asked, as they crowded around Elle to find out what days they had picked for the month.

Adam sighed. It was a really good thing the boss wasn't there. Worse, he was worried what the team would do to verify the bedding. One thing they took almost as seriously as their job, and that was the contests that involved money. Some offices had fantasy football, they had bets on each other's sex lives.

They were strange, but they were *'ohana*.

***

Emma tugged her T-shirt over her head, then grabbed her panties. After she pulled them on, her stomach rumbled. Her appetite was roaring to life now that she'd stepped back from work.

She felt better now after a shower, but her head was still fuzzy. Too many thoughts crowding her mind. She knew she was in a bad place, obsessing about the assignment, but she couldn't figure a way out of it.

Her brother had always told her to step back, look at the issue from another angle. If that failed, he told her to take a shower. It hadn't helped, although she didn't smell that bad anymore.

When her stomach grumbled again, she realized she needed to get something to eat. She went to her kitchen, but before she could open the fridge, there was a knock at her door. She frowned. Usually, the doorman told her if someone was coming up.

Another knock.

"Open up, Taylor. I know you're in there."

Del. Her heart skipped with delight, as she tried to fend off the inevitable dizziness she had around him. What was it about this man that just the sound of his voice made her want to giggle? It was one of the reasons she had done her best to stay away from him for most of the last two days.

She walked to the door but did not open it.

"I heard you walking to the door."

He was as bad as Sean and Randy. They could track a person's movements. It was probably from their training. All three of them had worked Special Ops in the military.

She knew he wouldn't go away, so with a sigh, she unlocked the door and opened it.

He had his mouth open to say something, but snapped it shut. He was probably going to yell at her. The man was always yelling at her one way or another. In emails, in texts, and the worst, in person. And *dammit*, a girl could only take so much. When he got all mouthy with her, she just wanted to kiss him.

She needed a therapist and maybe medication. Definitely medication.

When he continued to stare at her, she gave in. "What?"

His gaze slipped down her body, and she felt it as if he were touching her. When he met her gaze, he swallowed.

"Do you always answer the door dressed like that?" he asked, his voice sounding strangely strained.

She looked down and realized she wore only her massive shirt. Sure, she had on a pair of tiny little panties, but that was it. The man was making her lose her head.

"Come in."

She turned around, fighting the heat that was flaming her face. Seriously, she might have a one sixty IQ, but she just did not seem to be able to use any of her intelligence when he was around.

"I just got out of the shower. Give me a second."

She didn't look to see if he followed. He always did, for some odd reason. From the moment she hit him with that board, he always appeared and watched out for her. It was odd enough that Sean, and to an extent Randy and Jaime, kept an eye on her. She had been on her own so much in the last eleven years that she was accustomed to handling her life without intervention.

Emma grabbed a pair of board shorts and then rejoined Del in her living room. Jaime had been correct. He was a luscious piece of man meat. She had never seen him dressed up, but she liked him like this. A casual shirt, dark blue that brought out the gold in his brown eyes. He looked tired. They all were probably pretty tired, but she knew he wasn't sleeping well. It was there in his edgy expression and the dark circles under his eyes. She hadn't seen him ever look this way. But then, they had never dealt with a case like this.

He was looking over her notes and white board.

"You think you can find something this way? Some

connection?"

She nodded. "There is something there I am missing, but with only one murder and nothing else to go on, it has been slow going. And where were his other kills? Most of them had to be international."

He glanced sharply at her. "You think this isn't his first?"

She nodded. "This was too planned. Seriously, if someone wanted to come up with a plan to get away with murder, this would be one of the cases I would hold up as an example."

"Are you saying we can't catch him?"

She shook her head. "No, *you* can catch him. But it is going to take some kind of connection. That is what I have been looking for. The problem is there is not a good database worldwide of these things. They have them, and they are definitely hackable—" she broke off when he rolled his eyes. "Bloody hell, I didn't mean to tell you about that."

He sighed and shook his head. "Go on."

"Alright, well, I definitely think the tattoo has something to do with it, but I have yet to find any connection to it. And it could be a new element."

He nodded. "True."

He went back to studying the board. Her stomach rumbled loudly again.

"Get something to eat," he said. "I want to look some more of this over."

She hesitated, because she didn't like people looking over her work. It was usually a hodgepodge of things that made no sense to anyone. But she knew from experience that Del could make sense of her scribbles. Fighting the urge to explain the details, she walked into her kitchen.

The flat wasn't small by Honolulu standards, but most people from the mainland would find it tiny. Her kitchen overlooked his living room with a three person breakfast bar separating the two rooms. She grabbed a piece of pumpernickel bread and slathered some peanut butter on it.

"Do you want anything?"

"No thanks."

She poured herself a glass of milk and rejoined him in the living room. As she waited for the inevitable questions, she munched on her snack.

"You believe all this stuff?"

"Bloody hell, no."

His mouth curved and she tried not to react, but her hormones were an independent lot. Her hands grew so damp, she thought she might drop the glass. She set it down on the coffee table.

"Then why do you have it listed?"

"I am trying to work in his mind. I don't believe that much in analysis, but I do think that he does. He has a reason behind what he is doing. That, I cannot deny. No one orchestrates a murder like this, one that has all this symbolism. Especially where he left her."

"What about it?"

"She was in view of Diamond Head, which is considered sacred to the Hawaiians. It could be nothing, but with the goddess tattoo on her back, I would venture to guess wherever he leaves them is important. I also find it odd that he picked a goddess and killed her."

"Why?"

"In mythology throughout the world, women were often more powerful than men, or at least held the same level of power. Like here in Hawaii, you have Pele, a goddess who held her own and ruled the Earth while her lover ruled the seas. Or some similar sort of story."

"But she did not have Pele's face on her back."

"Well, no, but then Grace Singh was a science teacher."

He nodded again, and then looked at her. The moment stretched, and she tried not to fidget. Fidgeting was a sign of weakness according to Jaime.

"What?" she asked.

"Why do you live here?"

Okay, the conversation was turning weird. And when she noticed that, it was really, really odd. "Here? In Hawaii?"

"No. Here where the ocean is out your window every day."

She glanced out the massive windows that showed her a view of the Pacific. The light waves rolled in from beyond the islands, and she sighed. Sean had asked her the same question when she bought the condo. She finished off her snack and rubbed her hands together.

"I know it's odd."

He shook his head without taking his gaze from hers. "No. Not odd. Interesting."

There was something else in his voice, but she didn't really understand it.

"First of all, Sean picked the apartment. Secondly, I don't blame the ocean for my parents' death. That would be illogical."

"And you're not very illogical, are you?"

She shook her head, not taking her gaze from him as he approached her.

"See, that's where we differ."

"Oh?" It was the only thing she could say. He kept looking at her like…well, like he wanted to take a huge bite out of her.

"I have all kinds of illogical thoughts. All the time."

His voice had deepened. It set off alarm bells in her head. "Indeed?"

"Like right now, when you get that snippy tone in your voice. It makes me want to kiss you."

"I don't get a…" then her voice trailed off as she realized what he had just said. "Kiss me?"

He nodded as he stopped in front of her. "Yeah, I do. All the time. Have you noticed that I don't run the meetings anymore? I can't. All I can think is that I really, really want to kiss you."

Her brain went numb as heat spiraled through her.

"You don't want to kiss me."

He nodded again, his mouth kicking up on the right side. Damn him, and damn that crooked little smile. Every time she saw it, her bones seemed to liquefy. He cupped her face and bent down to brush his mouth over hers. And just like that, her world exploded around her. He deepened the kiss, thrusting his tongue into her mouth, as she slipped her hands up over his shoulders and around his neck. Pressing against her, she could feel the long length of his erection, and her body lit up like the Aloha Friday fireworks.

Yes, she wanted this. Now. He lifted her up and she wrapped her legs around him. Lust flashed through her as he sat her on the kitchen bar. She let her head fall back, and he attacked her neck. His lips, his mouth, his tongue. Lord. Every bit of her body ached, needed, begged for relief.

She slipped her fingers through all that dark brown hair of his, as he kissed his way up to her earlobe. He growled as he took it between his teeth. The vibration of the noise danced over her nerve endings and sent another wave of lust rushing through her body. Hell, she was still vibrating from the simple little bite on her ear. Then, it vibrated again, against her inner thigh.

Damn. It was his phone.

With much reluctance, she pulled away. He growled, the sound thrilling her, and tugged her back.

"Del, your phone."

It took him a long moment to open his eyes. When he did, she saw the barely suppressed hunger that made him look almost feral. Bloody hell, she had done that to him. Or with him, or something.

He didn't take his gaze from hers as he pulled out his phone and answered it.

"Delano."

Even if the person on the other end of the line didn't

know, she heard it there in his voice. Anger filled with sensual heat.

Then, in one moment, all the heat dissolved. Right there, she knew it was something bad.

"Okay. On my way down."

"What?" she asked as soon as he hung up.

He sighed, regret filling his gaze.

"Del?"

He shook his head. "We have another missing woman."

CHAPTER SIX

Even with taking a detour to try to avoid any reporters out front, it only took Del and Emma a few minutes to make it to TFH headquarters. Del glanced at his companion. The woman had a stubborn streak worse than his. After he dropped the bomb and ruined the mood, he had tried to convince her not to come with him. She had—of course—overruled him. Del really should have seen that coming. She'd been ignoring his orders since the moment they met.

They went in through a back entrance. Since it was already on the news, the media was probably already clamoring for information. Worst part of it was, if it wasn't for Grace Singh, some of them would not have paid a bit of attention.

Arriving in the squad room, they found his team seated at the table. Everyone turned at once as they walked in. There was a long beat of silence, and he realized they all knew he had been over at Emma's.

"So, we have a missing woman?" he asked.

"Yes, a Susan Tanaka" Adam said. There was no teasing or joking around. A missing woman, no matter if she was connected to their case or not, was important.

"When did she go missing?" Emma asked.

"They aren't sure." Adam punched a few buttons. The picture of a vivacious young Hawaiian woman, dressed in the costume of a dancer from one of the luau outfits, came into focus.

"Why aren't they sure? Her friends and family didn't know she was missing?" Del asked.

"She lives just off UH campus with a couple of girls, but they all have different schedules. Her family had no idea that she was missing, but they live in Washington State at the moment. So, they just thought she was fine."

"And no one noticed she'd gone missing?" Cat asked. "Not even her friends?"

"That's what they are saying," Adam said. "She took off this weekend from work, and skipped a couple of classes."

"She missed class and no one noticed?" Emma asked.

"Didn't you ever skip a class, Emma?" McGregor asked.

She shrugged. "I've never really been in school. It just seems odd to miss classes she's paying for."

Adam continued. "Her attendance is spotty at best. But, when she didn't show up for work today, her boss called one of her friends."

"Why is this on the news? Why didn't we get a report?"

"When one of the girls reported her missing to the campus police, and filed a report with HPD, she didn't get much notice. So she called Jin Phillips, thinking she might be able to help. With her reports on Grace Singh, her roommates hoped to at least get some leads. I think they were hoping that she was just off on her own, and the report would bring her forward."

"Fuck," Del said.

"Exactly. Instead of contacting us, she went on the air with it."

Del settled his hands on his hips, as he contemplated the coming shit storm. "It is going to be a madhouse."

A phone started ringing again. Adam shook his head. "Already is, Boss."

"Okay, Cat and I will go talk to the friends. You call

the parents to see if they heard anything. McGregor, Floyd, I need you to go talk to the employees out at Luau Paradise. Maybe one of them knew something about her. Adam, you hunt down the original officer who took the report. Maybe he or she can help give us a little background, especially on the state of her roommates' minds."

"What are you thinking?" Adam asked.

"Listen, this could very well be our worst nightmare. Or, she could have made herself disappear for any number of reasons. There is also a chance that all three of the girls cooked this up. They could be out to gain publicity. I don't think it likely, but let's cover every base we have here."

Everyone stood and started to prepare to leave, but Emma asked, "Hey, what about me?"

"Cat and I can drop you off at your condo." He looked at Adam. "Send her all the info you have on Susan right now. And, everyone tag her when you send me stuff."

"I can help with the girls," she insisted, following him into his office. "There might be something I can get from the interview that you would miss."

"No. You need to go do what you do best. Look at Susan and Grace. See if there is a connection someway."

"But—"

He knew one way to shut her up would be to kiss her, but she would probably belt him if he did that in front of everyone. Instead, he grabbed her by the forearms and forced her to look at him.

"I need you to do this. I need your expertise. If this is the same guy, you might be our best chance to save her. As of right now, we've lost at least three days. Going by Grace, we could have less than two weeks to find her. This is what I need from you right now. We have no evidence, but if you can zone in on something we might be able to find her."

She drew in a deep breath and nodded.

"Let's go. Everyone, keep us up to date. Maybe she just

decided to go off and play for awhile."

But deep down, in his gut, Del knew she hadn't.

"You don't think that," Emma said as they made their way to his truck.

"No. But, hey, maybe for once we'll get lucky."

"We can only hope," Cat said.

"Hope often leaves you shattered if you aren't careful," Emma said, as she slipped into the backseat of his pickup cab.

Cat let one eyebrow rise and Del ignored it. He knew that Emma's experiences taught her more than any of them would understand. And right now, he couldn't be distracted.

Susan Tanaka was depending on them.

* * *

After dropping Emma off, they drove to Susan's apartment. One knock and the door opened. The young woman on the other side of the door had swollen eyes, and she looked like she hadn't slept in at least three days. She was Asian American, with long honey brown hair and dressed in what Del considered the college uniform in Hawaii: a T-shirt and board shirts.

"Captain Martin Delano, TFH. This is Cat Kalakaua. Can we speak to you for a second?"

She studied his badge, then nodded. Stepping back, she waited until both he and Cat were in the tiny apartment before shutting the door. Another young lady, about the same age, blonde haired and blue eyed, sat on a futon-type couch. She looked like she had been crying also.

"My name is Diane Fung, and this is my roommate Bethany Brown," the first young woman said. "Please, sit down."

After they both sat down on the available chairs, Del said, "We wanted to talk to you about Susan."

Diane shook her head, her eyes filled with regret. "We tried to tell the police. We tried to tell them she had gone missing. We should have just refused to leave."

"The important thing is you tried, and we are here to help," Cat said, her voice in the same soothing tone Del had heard her use before. It didn't seem to help this time though.

"It still doesn't seem to be enough, though."

"I understand," Del said.

"No, you don't," Bethany said, her voice rising. "You don't know that we just *knew*."

Cat gave him a glance and stepped in to take over. Even with all his training with his younger sisters, this age usually still perplexed him. They weren't girls, but they still hadn't gained maturity.

"I can see that. College life…in each other's pockets, right? When I was your age, we used the buddy system. I always made sure that friends knew where I was going to be if I wasn't with them. Safety in numbers, and if you don't have them, make sure your friends know, right?"

Bethany sniffed into her tissue and nodded. "Yes. We are all so careful. You remember that rapist they caught a few months ago?"

Cat nodded as she glanced at Del. A serial rapist had been roaming the college parts of town, preying on tipsy college girls. It had taken two months to catch him. By the time they caught up with him, he had raped at least six girls.

"So we always check in. *Always*," Bethany said. "But she said she was going to the mainland. That's what she said. We assumed it was to see her parents, but when she didn't return, we got worried."

"And you tried to call her?"

Diane nodded. "Yes. It went straight to voicemail."

"You were worried that she disappeared when she didn't show up to work, not school."

Bethany offered him a sad smile. "Susan says that life was too short to worry about attendance all the time."

"But she wouldn't miss work," Diane said. "We're saving up to take a trip to Australia this summer. It is all she talked about. Missing work means missing out on money. She wants to see the Great Barrier Reef. We all do."

"Jin said she might be the victim of the *Akua* killer," Bethany said. "Is that true?"

He blinked, looked at Cat, then back at the girls. "The what?"

"That's what they are calling the man who killed that schoolteacher. The Goddess killer. Why do you think they call him that?"

"Do you think he abducted Susan?" Diane asked.

His mind went blank. They had kept that little bit of information to themselves and no one, not even her family, knew about the tattoo.

Cat stepped in when he fumbled. "We really don't know anything yet. It might all be a misunderstanding. If she caught a way to make money some other way and just forgot to tell you. So, remember, if you hear from her, you call us first. We'll make sure we call Jin and tell her all about it."

Both the girls nodded. They left them with their cards, hopeful they would stop talking to Jin, but he had a feeling they wouldn't. They were both genuinely upset, but Jin would use them, and in return, they would become celebrities of a sort.

"Did you let anyone know outside of TFH about this?" Cat asked as they walked down the hill to his truck.

He shook his head. "We need to check in with everyone on the team. This was not supposed to leave the office."

If it did, they would lose that tiny leverage they had right now.

* * *

"Have you made it out here for a luau?" Marcus asked as Graeme pulled into the parking lot.

He shook his head. "I keep meaning to, but I never seem to find the time. We should do a TFH night here or something."

"Well, without Emma. She doesn't like crowds."

Graeme chuckled. "Oh, she will deal with them. Don't you remember her going on and on about Disneyland a few months back? Her brother took her and she would not shut the hell up about it. Besides, I have a feeling if Del is with her, it won't bother her much."

Graeme parked up front and they both got out of the truck. It was so damned hot out today. Hawaii usually had mild temps even through the summer, but the trades weren't really great today. Add in the higher than usual temps, and it was making him long for Scotland in the dead of winter.

"Damn bloody heat."

Marcus chuckled. "Dude, you're going to have to chop off all your Goldilocks."

He grunted but didn't respond. He walked into the pavilion area. He lived over on the North Shore, and hadn't made it out to what some called the West End of Oahu that much. It was drier, and while all traffic on Oahu sucked, it could particularly suck on the West End. One downed pole over the highway, and people were cut off.

This area was populated by newer homes and condos, along with Disney's newest resort.

"Can I help you?" a young woman dressed in a luau costume asked.

"We need to talk to the manager, or someone in charge of the dancers," he said as they both flashed their badges.

She nodded. "This way."

She led them to a tiny hut that looked like it would be blown away in a stiff breeze, but once they stepped inside, it was all modern.

"Danny, these policemen need to talk to you," she said.

A tall Hawaiian man stepped out of the back room giving them a smile. He wasn't as tall as either of them, but he was built like a stone statue. And apparently, he had no problem walking around half naked.

"Danny Aiona. How can I help you?"

"We're looking for some information about Susan Tanaka."

His smile faded. "Of course. I can't tell you much about her. I'm the supervisor, and therefore the enemy, but she's a good girl. Always on time, never misses work. That's why I was so surprised."

"Do you know if she was seeing anyone?" Marcus asked.

"No. But then, the girls don't share with me. Let me get some of the girls here so you can talk to them. They'll definitely know more than I do."

"Thanks," Graeme said.

He picked up the phone and punched a couple buttons. "Hey, Lani, could anyone who knows Susan well come to the office? There are some policemen who would like to speak to them. Thanks."

He hung up and smiled at them again. "So, how's Cat Kalakaua doing?"

"You know Cat?" Graeme asked.

He chuckled. "We went to school together, and she gave me my first speeding ticket."

"So, got any horrible stories about her?" Marcus asked.

"Many."

* * *

Charity had Jack Johnson's latest single blasting in the lab when Del showed up.

"About time you got back," she said. He offered her a cup of coffee and she smiled. The team members of TFH knew just how to get her to work for them.

"What do you have for me?" he asked.

She clicked a few buttons. "What I have is a possible bastard sighting."

The screen showed an SUV roll to a stop.

"I went back and found out that this SUV stopped somewhere right off McCully."

"He didn't park on the bridge?" Del asked, obviously

looking at the screen.

She shook her head. "There is no parking on the bridge, so he might have been worried that he would draw more attention to himself."

She punched a few more keys, and the video picked up someone walking along the street, then turning onto the bridge. There was a large bundle over his shoulder, but it could have been anything. Then, he was out of frame.

"That's all I have."

"Could you follow the SUV after it left?"

She nodded and brought up that bit. "You can watch him here…then he pulls over here and leaves it. He walks into that alley and just disappears."

"*Fuck.*"

"Oh, but I have something for you."

She blew up the screen. "Looked up the license plate and guess where it is now?"

He looked at her.

"It was impounded. It is being sent over, and I will get my grubby hands on it tonight."

He kissed her cheek. "You *are* an ebony queen."

She smiled. "And don't you forget it, boss man."

"Let me know what you find."

"Of course," she said, sipping on her coffee as she walked out of her office. She had a car to take apart and play with. She needed to change.

* * *

Del walked into the squad room just as his phone chimed. It was McGregor.

"Yeah, I have you on speaker."

"Marcus and I talked to a few friends of hers here at work. Some of them had no idea she was missing, but there were one or two who claimed that Susan was involved with a man."

He looked at Cat, who nodded. Damn, he hated when she was right, but maybe she was just off with the new man having fun.

"That's news to us. Her roommates didn't know about a man."

"She just met him recently. Called him Sugar Daddy when she talked to him on the phone. She told a few of the girls here that she was going away with him for a few days."

"Interesting. Did they say why she might not have told her roommates?"

"Not sure." Marcus said. "Although one of them gave us the idea that the man was older, and something about one of her roommates might be jealous. Other than that, nothing."

"Okay. Come back here and we can mobilize with HPD."

"Oh, Cat, we met Danny Aiona today," McGregor said.

Her eyes narrowed. "Yeah, so?"

"He had a lot of interesting things to share about you."

She opened her mouth to argue, but Del pushed on. They didn't have time for this shit.

"Quick question. Did either of you mention the tattoo to anyone?"

"Nope," McGregor said.

"I thought we were keeping that under wraps," Marcus said.

"We are, but somehow someone let it leak. Or something. The press is calling it the *Akua* Killer. The Goddess Killer, in other words."

"Well, *fuck* us. Neither of us gave it away," McGregor said.

"Okay. Get back here as soon as you can, and we'll go over some things."

He clicked off the phone just as Adam came breezing back into the squad room.

"Hey, Boss. Talked to the parents. Nothing. They had no idea she was missing. They usually talk to her about once a week, but her parents were out of town all of last week. They went on a cruise, so they didn't have good contact with her."

"And that would have been planned months in advance. Something Susan would have known about and might tell her boyfriend," Cat said.

"Are there things you would tell your boyfriend and not your friends?" Del asked.

She snorted. "Yeah, and the other way around too. Young women at that age can really cause problems with relationships. Plus, if he is older, there's a chance he's married. He might have insisted on it for that reason." She shrugged. "Maybe it's a simple misunderstanding."

He looked at her, and knew from her expression, she didn't believe it. He glanced at Adam.

"Yeah, I am going to err on the side of caution," Adam said. "The woman has been missing several days, and what did Emma say? She thought for sure he already had another woman?"

He nodded. It was one of those times he wished she had been wrong. He was betting that she wished that, too.

"Did you reveal anything about the tattoo to her parents or anyone?"

Adam shook his head. "I thought we were keeping it out of the press. All I asked them was about her feelings about tattoos."

"We were. And without her parents knowing, we have a problem."

"Why?" Adam asked.

"Well, Jin is calling him the *Akua* Killer."

"*Fuck.*"

"Yeah."

"You don't think Emma told anyone, do you?" Cat asked.

He shook his head. "Do you think she would willingly talk to a person?"

Cat chuckled. "No, I guess not."

"I'll double check with her, but I think we might have a really big issue here," he said as comprehension lit Adam's eyes.

"*Fuck*, we might have a leak somewhere."

"Bingo," he said. "And, if we lose the killer because of this, whoever leaked the info is going to wish he had never been born."

Del would definitely make sure of it.

CHAPTER SEVEN

Two days of hunting for the college student did not give them anything. The entire police force, the UH college campus, and the majority of Oahu had come together again to search for the young woman. They had covered the island and found nothing. The idea that this young woman had just disappeared off the island with no trace was absurd. Worse, after checking all the airlines and going through hours of security recordings, they knew she had not flown off the island. Other than by boat, that woman could not have left. Del's irritation with the newswoman continued to grow as they watched the update she was giving on the news.

"Still no leads in the investigation, even with TFH in control of it. The amount of money spent on the task force is exorbitant, and it has led many to question if they are worth the price."

"Turn it off," Del said. "I can't deal with that woman any more."

Adam shook his head. "She isn't far off, Boss."

He looked at his friend. "What? You think we deserve that shit?"

"No. But I know a lot of people are questioning us."

"Let me guess. A couple of the asses who didn't get my job?"

He nodded. "I'm not saying it's all true, but damn, it's fucking frustrating."

Del couldn't disagree with that. Every lead had dried up. No one knew who she was dating. They had yet to find a traffic cam video of her leaving the Luau Paradise show that night. On top of that, they had hoped to find something in the abandoned car, but the only thing Charity found were strands of Grace Singh's hair and carpet fibers. If they found the guy, then they might be able to connect him.

"Any word from Emma?" Adam asked.

He settled his hands on his hips. "I texted her an hour ago. She texted back BO."

"BO?" Adam asked.

"Bugger off."

"So, nothing in that realm and now this crap. I'm not sure how much more we can take, Boss. It seems every inch of this island has been searched."

"That's impossible, knowing some of the areas around here. The hiking trails alone lead to all kinds of places that have not been searched. Our problem is the lead time he has on us. Not knowing where and when she disappeared doesn't help. He is a crafty bastard."

Adam nodded. Del looked out his window. The sun was setting and another day had disappeared. Since they had the National Guard helping in the rescue, he had some of his time back, and they could pursue leads. Well, if they had any leads that is. Right now they had next to nothing. Even another visit with Susan's friends yielded nothing. With Jin Phillips fueling the fires, it had caused even more scrutiny of his team.

"Why don't you go home, Boss?"

He glanced at Adam. "Sick of me?"

"Well, there has been a discussion about your smell."

He chuckled. "I've had showers here and changes of clothes, but getting out of the office might do me some good."

"You have the bike here, right? Go for a drive, clear your head. I'll call if there is anything."

"Make sure you ping me as soon as you hear."

Adam nodded, but they both knew there would be nothing. Not tonight. They both had a sense about these things, unfortunately.

"You're doing everything you can. Take an hour or two, come back refreshed."

So, less than ten minutes later, he was on his bike, but he didn't head out to Hawaii Kai. Instead, he found himself parking his Harley by Emma's condo. Like last time, he flashed his badge and went up. He knocked, expecting her to take her time coming to the door. Instead, it flung open.

He blinked at the vision before him. What the hell had happened? She was a mess. Her hair was sticking up on one side of her head. It was as if she had twisted it around her finger over and over, a habit when she was concentrating. It was easy to see she hadn't had any sleep. The delicate flesh beneath her eyes was bruised. Del was pretty sure she probably hadn't been eating either.

"Any word?" she demanded.

It hit him, and he realized that she had been waiting just as they had. He shook his head and she stepped back. "I thought you might call if something broke."

"Nothing has."

She emitted a sound of disgust, then turned on her heel and marched into the living room. He followed, then stopped as soon as the room came into view. Good God, it looked like a bomb had gone off. When Emma started working, some things would go to hell. Her clothes, and there would be research crap all over the place. But…this was a whole other level of chaos. The usual papers and books littered the floor and tables. Candy wrappers, empty energy drink containers, plus takeout containers were stacked everywhere else.

"What is going on here?"

She glanced around and shrugged. "I've been working. I have yet to find anything between the two women. But, I have been finding some interesting things in Japan. They had a couple of killings last year. It took a bit of digging, and I still need to get more background, but a few reports talk about some women and tattoos."

She was talking too fast—almost manic. He should have made Sean come over and check on her. With the press hounding his every step, he'd avoided leading them to Emma's door. Her brother should have been stopping by though. Sean knew she was working on this case and knew she could lapse into an episode.

"They probably had more than just a few."

"I meant like these. Both of the women were tattooed. I am still searching for more information, but I haven't found what the tats were of or if it had the same MO."

She stuck the pencil in her mouth and started typing on her computer. He knew that crazed look in her eyes, and the use of run on sentences. It was when she was about to go into the deep end. Too much info and too much to think about. All of it became a mass of unending thoughts that she could not seem to split apart. She could continue on like this until she had a meltdown. She was brilliant, but this was one of those times when she needed someone to push back. Del elected himself as that person for the night.

"Hey, are you hungry?"

It took her a second to turn to face him. When she did, it took more than just a moment for her gaze to focus on him. "What?"

"Eat, as in have food?"

She shook her head. "I'm fine. I had Skittles for breakfast."

He shook his head. "You eat like a teenager."

"What does that have to do with the investigation?"

He grabbed her by the arm and pulled her away from her laptop. "Come on. Let's go eat."

"I think I have things here. And I have work. Lots of work. I have to read over the reports as soon as I get them sent to me. I must be here."

There was a tinge of desperation in her voice, and he knew it well. Their first case had affected her like this. She'd almost lost it then, but he knew how to reel her back from the edge.

"Most of your food is probably unhealthy."

"How do you know that?"

"You just told me you had Skittles for breakfast, and there are enough empty energy drink containers to fuel a football team for weeks. You need real food."

She dug in her heels. Panic was definitely setting in. It shimmered in her voice. "We could order in."

"No. We need to go out."

"Need?"

"Yeah. Fresh air will do you good, and because your bed is just a few feet away."

She yanked her arm away from him. "So?"

The woman knew just how to push every last one of his buttons. One of these days, the two of them were going to have it out, but it wasn't the right time.

"I am in the mood to finish that kiss I started the other day."

She opened her mouth, then snapped it shut.

"Yeah, there's that."

She suddenly looked wary of him. "You haven't said anything since then."

"We've both been too busy, other things in the way."

"But you don't want to act on it?"

He could give her a line, but he didn't. He couldn't. Del was starting to realize just how important she was to him.

"Yeah. I would give anything to strip those clothes off you and kiss every inch of your sweet, soft skin."

"What's stopping you?"

"We aren't ready."

She frowned. "We aren't?"

"No. Now, let's go eat."

She crossed her arms beneath her breasts. "Not really hungry."

"Okay, let's just go for a ride. Get some long pants on."

"On your Harley?"

He nodded and held his breath. When she got set on a path, it was very hard to divert her, unless he physically carried her out of her condo. But he didn't want to do that.

Then, inch-by-inch, her mouth curved.

"That sounds brilliant."

She hurried away and Del started to realize that making her smile had given him a high he had never experienced before. Just the sight of her happiness had his hormones humming, and his mood suddenly seemed lighter.

Damn, he was in a lot of trouble but, at the moment, he didn't really care.

* * *

Emma hated to admit it, but Del had been correct. The ride through the night had lifted her spirits and eased her mind. By the time they stopped to eat, it was already dark. Emma had enjoyed the fast trip up Pali Highway, then back down into Honolulu. She couldn't remember ever just going for a ride for fun, and especially not on a Harley. Her Moped just did not measure up. They parked at the Fort DeRussy parking garage and walked over to Wailana Coffeehouse.

Once they were seated, Del looked over the menu.

"What are you going to have?"

"Roast turkey sandwich. It's not as good as Randy's, but it still tastes pretty good."

He glanced up. "Randy cooks?"

"Well, some. He seems to be in charge of Thanksgiving, but he's also made roast turkey sandwiches for Sunday dinner before. They are amazing. All three of them have their specialties. Sean is amazing with a grill, and Jaime is the baker."

He opened his mouth to say something, but the waitress showed up.

"Hey, Emma. The usual?"

She nodded. "Sure thing, Peg. And some hot tea, please."

Del looked at her, and then at the waitress. "I'll take a burger, medium, a glass of water, and coffee, no cream."

"I'll get it right to you," she said with a smile, and left them alone.

"Come here often?"

Emma chuckled. "While this is a cosmopolitan city, there aren't a lot of places that cater to insomniacs, and it took me awhile to find a place that wasn't loud and close to my condo."

He nodded and waited to continue as Peg brought them their drinks.

"So, how do you handle your brother's lifestyle?"

She shrugged. "It is a little different, but then, what do I know about family? My father and mother were…well odd. Add in the fact that my father never told me I had an older brother, so it doesn't really give me a good basis. But, Sean is the only family I have left, and I really want him happy."

"Yeah, I got that idea during the takedown of Letov."

Those days, to her, were still a horrific memory. Having a deadly terrorist plotting to kill her brother had consumed her. Saving him had been her only goal for months. The idea that they had been brought together by Letov to punish Sean was just icing on the cake for her. He had wanted to break both of them, but what the bastard had done was bring them together.

"But, they are really happy, so I don't have an issue with it. I mean, so what three people live together. Who cares? Well, there is one problem."

"What's that?"

"I have to text before I come over."

"That's Sean's rule?"

"No, mine." She sipped her tea. "If you ever eat over there, you will be glad to know that the kitchen counter has been cleaned with the strongest antibacterial cleanser there is. I insisted on it."

He snorted. "So, walked in on something, did you?"

"There are just some things a sister does not ever want to see. I mean, how do I get that out of my memory?"

He said nothing, but smiled at her. Something tickled at the back of her throat, as she felt her body heat. His eyes had turned darker…warmer. It was harder to ignore these feelings after that kiss. Before, she was convinced that he wasn't interested in her. Now though, she wondered what was going through his mind.

"What?"

He shrugged. "It's been a long time since we talked like this."

When she had first settled in Hawaii, she had stayed at the Hilton Hawaiian Village. It suited her needs, and she liked that she could get to know where she lived before finding a place.

When Del first started to pop up to her room, she had thought he was doing it to be nice. Then, she realized she'd started counting on those early morning chats. She didn't know a lot of people, and she hated to socialize, but with Del, she hadn't minded.

Coffee in the mornings together had been one of her very few social outlets. That had all stopped when they had their blowup at work.

"Oh."

"I missed this."

She hadn't realized how much she had come to depend on those chats until they had stopped. She had been too much of a coward to seek him out though. She didn't really want to face her attraction to him. Not now. And not then.

She didn't respond because she couldn't. Emma just didn't have it in her to talk about feelings, especially these. She was still raw from their blowup and while they had sort of made up, she wasn't sure how long it would last.

"And then, I had some bad moments when I thought you might be dating Drew."

She shook her head. "Dead Guy Drew?"

"I didn't know you knew about his nickname."

"Just like I know the team calls me Beautiful Mind."

He made a face.

She smiled. "No, really, I don't mind. It's kind of cool."

"You think it's cool you have a nickname like that?"

"At first I was kind of upset, but when I talked to Sean, he explained it was their way of making me part of the group. He said in situations like the one we work in, nicknames are kind of their way of accepting me. Like how everyone calls Graeme Goldilocks."

"I thought that maybe you would go out with him."

"Him? Graeme?" It took her a moment to comprehend what he was talking about. "Oh, Drew? Because we're both odd?"

He blinked. "No. I thought because you had common interests."

"I don't like dead people."

"That's good to hear," Peg said, as she set their plates in front of them. "Anything else?"

"I'm fine," she said.

Del agreed. Peg left them alone again and Emma's stomach grumbled.

"So, you thought I was dating him?"

"You two seemed to spend a lot of time together when you first started working there."

That much was true. When she first started working at Task Force Hawaii, she and Drew had hit if off. Both of them were gamers, and he had been a soothing balm to her libido. She'd had no feelings for him other than those of a friend. With her hormones working overtime, she had needed the distraction. Drew had needed someone to talk to about his own obsession.

Emma rolled her eyes. "I think he just wanted to get the low down on Cat."

"Cat? My Cat?"

She blinked at his tone. "She's yours?"

"Not like that. I mean, on my team."

"Yeah. I have a feeling he's been very interested in her for a very long time. For some reason, he thought he could get information from me."

"How do you know that?"

"That he wanted information from me?"

"No, that he's interested in Cat."

"Well, on the whole, asking me for information was a tipoff, Del."

He looked up from his burger and stared at her.

"What?"

"You hardly ever call me by my nickname."

She shrugged.

"So, back to Drew."

"What about him?"

"It was just his questions?"

"No. Whenever he would talk to her, his eyes would dilate."

He stopped drinking his water and looked at her. "What?"

"When a person is attracted, his eyes can dilate."

"Oh. So, you think the feeling is mutual?"

She frowned as she thought about it. "I don't know. I just noticed it with Drew because he kept dropping things and running into walls and tables when she was around. I thought he had a concussion, so I looked closely at his eyes."

"That would definitely be an opposite-attracts kind of thing."

"Like you kissing me?" She asked.

"We are not opposites."

She rolled her eyes. "You don't have to pretend you don't think I'm odd."

"Odd." He cocked his head to the side. "Not what I would call you."

She snorted. "Then you're the only one."

"No. I would call you quirky. I like quirky."

"The nice way of calling me odd. That's okay."

"Why is it okay?"

"I have never fit in, and I am at a place that I am okay with it. Some people will never fit in with the crowd, but that also makes me very unique."

"You are definitely unique. And, I disagree that we aren't the same."

"Indeed? What do we have in common?"

"Other than we apparently both like to ride a Harley at night around the island?"

"Who doesn't like doing that?"

"You would be surprised. My sister for one person."

"Marlena?"

She had learned about his sisters over the last few months. Emma had soaked up any bit of information about his life, his normal life. She might have accepted that she would never fit in, but it didn't mean she didn't want to know more about the man.

"She freaked when I took her up on Pali Highway."

"Let me guess, she didn't want to hold on tight enough?"

He nodded.

She chuckled. "Del, your sister didn't want to hold on to you."

He frowned. "Why not?"

He was very smart when it came to his job, but he had a hard time understanding women. She had seen it more than once.

"I held on to you because, well...I liked it. Your sister does not. Now, if you had been another man she was interested in—"

"Stop right there. My sisters are all virgins and have no sexual feelings."

She blinked. "Is that a fact?"

"You want to talk about that scene in your brother's

kitchen again?"

"Truce," she said with a smile.

"There is something else we have in common."

"Yeah, what's that?"

"I think both of us are tenacious. We will not give up when we get our teeth into something."

She thought about that for a second, then she smiled. "You might just be right—for once."

***

Del walked her to her condo. It had been ingrained in him during his youth to look after his date. And that was what this was. He wasn't sure how Emma looked at it, but he was counting this as their first official date.

They arrived at her door. Del watched as she unlocked and opened it.

"You coming in?"

He smiled. "I'd like to, but no."

She frowned, and, for some odd reason, that made him happy. Maybe knowing she was disappointed that they were not going to spend the night together was the reason.

"You want to explain to me why?"

She was standing in the doorway, the light from her hallway lighting a halo around her head. From the moment they had met, she had knocked him off balance. Like right now while she looked at him with those mermaid eyes of hers, he felt slightly dizzy.

"It's hard to explain."

"Whatever."

She turned to leave, but he caught her arm, then slowly drew her closer.

"I'll try to explain, though," he said, slipping his arms around her waist and enjoying the feel of her pressed up against him. "I think we both need to get used to the idea of this, and I am not too sure that we should just jump in."

She pulled her full bottom lip between her teeth and he groaned. He couldn't resist a taste, just one. He swooped in, taking her mouth in an open-mouthed, carnal kiss. He did his best, trying to pour in all the feelings that had been haunting him for months. Lust being the primary one. By the time he pulled back, he knew she did not have a doubt about his intentions. Hell, his own head was swimming from the simple kiss.

"Are you sure you want to wait?" she asked, her voice husky with desire.

He chuckled. "Yeah. We have important work we do, and you are a contractor with me. It could really cause problems at work if we are not completely sure."

She sighed. "I hate when you make sense."

"Yeah, it kind of bites."

She rose to her tiptoes and brushed her mouth over his before he let her go.

"Good night, Del."

"Night."

He waited until he heard her lock the door before he turned to walk to the elevator. He could head home, but he knew he wouldn't get much sleep. The dual worry of the missing girl and his growing attraction to Emma would keep him up and going for hours.

When he got on his bike, he headed back to the office. At least there he might be able to find something else to keep him busy.

* * *

Jin Phillips arrived at her small house in Aiea and found a manila envelope on the front step. It was well past one in the morning, so she didn't know how long it had been sitting out there.

She glanced down the street, then back up the other way and saw nothing. She picked it up, unlocked her door, then slipped inside. After shutting and locking it, she walked to her kitchen.

It was a small house, but she wouldn't be there for long. She knew this story was going to be big, and she was in front of it before everyone else. Of course, no one had found any information out in the last few days. Frustrated didn't even cover it.

She turned on a light and looked at the package. It was very light, as if it might not even have anything inside. Although, the last little bit about the goddess tattoo had been dead on the money. A very nasty phone conversation with Adam had confirmed there was something to it. So, she wouldn't turn up her nose at any help.

The envelope had her name and a little note written on it.

Ms. Phillips. If you want to know more about the Akua killer, please look inside.

Jin knew it might be a trick. Many of her colleagues didn't like her. They found her too pushy, too loud…just too much. She'd even had a problem with one other reporter because he found out that she was half Asian, half African American.

She pushed the thought of that asshole aside and carefully opened up the package, which held only a note.

Each woman had a Sugar Daddy, and he made sure he was the last.

CHAPTER EIGHT

The next three days, Emma worked nonstop looking for some kind of pattern, a connection, anything. Del had called daily, and she had answered. More of it had to do with the fact she wanted to be kept in the loop about Susan. The idea of what the young woman was going through, of what that monster was doing to her...Emma shivered. It was what nightmares were made of.

She stepped back from her whiteboard and looked over what she had written. Bloody hell, she knew it was connected, that there *had* to be something, anything. But so far, she had not found it. An idea was there, but it danced right on the outskirts of her thought process.

She noticed a note she had written down and she grabbed it up. She wanted to ask Adam about the owner of the SUV. She knew that it had been reported stolen hours before Grace Singh was found, but something was off in the statement.

She picked up her mobile to call Adam, but her doorbell rang. Del usually banged on her door like a gorilla, but maybe he was trying something new. When she looked through the peephole and found Jaime standing there smiling, she sighed. Why did she feel so…disappointed? And irritated. She was definitely irritated, but not with Jaime. Mainly, with her brother. He probably was worried about her, so he sent Jaime over to check up on her.

She opened the door and Jaime laughed. "Don't ever go into diplomacy, love, you would never make it."

Emma snorted, then chuckled. They had started off rocky in their relationship. She hadn't trusted the former MI-6 spy because of her past. The feeling had been mutual for Jaime. But, because they both loved Sean, they had learned to get along. Emma was certain there were a lot of times that Jaime was just thankful to have another woman around to talk to.

She was dressed like she had spent her entire life in Hawaii. The halter dress was blue, one of Jaime's favorite colors, which contrasted nicely with her ebony skin. White hibiscus flowers decorated the fabric and, as always, it fit her perfectly. It clung to her body as if it had been custom made for her. And…she had one of those bodies all men seemed to like. Full chested, full hipped, and very feminine. She always made Emma feel like a twelve-year-old boy. Of course, since Emma was wearing a pair of board shorts and an Iron Man T-shirt, there was probably a reason for that.

"Come on in. What did Sean make you come here for?"

Jaime stepped over the threshold. She was holding a reusable grocery bag. "First of all, he did not *make* me come."

"Then why are you here?"

"I'm just checking up on you, and I brought you food." She pulled a plastic container from the bag, then walked into Emma's kitchen. She opened the fridge. "Randy is convinced you don't eat enough, and from the looks of this, you don't."

She made a face. She probably had several energy drinks and molded over fruit in there. "I order in a lot."

Jamie shut the fridge and turned around. "Well, a good home-cooked meal wouldn't hurt you every now and then."

Emma couldn't argue with that. "What is it?"

"Randy's chicken and dumplings. Rain is coming, so he thought you might be in the mood."

She didn't say anything as she started going through her email. After all the years that she had to look after herself, she still didn't know how to react to their actions. It was really sweet of them how they all looked out for her. It didn't make it any easier for her to say thank you, or explain just how much it meant to her.

"Was there anything else?" she asked.

"Here's your coat, what's your hurry?"

Emma looked up. "What?"

"It's an old joke." Emma said nothing. "Never mind. I just wanted to talk to you for a bit."

She studied the woman, then panic hit her out of nowhere. "What? What's going on? You all are not going back in the field?"

The three of them had been spies and then security detail before they had decided to settle down in Hawaii. They had been doing quite a bit of consulting, and Sean had assured her they would never do the undercover work again. All of them had too many close calls in the past.

Jaime shook her head. "Oh, no. No, love, I didn't mean to worry you."

"Are you sure? Sean has a tendency to leave things out that I might worry about."

He was always trying to protect her, and it wasn't something she was used to. She'd been on her own since she was fifteen, when she was left without her parents. Even before that, she was on her own a lot. They tended to move frequently because of her father's work and her mother...well, her mother had been a different kind of mother.

"I promise. I don't want to, and if either of those idiots

even thought about it, I would definitely put my foot down. I like not having to look behind me all the time, and I am enjoying life too much. But I have something else on my mind." There was a gleam in her eyes that set alarm bells off. "I have been thinking about you...and a certain team leader."

Emma blinked. "What?"

"Emma, don't even try to play dumb with me. I know you fancy him."

"What woman wouldn't? Why are you asking me this again?"

"Defensive answers make me more interested."

Emma sighed. "All right. I have had a crush on him. And, it's truly embarrassing when he looks at me with those eyes of his..." She closed her eyes and shivered. When she opened them, she found Jaime smiling at her.

"Yes, I had an idea over the last couple of months that you were at least interested in him."

"You think he's out of my league."

"Oh, no, love, you are out of his."

"Why would you say that?"

"You're a woman. We are the far superior sex."

Emma smiled. "That's true. I just never thought he would be interested in me. Until he kissed me the other day. Then he took me for a ride on his Harley."

Jaime sat down on the sofa and smiled. "Do tell."

She opened her mouth, then shut it. "I'm not really good at the girl stuff."

"You mean gossiping and the like?" Emma nodded. "I can understand that. I only did it on the job. It's not like I had a lot of time for gossip when I was younger."

Then it hit Emma. They had more in common than she had previously realized.

"We both grew up on the streets."

Jaime nodded. "And, at a very early age, we had to take on responsibilities that children should not ever have to handle."

"I was fifteen."

"And sheltered."

"Not *that* sheltered."

Jaime cocked her head. "Indeed?"

"Yeah, I wasn't a virginal saint, and I am definitely not one now. I lived like a normal person every now and then. I had a few...nights of fun."

"But then, you would be on the move again."

She shrugged. "It's weird, I thought I would end up in Thailand or possibly in England. Sean found some properties we own in both places after going through Dad's mess of finances." Half brother and half sister had not met until they were adults. Emma had not known her father had left her so much money until Sean started going through everything. "When Sean brought me here, it felt like…"

"Home."

Emma nodded.

"Me too. Weird, because I love the seasons, but there is just something that felt right here. I had always thought it was Sean that drew me to Hawaii, and I know he is part of it. But here, I feel whole."

Emma sighed. "Yes. It makes me feel as if I belong."

"And Del helps with that."

"In a way. He doesn't think I'm weird. He says I'm quirky."

Jaime's lips twitched. "Is that a fact?"

"He also said he and I are a lot alike because we are both stubborn about completing projects."

Jaime pursed her lips. "You know, he might have something there. And tell me this. What was his kiss like?"

The rush of the memory hit her with full force. Her head started to spin as her pulse increased. Emma felt her mouth curve.

"He made my brain melt."

"Then he is definitely worth a try."

Emma sighed. "Unfortunately, he gave me all this bunk

about wanting to take it slowly because we work together, and we need to be sure."

Jaime blinked. "He said that to you?"

Emma nodded.

"Oh, love, be careful of that one."

"I don't know why it is so important to wait. Sex is sex. A basic human need, and a good way to release some stress."

"True."

"And the exercise benefits are wonderful.

"But, Del just doesn't want sex, Emma. He wants more from the sound of it."

She pulled her bottom lip between her teeth. It was something that had been worrying her the last few days.

"I don't know if I can do that."

"Why not?"

"I know it's hard for you to understand this, but I don't handle emotions well. Relationships are hard for me. All of them, not just the sexual ones."

"But you do fine with Randy, Sean, and me."

"You have no idea how difficult it is for me. All that…emotion. Sean always wants to hug me."

Jaime gave her an understanding smile.

"Maybe that's why Del wants to go slowly. He wants to give you time to get used to it."

Her throat ached all of a sudden, and she felt her eyes burn. For months, she'd convinced herself that nothing would ever happen. They were too different, too…volatile together. But thinking about the fact that he wanted to try to have a relationship with her, or at least go on a date or two, almost overwhelmed her.

"Emma, are you all right?"

She nodded.

"Tell me," Jaime said, coming around the breakfast bar to slip her arm around Emma's shoulders.

"I don't think I can, Jaime." She looked at her. "I have feelings for him, but I am not good at expressing them.

And I have a tendency to upset people with my bluntness."

"Del doesn't seem to mind that."

"Long term is not good for me. Relationships are not good for me. I don't know how to do them. Other people always say they understand and I believe they try but after awhile they get frustrated with my behavior."

"What do you mean?"

"People never say what they mean. They always speak in half truths, and I can't understand them. If there was a blueprint, or directions…I could handle that."

"Oh, Emma," Jaime said, a light chuckle dancing through her voice. "Believe me, I understand. I almost lost your brother because of it."

She looked at her.

"I had a plan. Love wasn't supposed to happen so fast for me, so early in my life. So, when he asked for marriage…I said no. I paid for it. And, the result of it is that the three of us found each other."

"I don't have the same emotions that other people do."

"No, Emma, you have more. You have been through so much in your life, that the only way you could deal with some of it was to file it away. It helped you through it, but it also makes you very vulnerable. You had to protect yourself. And I think a lot of stimuli is bad for you. Big crowds, too much activity…I've seen you. Sometimes you can deal with them, especially when Sean is around. And, I think the right man would make it easier for you to let some of that out. Del is the kind of guy who could comfort you when it gets to be too much."

She nodded.

"Now, let me help you clean this place up, and good God, woman, take a shower."

Emma smiled. "Thanks, Jaime."

"Anytime. We women have to stick together."

* * *

After some snacks Jaime had foisted on her, Emma

was feeling much better.

"Make sure you get some rest, Emma. Sean is very worried about you."

"I'll make a note to call him every day. Or at least text him."

Jaime picked up her purse. "And remember what I said about Del. Think about giving the man a chance."

After she was gone, Emma went to the board again and looked at it. Then...something caught her eye. Goddesses. What was the word she saw in the Japanese report...*kami*.

There had been a report about a woman who had been attacked. Or, was she killed...?

Emma pulled up the document and felt the spark of excitement. She had a lead. Not much of one, but she had one nonetheless.

She picked up her laptop and went to her lanai. Settling in the chair for a research session, she got to work.

* * *

Jaime was attacked, and not in her favorite way, when she walked through the door.

"So?" Sean asked as Randy was coming up behind him. How on God's green earth did she bag two delicious men like these? And when did they actually turn into such nervous Nellies?

"She's fine. She's working on this case, and I take it that she's pretty focused on that. They all seem to be. With Susan Tanaka still missing, Emma is doing everything she can to find more info out, make the connections. You know how she gets. Factor in the little romance on the side, then she's got a lot to handle."

She tried to walk by the guys, but Sean grabbed her and spun her around. "Romance?"

"I think she and Del are having a little flirt going on. That's all."

She knew it was more than that. A man like Martin Delano did not wait, unless he thought it was important.

"I'll have a talk with him," Sean said as Randy nodded.

"No, you will not. Your sister is almost twenty-seven years old. She does not need her brother and his boyfriend roughing up a potential...date."

She had almost said lover, but thankfully stopped in time. Lord knows what Sean would have done if she had said that.

"She's doing okay then?"

Jaime nodded as she cupped his face. "She's fine, love. In fact, I think she's finding her place in the world. She loves working with TFH. It gives her life purpose. I told her to call you soon and she promised."

He nodded, and she turned to walk away. She held the little bag of lingerie she had just spent entirely too much money on. "Now, I bought this teeny, tiny maid's uniform if there is anyone interested in role playing tonight."

She started walking up the stairs, and laughed when she heard the footsteps rushing up behind her. Men were so easy.

* * *

Emma rushed to TFH headquarters with her news.

"What has your hair on fire, lass?" McGregor asked as she dashed through the door.

"Hey, is Del around? I think I have some connections."

"He's got company," he said as he bent his head to the office.

She saw the newswoman who had been such a bitch the last few weeks in there. It was at that point, she realized they had shut down all of the computers.

"Why is he talking to her?"

"No reason to be jealous, love. He was ordered to talk to her."

She frowned at McGregor. The giant Scot was often an ass, but she liked him. Now, he was just confusing her.

"What are you talking about?"

"He's not *interested* in her."

She hadn't even thought about that. Emma looked back at the window and found Del staring at her. There was a little smile curving his lips, and she felt her heart jump a beat. Bloody hell, he was barely trying and she was melting.

"See, there, he only has eyes for you."

Without looking, she smacked McGregor on the back of the head.

"Bloody hell. What was that for?"

"Behave or I'll tell Elle how you look at her when you think no one sees you."

He frowned at her. "I do not."

She looked at him. "Yes, you do. Remember, I have a photographic memory, and I always remember dates. It was September third, and she dropped something in the hallway. You stood there staring at her arse. So, stop being a wanker, or I will tell her."

"Tell who what?" an annoying voice said from behind her. Emma turned around and found the newswoman behind her. Del was standing behind Jin looking irritated. With her possibly?

"It was personal, so none of your business."

Jin faltered a bit. Apparently, bitchy newswoman didn't get rude answers that often. "And you would be?"

"Still, none of your business."

McGregor coughed, and Emma had a sneaking suspicion that he was trying not to laugh.

"Well, you put me in my place."

"Actually, I believe that your place lies beyond the doors outside of our squad room, but that is just a personal opinion."

Her eyebrows shot up. "Well, I guess that is the end of this discussion. Thank you for your time, Captain Delano."

She offered Del her hand, and a flirty smile that made Emma want to smack it off her. What the hell did the woman think she was doing?

"Doona fash yourself, lass," McGregor whispered as they watched Del walk Jin out of the building. *Don't worry.*

"What makes you think I'm worried?"

"Because you look like you wanted to tear out her heart and dine on it with a nice bottle of red wine."

She closed her eyes. "I was that obvious?"

He chuckled and she opened her eyes. "Doona worry, love. I think he feels the same way."

As Del made his way back, Adam joined him. "Hey, Emma, you have something?"

"Something." Her mind started work again. *Goddesses*. "Oh, yes. The reason I am here."

"What do you have?" Del asked.

"I have a killer. Or, at least a profile. If I am right, this bastard has been doing this a very long time."

* * *

The reporter was proving to be the most wonderful asset. Only in America would he be able to use a reporter so easily. He only had a few more days before he would lose his *special friend*.

A wail rose up. She was awake again. With anticipation singing in his blood, he went back to work.

MELISSA SCHROEDER

CHAPTER NINE

It took a good ten minutes to get everyone into the squad room. Emma and Adam were working on bringing up her research on the big screen as everyone took their seats.

"So, tell us, Beautiful Mind, what do you have?" Marcus said.

She slanted a look at Del, and he had to fight the smile. The woman liked to be right. It was another trait they both shared.

"I started going through reports in the last two years in this area."

"We haven't had any murders like this one," Drew said.

Another look from her. Okay, so he got what she meant. Drew was a geek, but he didn't have a lot of common sense.

"I am talking about the Pacific Rim area. It was hard because there were several different languages to sort out." She clicked on a few buttons. "I found two that caught my interest in Japan. Both of them had tattoos when they were found, but they did not have them before they were abducted. Same MO. Two to three weeks, then they were found just a few hours old."

"No suspects?" Del asked.

"Not really. But these two had something that we heard with Susan's situation. There was a mysterious man the women were dating. The one thing that stood out was that he was Gaijin—an outsider."

"So, definitely not from Japan," Adam murmured.

She nodded. "I am guessing he was white, but not sure if he was from the US or somewhere else. He could have been European. No one, from what I could figure out had talked to the man, so I am assuming he was labeled because he was white. One thing was for sure, he had money from what they said. A friend claimed the first woman, Grace, had gotten quite a lot of jewelry from her mystery man."

"Maybe he has something against Asian women?" Del asked.

She shrugged. "I don't deal with that kind of thing. I just deal with the MO and connections. But, it could be that he found it easier to move about in these societies."

"Even if he is Gaijin?" Adam asked.

She nodded. "Think about it. First, some of the women might not tell family about their new boyfriend. Secondly, he probably found women who were attracted to men with a lot of money. These two came from very simple backgrounds. A man who promises to take care of them might be irresistible. Convincing them not to tell anyone much about their new boyfriend might not be that difficult. It would definitely be less difficult than dating a woman who would want to show him off to her family."

"So, you found those two? That's it?" Del was kind of disappointed. Two women who had been murdered and tattooed might be a lead, but it would take a lot to convince others of the connection.

She shook her head. "No, there are others." She clicked a few more buttons. More case files appeared with pictures. "First, there was this woman. She was found in Japan, and had a tattoo when she was found. As did this woman in Korea. But both of their tattoos faded in a few hours of them being found."

"So, they had tattoos, but they disappeared?" McGregor asked.

She nodded. "Which means he had not perfected his

work at that point."

"Why did they fade?"

"Because he killed them too fast," Elle said. "I remember now. There was another case like this with a traffic victim here. The woman was on her way home from the tattoo artist when she was killed in an accident."

Emma nodded. "Exactly. That's why I remembered, because you told me about it."

"Why would it fade?" Del asked.

She motioned to Elle to explain it.

"Well, we...I mean all of you have tattoos. It takes a while to heal. About two weeks to be precise. Blood must flow to the marked skin for it to heal and leave the tattoo. If the person dies, then the tattoo cannot cure properly. Depending on the length of time between getting the ink and her death will determine how long it stays."

"It fades, just like this woman's." Emma punched a few buttons. When she was onto something big, whether it was working out a glitch in a computer system, or one of their cases, she glowed. "And these two women in Korea. I wouldn't have connected them all if the MO had not been similar. Apparently, in each of these cases, they were gone for a week."

"He was working it out...testing his theory?" Cat asked. "That's sick."

"It wasn't like we were going to be dealing with a person who is all there. And because of this, I linked one more to him. There was another woman found in Korea, no tattoo, but she had been missing for over a month. Also, she was not posed, and was found in a wooded area. I am not sure she would have been found if a hiker hadn't stumbled over her body."

"What do you think that was about?" Adam asked.

"I think there is a good chance that she was his original test case. Although, I am not entirely sure that this was his first foray into killing. There is a chance that he slowly worked out his plans for killing women over years.

Attempted rapes will be something to look at, of course. There is a very good chance that he killed animals as a child."

Elle nodded. "Serial killers often start out torturing animals early in their life. Did they find any DNA?"

Emma shook her head. "This bastard is clever. He knew just what to do and how to do it."

"Why Hawaii? And why Japan and Korea?" Del asked.

"You'd have to ask a profiler that and, without any other kind of data, it would be hard for me to guess. He could have just been in the areas and took the time to kill. That's why I think you should check out all these places the women lived and worked. If you can find a connection to someone who traveled the same route, that would help."

"Not piling on that much work, are you, lass?"

She didn't smile. "It shouldn't be too hard. The last woman in Japan was killed three months before Grace Singh disappeared. Looking at who came in from Japan during those months, then you can narrow it down from there. More than likely white, and male, old enough for something like this, but not too old—or at least in good shape. And money. Lots of money."

"Yeah, he would have to be able to carry dead weight, and that is never easy," Marcus said.

"I sent everything to your phones. I need to do some more looking on my end to see if he has been anywhere else, or if anything with goddesses has been mentioned."

"Another thing," Marcus mentioned. "Three in each place."

"That we know of right now. That's why I want to do some research."

"It could have something to do with the trinity. Three." This from McGregor.

Everyone turned to him.

"Explain," Del said.

"The trinity goes back into all mythology and through

Christian history. In the Christian church, you have the Father, Son, and Holy Ghost."

"And other mythology...that makes sense," Emma said. He could tell from the look in her eye, and the distraction in her tone, that she was already thinking through something.

"Yes, and the Fates...the three with control," Elle said.

McGregor glanced at his nemesis. "Do you mean to tell me I have something to contribute?"

Elle said nothing to that.

"Okay, so we might have someone working the trinity, finding three women, then moving on," Del said.

"And he spends time with them," Elle said.

"Except everyone said that Grace wasn't seeing anyone," Floyd stated. "Her coworkers, her friends, family...they said she hadn't been on a date in months."

"But, she was out the night she disappeared...and not with friends," Cat said. She looked at Adam. "Traditional?"

"Yes, and her mother is Korean."

"What does that mean?" Del asked.

Cat explained, "It means that her parents might not have been happy with her dating a white man. Many very traditional Asian parents do not want their children dating outside of their own ethnicity. Heck, even one boyfriend's mother had issues with me because I have only Hawaiian and Japanese in my blood. They were Chinese. It isn't always an issue, and one that isn't that big these days, but some parents hold onto their traditions. But there was a diversion into another race at some point because Singh is Indian and not Korean."

"True, although they could have changed it along the way. And, she was definitely a woman who worried about her parents. She lived with them, took care of them. They were quite a bit older than she was," Adam said. "There's a very good chance that she didn't tell them."

"But, she's dead. Why would her friends hold back?"

Del asked.

"Not sure. It could be a way of protecting her reputation. Were they all Asian?" Emma asked.

He nodded. "But there was one teacher that I could not get a hold of. She had an emergency with a family member back on the mainland. In fact, she could be back, so maybe she has something."

"We need to look at all of the men in her life," Del said. "Everything, from the men she worked with to the mailman on her route."

Emma shook her head. "He won't be *in her life* as you call it. This bastard is rich."

"Why do you say rich?" Drew asked.

Del answered for her, as he kept her gaze. "He arrived on the island within the last few months and found a house that is isolated. Not that easy to do. And remember, Susan called the man she was seeing *Sugar Daddy*. But…they just said he was older."

Cat chuckled. "Anyone over thirty is old to those girls. They're in college."

"I'll get hold of that other teacher, see if she knew anything," Adam said, heading to his office.

"Elle, I sent you the forensic reports and translated them for you. I didn't know if you read Korean or Japanese."

"Speak, that I can do, reading…another matter altogether. Thank you." She looked at Drew. "Let's go."

As Elle and Drew were walking away, Del noticed Emma was picking up her things.

"Cat, you and McGregor go check on the status of the search. I know it was bare bones right now, but with this tropical system moving in, I thought it would be good to get another rundown. Marcus, you speak a little Japanese, yes?"

"Could you call any of your contacts in Japan, see what you can find out about the status of those murders? See if you can discover what they didn't put in those reports?"

He nodded. "I have a couple of buddies stationed there right now. One I served with actually stayed on, married a sweet little Japanese woman. And—he has something to do with the police or something over there. I'll dig up his info."

When the others went off to do his bidding, Del turned to talk to Emma, and realized she was on her way out the door. She was in the hallway before he caught up with her.

"Hey, that was some great work," he said, feeling like an idiot.

For a moment, she just stared at him. Of course she knew it was good work. The woman was a genius. She didn't need him to tell her that she had done a good job. But still, her eyes lit up and her cheeks turned pink.

"Thank you. I still need to work some of it out."

He nodded. "So, how about dinner?"

"No, I already have something to eat."

Again, she just stared at him, and he had to fight the urge to roll his eyes. "I'm asking you out."

"Oh." Then she said nothing.

"Yes, no?"

She sighed. "I really want to work on this."

"I could bring food by your apartment."

Now he was just being pathetic. He heard the desperation in his own voice. Apparently, she didn't pick up on it. She frowned at him.

"I said I already had food to eat." The woman was not being stupid, she just had other things on her mind. It was the way she worked. And it was one of the things about her he admired. But it didn't make it easy to romance her.

"I wanted to bring you dinner so we could share it."

"Oh."

"Yeah, oh."

"Randy sent over chicken and dumplings. Do you like that?"

"Homemade chicken and dumplings?" She nodded. "You got it. Seven?"

She nodded again and offered him a shy smile. She turned and started down the hallway again, but turned back around to hurry back to him. Rising to her tiptoes, she brushed her mouth over his cheek. Then she was rushing out of the building.

He stood there for a long time, his heart in his throat. A little peck on the cheek and he was…enchanted.

Damn, he had it bad, but he couldn't remember why he should be bothered by it, and he didn't want to. He had people to call, a mayor and a governor who wanted updates and all he cared about was having dinner with Emma.

***

Emma had the chicken and dumplings on the stove simmering when she heard a knock at the door. This time she knew it was Del.

She hurried to the door and looked through the peephole. When she saw him, her heartbeat danced. She opened the door. He had a few drops of rain in his hair. He smiled at her.

"Hey."

That one little word made her mind melt. Not the word itself, but the way he said it. His deep voice rolled over it, as if he were saying more than a greeting.

"Hey."

"Wanna let me come in?"

She felt her face heat as she stepped back to give him room to walk in.

He did, as he pulled off his jacket. He was still wearing his gun. She knew that he kept it with him most of the time. It was as usual to see him wear it as a shirt. And there was part of her that found it damned sexy. Not the gun, because she really didn't like them. But the way he wore it. It probably had something to do with anthropological meaning. Protection or something.

Good lord. Or something? Yep, he was killing her brain cells each time he kissed her.

"I hadn't noticed it started raining."

"Just a light drizzle right now, but soon, it will be a mess." He drew in a deep breath as she took his coat and hung it on her coat rack. "Damn, that smells good."

She smiled. "Jaime brought it by today. Apparently, the guys are worried that I don't eat enough."

"I wonder about that myself."

"I eat. And I do have a high metabolism."

He walked into her living room. "It still looks like something exploded in here."

She chuckled. "Do you want a beer?"

"You have beer?"

She shrugged. "Randy likes to have a beer every now and then. I keep it on hand."

He shook his head. "We might get a call because of the weather."

"It's supposed to be that bad?"

"No, but there is going to be a ton of rain, and that can lead to flooding. Remember what happened with the water main breaking and spilling all the sewage into Waikiki a few months ago?" She nodded. "So, you know that anything can happen around here when we get any kind of rain. They always need folks to help."

She nodded as she rose up on her tiptoes to get a couple of bowls from her cupboard. Del stepped in behind her and set his hands on her waist. She could smell him then, the rich scent of his aftershave, and the clean scent of rain clung to him.

He lifted one hand from her waist and brushed her hair over her shoulder. Bending his head down to her neck, he nuzzled her. His breath was warm against her neck.

"It's been a long few days since we have been alone."

She nodded as she set the bowls on the counter. He stepped closer, pressing against her. She could feel his erection against her rear end. He nipped at the nape of her neck.

"I used to have fantasies about your neck. Still do."

Heat flared low in her belly, as she felt her body respond to his words, and whatever he was doing to her neck.

"My neck. How odd."

He chuckled, pressing his mouth against her flesh. The vibration of it filtered over her. She shivered in response. Good lord, they both had their clothes on and she was melting right there. Every hormone in her body was screaming for relief, and he had barely touched her.

"I really wanted to know what it tasted like. Especially now that it covers it."

She wanted to say something, but she couldn't. Her throat had gone unbearably dry. Her body throbbed with need. It was embarrassing that all he had to do was tease her just a little, and she was ready to rip her clothes off and jump him.

With a sigh, he stepped away and turned her. He leaned his forehead against hers. "You test my control, Emma."

"I don't know what I am doing to you."

Humor softened the features of his face. He had such a pretty face. "I know. That makes you even more enticing."

He kissed her then, with the rain tapping against her window, and the smell of supper surrounding her. And right there, she realized she was in love with him. Nothing in life had prepared her for it, and she doubted anyone could prepare for this. This bigger than life man had snuck in and stolen her heart. When he pulled back, he looked at her. His brow furrowed.

"Emma? Are you okay?"

She shook her head. "Not sure, but I will be at some point."

He opened his mouth to respond, but his phone went off.

"Gotta get that."

"Of course," she said.

He answered and listened. The lightness in his eyes dimmed, and the warmth of the room seemed to seep away. "Where?"

"Okay. Can you pick me up? I have my bike and I am at Emma's."

He hung up and sighed.

"They found Susan?" she asked, not really wanting to know.

Del shook his head. "No. Her cell phone just went on though."

He hesitated and she shook her head. "Go. Come here when you are done."

He nodded and grabbed his jacket off the coat rack. Then he turned around and came back her.

"Stay here. Please."

She smiled. "No worries. I have some more work to do."

He kissed her. The sweetness of it stole over her, tugged at her heart, and captured her soul. If she had not been in love with him before, she would have fallen right on the ground at his feet. He pulled back and she wanted to protest, but could not. They both had work to do.

"I'll call."

She shook her head. "Just come back."

Comprehension came fast and his mouth curved. Her heart warmed at the sight.

He kissed her quick, hot and hard, then he was gone. She walked to the window and looked out over the water. She could see the outer bands of the storm approach. She prayed it was just a phone and not the woman.

CHAPTER TEN

Del's nerves were raw, and his head pounding by the time Adam took the exit to Ko'olau Golf Course. Lights lit up the night, as Adam followed the directions of the HPD officer in charge of controlling the traffic in and out of the parking lot. The rain slashed at the windows, coming down so hard, it bounced off the hood of Adam's TFH pickup.

"I can't help but think this is planned," Adam said as he drove to the back corner of the parking lot where everyone had assembled.

"You mean because of the storm?" Del nodded. "Yeah, might be. If this is one guy doing all these killings, I could see him getting particular joy out of this. It's a mess out here; the storm will make it difficult."

"Add in that he wants to make sure there is no evidence, and this kind of storm would definitely ensure nothing would be left. Still, it hasn't been two weeks, so I wonder if this was all sped up because of the storm."

"It might be. Emma has gotten a little more information tonight, things she put together since the meeting this morning. She is going to focus on the goddesses and the deity aspect. She thinks that might pop up in some other reports. Even if he didn't tattoo them, there is always the chance she could find another connection. Writings, postings to social media. I don't know why the hell people are surprised when their social media posts take them down."

Adam nodded. "I looked over some of those things she sent me. I also talked to Tamilya Avery."

"You mean the woman who works for Conner Dillon?"

Conner Dillon was a former FBI agent who now ran one of the most reputable security firms in the world.

Adam nodded. "She's former FBI and used to be a profiler. She agreed with Emma's assessment. She said she'd hunt around, see if any of her old colleagues had heard anything, but she hadn't heard anything herself."

"I hate to say it, but I have a feeling the governor is going want to call the FBI in."

"Well, that's what we are now. Their…go between."

Del tossed him a look as he put the pickup in park. "Like they will see it that way. You know they'll want to take over the entire thing."

Adam shrugged, but said nothing else as he turned off his truck. Del knew his friend was trying to come up with something to lead to the real question he wanted to ask.

"Spit it out."

He cleared his throat. "So, you're like an item now?"

He glanced at his second-in-command. Del could tell Adam was trying to keep his voice professional. More than likely it was because his friend knew Del did not do "talks." He said nothing.

"You just might want to let people know, because there are a couple of guys in HPD who have a thing for her," Adam said.

Del grumbled and tried not to show any other reaction. Still, he felt his temper heating at the thought of HPD officers checking out Emma. She had no interest in them, and more than likely had no idea that they were attracted to her. Still, it didn't sit well with him. "Especially Drew."

That made him chuckle. "No, he doesn't have interest in her. His eye is wandering to another member of the team."

Adam frowned. "Elle is too old for him."

"First, she would kick your ass, or arse as she likes to say, if she heard you."

"She's almost thirty-seven, but I was talking more about maturity."

Del nodded. "Either way, you're wrong. He has a crush on Cat according to Emma."

"Cat," Adam said with a laugh. "No way."

He shrugged. "She said something about his eyes dilating."

Adam pursed his lips. "Yeah, he does follow her around a lot. But that doesn't mean you're getting out of talking about Emma."

"I think I did because we're here, and I'm the boss. I don't talk about my feelings. I just punch things."

Adam reached into his back seat and grabbed a couple of rain ponchos with the TFH logo on them. "Hey, not my fault you told me to pick you up at her condo."

Del tugged the poncho over his head and looked at Adam. He was spending an inordinate amount of time pulling the poncho over his head. Then it hit him.

"Aw, *fuck*, I was on speaker," Del said shaking his head. "You should have told me."

"Not my fault. You know every time I call there is a chance you're on speaker."

"That doesn't excuse you."

He shrugged. "Not changing what happened. Some people lost bets tonight."

"On what? We were just going to have dinner."

"You mean you haven't…"

"Good God, are you a woman? Why is this important to you?"

Adam chuckled. "You're *'ohana*, Boss. Whether you like it or not, we are all in your business. We share."

Del rolled his eyes and stepped out of the truck. The place was flooded with lights, and he saw his team at the very back of the lot, not too far from where the path to the Likeke Falls started. They made their way over as McGregor was handing out a few umbrellas, although the banyan trees were shielding them from some of it.

"Left just in range I take it?" Del asked.

Adam nodded. "Yeah. One more foot and we wouldn't have been able to track it."

They reached the team, and he heard more HPD showing up behind him. Cars parking, feet stomping, everybody they could spare. It was harder on a night like tonight because the possibility of flooding always came with a tropical system. And tonight, there was a good chance some of Honolulu would be under water. HPD would be called in to help, so they might lose some of the searchers if the storm turned worse.

His team looked at him expectantly. Del looked at Adam.

"We have to redo the bets," Adam said. "Just dinner."

He frowned, and then growled. "Wait, are you saying the bets were on my sex life?"

Cat shrugged. "We do it all the time."

"Yeah, remember when that Frenchman was here for a conference and he kept sniffing around Elle?" Marcus asked.

"None of us won that one," Adam said.

"Good God. I can't believe you all spend so much time worrying about what other people are doing or not doing. Or who."

Cat shrugged. "You're *'ohana*, Boss. Just gotta accept this is going to happen."

"I don't have to accept anything. All the money is being donated to the Humane Society of Hawaii."

There was grumbling, but he cut it off with a look.

"So, anything?" he asked.

Marcus held up an evidence bag that contained the phone.

"Got the phone. Since it was turned off, the tech probably won't be able to find anything on it in the way of

GPS or anything. There's also some fabric with it. It was laying on top."

He took the bag and turned it over. The moment he saw the fabric covered in blood, his own ran cold.

"Not a good sign," Adam said.

"No." If the fabric had been torn, it could have been left due to an accident. But this fabric was cut with a pair of scissors. Someone had taken the time to cut it in a small four-by-four inch square. It must have been soaked with blood, because it was still stained even after all the rain.

"I worked up a search area," Floyd said. He was the most logical, since he'd worked rescue at one time. He held up his tablet, which he had in plastic to protect it from the rain. "Right now, I think we should go along the path. We can send a few officers out to the golf course, but I think that we should concentrate most of us in this area. There's a reason he left her phone here."

Del nodded just as Captain Pham walked up to join them. The seasoned commander had a grim expression. His years in HPD probably told him this was a recovery, not a rescue.

"What do you need from us?"

"Marcus worked up a search area. If the weather gets too dangerous, we'll pull back, so make sure each team has a walkie-talkie. I would hate to have our rescue of a victim turn into trying to rescue one of our own. So, just in case, we need to make sure we have them. Once you get past here, the cell coverage dies."

Captain Pham nodded, and he and Floyd went off.

"It might just be a warning. It's early, Boss," Cat said. But even as she said it, he could tell she didn't believe it. He saw Elle walking up the long path.

"We don't have a body," he said. The *yet* was implied, and he knew everyone heard it in their heads. All the signs were bad, but he still didn't want to give up hope. There was still a tiny chance she was alive.

She nodded. "Yes, but if there is a chance you find a

girl instead of a body, I wanted to be here."

He knew what she wanted…what they all wanted. They wanted Susan to be safe, to not have gone through the horrors that Grace Singh had endured. But wishes don't always come true, especially when dealing with their business.

They walked along the path, looking for any kind of evidence. The hiking trail was muddy and slick in the best of conditions. With the tropical system moving through the islands, the path was a mess. While they were minutes from Pali Highway on one side and H-3 on the other, they were thrust into the middle of a jungle the moment they set foot on the path. Plants, trees, and bushes covered the area. Some of it helped shield them from the worst of the rain, but it didn't make it easy to get down the path.

Less than thirty minutes later, he heard a shout. They all hurried in the direction of where the shout had sounded. Shoes pounded through the wet mud; the sound of splashing filled the air around them. He knew the path well, had hiked it. But, it was a different feel at night, with rain pounding away at them, and the fear of finding another dead girl.

He made it through to a clearing. The Likeke Falls roared thanks to the rain still falling. There, on a huge rock at the bottom of the falls, lay Susan Tanaka.

Stripped of her clothing, she was positioned with her arms spread out, and with her feet one on top of the other—as if she'd been crucified.

"Holy Mother of God," Elle said from beside him.

He turned to look at her. The horror he heard in her voice was easy to see on her face. Del turned back to Susan's body. Her skin had been marred by the same kind of burn marks as Grace Singh's had, and her eyes were opened. The way she was posed, her eyes were looking up at the top of the falls, as if the waters were the answer to her prayers.

Unfortunately, no prayers were answered tonight.

* * *

Emma stared out her floor-to-ceiling window and watched the rain beat against her lanai. Usually, this kind of weather was conducive to work. Emma thrived when she could shut the world out and just concentrate. The pounding of the rain helped with that. The regular rhythm seemed to allow her to think and just delve into her work. Tonight, it had not helped at all.

In the hours since Del had left, she'd attempted to work several times, but found herself at a loss. Worry about Del, about the team, and what they would find…she couldn't think straight. She had left the television off and had avoided the Internet as much as possible. She did not want to know about the woman from anyone but Del.

About an hour after he left, Del had sent her a text. It had only been Susan's name, but she knew what it meant. It was something that she had been expecting from the moment he left. Her stomach knotted and her head throbbed. They had failed to save Susan, and she had suffered because of it.

After that, she tried to throw herself into work, with the idea that she would catch the bastard, but she couldn't bloody concentrate. All she could think about was Del and what he was experiencing.

When the knock sounded at her door after two in the morning, she knew who it was before she checked. She opened the door and he stood there, drenched, looking so bloody tired. He must have come right from the scene. Mud caked his shirt, jeans, and boots.

"Come in," she said, stepping back.

He shook his head. "I'll get everything wet. I just wanted to stop by to let you know that I was getting my bike."

She glanced outside. The rain was still coming down in torrents. It actually appeared to be growing heavier by the minute. When she looked back at him, her protective gene kicked in. There was no way she could let him go back out in that weather. He definitely shouldn't be driving in it, even on the best of nights, but tonight, she knew his mind wouldn't be on driving. She could see the emptiness in his eyes. Her chest hurt, and she realized her heart was aching. For the woman who had been lost, but mostly for the man who stood before her.

Emma couldn't fathom what he was feeling at the moment. He had hoped, up until that very last moment, that they would find her. It was Del's way. There was always a way out of every situation in his opinion. Because of her past, Emma had always planned for the worst. It kept her prepared for the inevitable disappointments that came along the way.

"You can't go back out in this. Come in," she said, grabbing onto his sleeve and tugging him through the doorway.

She shut the door and locked it. She could smell it then, the sweet Hawaiian rain—it always smelled of flowers. But tonight, there was a tint of Del to that scent. Masculine overtones with the fragrant tropical flowers. Emma knew she would never forget that smell as long as she lived.

"I'm wet," he said, but she ignored him again. After that, he said nothing else, which worried her more.

She helped him off with the soaking jacket and hung it on her coat rack. She knew he hadn't probably had anything in his stomach for hours, and that couldn't be good, considering the amount of energy he had been using.

"Are you hungry?" she asked.

He shook his head. Her worry increased. Usually, Del would have put up a fight. It was one of the things she loved about him. Fighting was kind of like foreplay to an extent. At the moment, he acted like he hadn't even noticed that she was undressing him.

She helped him off with his shoes, putting them in her kitchen on the tiled floor, so they didn't stain her carpet.

When she straightened, he wasn't even looking at her. It was as if he was looking straight through her. Goosebumps rose over her flesh. He wasn't even in there, not mentally.

"Well, let's get you in the shower. You're soaking wet."

Again, nothing. He kept quiet as she led him to her room, then into her bathroom. She turned the shower on so it had time to heat up. He just looked at her. He roused himself, then looked around. When he met her gaze again, he was even more remote.

"I really should leave."

She crossed her arms and shook her head. "I said no."

And without any other comments, she first took off his shoulder holster, setting it down on the bathroom counter. Then, she helped him out of his clothes. His skin was cold to the touch, and she was worried that he might be going into shock of some sort. She ignored the little skip of her heartbeat when she finally had him nude. The man was amazing. All long, lean muscle, tats on his shoulders, one for Special Forces, the other of American and Italian flags. He had just enough hair on his chest, and she liked the way it narrowed down to a long path that bisected his abs. She hesitated for just a moment. Emma wasn't especially modest, but it was the first time he would see her naked. Del wasn't really paying attention at the moment, so she shrugged inwardly and peeled off her clothes. After stepping into the shower, she tugged him into the stall with her.

He said nothing as he turned his back to her. Well, that was fine with her. Bloody hell, the man had an ass on him. All that working out definitely had paid off. Hell, his entire back was sculpted. She should feel guilty scoping out his body when he was in this condition, but she couldn't help herself.

He placed his hands on the tile and bent his head down, letting the water slide all over him. She sighed in appreciation. She grabbed a pouf, some soap, and lathered it up. Del said nothing as she rubbed it over his skin, but he sighed. The muscles beneath her hands relaxed, as she continued to scrub and massage him. She washed him, hoping to cleanse his mind of the horrors he had seen tonight. Emma knew it was probably not going to help much, but she had to try.

He turned to face her. Water splashed down on both of them as he watched her. He had his cop face on.

"I really should go," he repeated.

She studied him for a long moment, then raised her hand to his cheek. "I don't want you to though. I want you to stay here."

He stared at her for a long moment, the seconds ticking by. She knew he was having some kind of internal battle, then he groaned and grabbed her. There would be no denying him. She wanted him, needed to be the person who filled the void that had been left by the night's events. She dropped the pouf and went easily into his arms. He cupped her face in both hands, and kissed her.

If he had enticed and teased her before, this kiss shattered her. His passion crashed through her as she surrendered to him, her body immediately responding to it. He slanted his mouth over hers again and again, driving his tongue into her mouth repeatedly. She pressed against him, his erection hard against her stomach. He reached behind him and turned off the water, before he picked her up. She wrapped her legs around him, and he carried her out into her bedroom. He'd grabbed a towel on the way out of the bathroom.

He threw it down on top of the mattress, before he dropped her onto it. He turned away for a moment, and she realized he was looking for his wallet.

"Top drawer, Del," she said.

He wrenched the drawer open, and pulled out the box. Opening it, he let the condoms fall on the bed beside her. Then, he turned back to her. In that moment, she felt a sharp ping of panic. He looked so different…this man. He was determined and hungry. It was beyond the cop face. This was a man intent on ravishing her, on taking her to ease his pain. Emma knew she could not reject him. She could not even comprehend how to say no to him. Instead, she held her hand out to him. He groaned and bent his head in surrender.

In that next moment, he was on top of her, unleashing the storm he had been holding back. He pressed against her, as she rose up against him. They were slick, and so delightfully lost in that moment.

He kissed his way down her body, treating her as if she were a delicacy he had been craving. He consumed her, fed on her, teasing first her nipples and breasts, then moving further down her stomach. He nipped at her belly, his large hands skimming over her flesh as he tortured her with his mouth. Hell, the man was lethal with his tongue. When he reached her sex, he set a hand on each inner thigh and moved them further apart, then he feasted on her. He slipped his tongue into her pussy, over and over again, grazing her clit with his teeth. As he did, he slid his massive hands beneath her rear end and lifted her. At the same time, he pressed his thumbs inside of her.

Her first orgasm hit her so hard and fast, she wasn't prepared for it. She screamed his name as her body exploded with release. She shivered and moaned as it lanced through her, sure that she wouldn't be able to stand another one. Del had other ideas.

He continued his sensual assault. Using his mouth, his hands, and his tongue, he pushed her to more pleasure. He built her up, again and again, taking her to the edge and teasing her until she lost all sense of time and balance. Relentless in his pursuit, he brought her to orgasm twice more before he relented.

He pulled away for only a second, and she heard the crinkle of foil, then he bent down to start kissing his way back up her body. He rose to his knees and grabbed hold of her hips. With one, hard movement, he thrust himself into her.

This was it, that moment that she had been craving since they first met. She looked up at him and their gazes collided. This wasn't easy, never would be. But she could see the passion he felt for her, right there in his gaze. When he started to move, he leaned down, kissing her, letting her taste her arousal on his tongue. Ruthlessly, he pummeled into her, and she reveled in it. The connection, the way it felt to have this one person with her, in this moment. It wasn't just good sex. It was making love with wild abandon, and she delighted in every second of it.

Just as he increased his rhythm, she felt another orgasm approaching. Her body tightened, every nerve shimmering. In the next instant, it washed over her, more powerful than her first three.

"Del," she moaned, bowing up against him. He thrust into her core one last time, then shouted her name as he joined her in ecstasy.

Moments later, he collapsed on top of her, and she wrapped her legs and arms around him. His heart beat out a tattoo against her chest, as she could feel his breath against her flesh.

He rose up to look down at her. The scary look was gone, but the connection was still there. He looked like he was searching for words to say, something to make things better. What Del didn't understand was that he had given her more than any other person in the world.

She smiled and kissed him. "Don't think. Just rest."

Then, he relaxed, a small smile curving his lips as he snuggled in closer to her. She knew that for right now, it was enough for both of them.

CHAPTER ELEVEN

Emma lay half on and half off of Del. As he ran his fingers up and down her delicate spine, he realized that he had needed to see her tonight. His first thought had been to go home, then call. He was too raw, too sick of the entire mess. He hadn't wanted to expose her to his nasty mood. They'd had one chance, that one slim chance, to save Susan. They had failed. As he helped with the transportation of the body, he had felt the cloak of responsibility hanging around his shoulders. He had been hired to do a job that was supposed to deal more with threats from outside of Hawaii. This was a whole other bag, and tonight he had wondered if those bastards were right. Maybe he shouldn't be in charge and just maybe, he should resign.

When he had finished at TFH headquarters, he had just wanted to go home, drink some whiskey, and brood.

But something made him come to her condo, walk past the guard to the elevator, then knock on her door. The moment he saw her, he knew she was all that was good in his life. At the moment, he didn't want to taint what he felt for her. The evilness of the investigation had weighed so heavily on him. Emma had seen enough of evil in her lifetime. He had exposed her to it in the investigation, but he had wanted to save her from his own mood. So, he had decided to just tell her everything and then go home. As usual, she had disagreed. Del was damned thankful she had.

The rain was barely a patter against the windows. He missed that in Hawaii. He loved the sunny days and balmy nights, but every now and then, Del wanted a big storm. He just wished it hadn't arrived with the death of Susan Tanaka.

"You think almost as much as I do," Emma mumbled.

He smiled. "I don't think there's anyone who can think as much as you do."

She raised her head and looked at him. Damn, she was beautiful. Probably not in the most traditional way, but she had been taking his breath away since the day they met. Her silky hair lay across his chest, and she had the most amazing green eyes. Long black lashes made them even more remarkable. They blazed brilliantly against her honeyed skin. He couldn't imagine her on her own when she was fifteen years old. With her issues, how had she survived?

"Now what are you thinking?"

"What was it like?"

She frowned. "The sex?"

He chuckled. "No. After your parents died."

Emma stilled and didn't say anything for a long time. In the six months he had known her, she had never talked about it. The long moment stretched. Now, he felt he had stepped over some invisible line. "Never mind."

"No. I want to tell you. Just, you have to know *everything*."

He didn't know if he was ready for that, or even what it meant. Seeing the stark honesty in her gaze, he wouldn't deny her. She needed to tell him and he needed to listen.

"Okay."

"You know that they died in the Boxing Day Tsunami?"

He nodded.

She laid her head down on his chest again before she

started speaking again.

"We were on the beach that morning. It was so pretty and we rarely went. Mum never did like the beach. Dad wanted to go though. We had spent the holidays in Phuket, mainly because my father had work there. I can't remember much before the wave came sliding over the ocean and hit. Which is odd for me. I have a photographic memory for the most part. I can remember what I was eating the day I turned thirteen, and I can remember the exact moment I fell down on the bike when my dad was teaching me how to ride when I was seven. For some reason, I can't remember that morning. No matter how many times I try to think back, it's a mystery to me. All the laughter—because I do remember that—is just a sound there in my head. I can't remember how my mother looked or what my father was wearing. I try and try and try, but it never comes to me."

She didn't continue for a second, then he felt the wetness on his chest.

"Hey," he said as he urged her to sit up. "Don't cry."

She shook her head. "No. I have never told anyone this really. Sean has always been afraid to ask, I think. But, I *need* to tell you."

He nodded as he brushed away her tears with the backs of his fingers. It broke his heart, but he had asked, and she was going to share something with him she hadn't shared with anyone else.

"And so, I can't remember anything before that sound, the rushing of water, and the shouting. What I do remember was running. I ran so fast I thought my legs would fall off."

She wiped away the tears.

"What were your parents like?"

"They were just my parents. They weren't particularly good at parenting, but they tried their best. My father—well he was a goofball. He had the most horrible sense of humor. My mum, she…she was like me."

"Beautiful."

She rolled her eyes, but he didn't miss the tiny smile, and it made his heart sing.

"The one thing I remember most is my father pushing my mother up, so she could get on the tree. The water was so loud behind us, or maybe it wasn't. Maybe I imagined that because of the threat. Then my mother was urging me up higher on the tree, so that the man on the balcony could grab me. I made it up and over and turned to watch my mother do the same. In that instant, the wave came through and they were both gone. The last thing I remember about my parents was watching them die."

Jesus, and she had been fifteen years old, alone in the world, and in the middle of a natural disaster no one was prepared for. He knew she had an eidetic memory. She remembered just about everything she saw. For that to be the last memory of her parents…he couldn't even imagine what that must have been like.

"After that, I survived, just like everyone else."

He shook his head. "You thrived, Emma."

She sniffed. "Don't think I'm special because I survived the tsunami. Thousands of us did it. Not just me."

"I don't." She laughed, albeit it was watery, but a laugh nonetheless. "You didn't just survive. You made a place for yourself in this world. It isn't conventional, and you definitely have your issues, but look at you. You never let it change the way you are."

"It did, in a way. I had quirks that became even more pronounced as time went on. And for a very long time, I didn't trust anyone. I am not that same girl."

He heard the regret in her voice, and he had those too. He hurt for the girl who had watched her entire world wash away, and he hurt for the woman who had lived without any real connections until this last year. But he couldn't hold back because he also heard a tinge of shame.

"I'm sure you're not the same girl. I lost my father

when I was eighteen. It wasn't easy, and I know it affected some of my choices in life, just as your experience did. But, babe, look at you. You survived the worst tsunami in recorded history. And what do you do? You live in a condo that overlooks an ocean. You *are* brave."

She said nothing for a long moment, and he thought she was going to start crying again. Then, something shifted in her features, and her mouth curved, and a moment later, she was laughing.

"Does anyone know how sweet you are?"

For a second, he couldn't really come up with anything to say to that. She thought he was sweet? He opened his mouth, then grunted when she gave him an attack hug.

"I have never told anyone that story. I am so glad that it was you."

She had *shared* it with him, and he would never forget that. She might have told people that she had lost her parents, but that horror, reliving it so he could know what she had gone through, she had shared a piece of her soul with him. She had laid herself bare to satisfy him.

He knew then and there, she had his heart. Oh, he should have seen it coming, should have known she was going to be trouble when she broke his nose on their first meeting. He never would have known she would be the *one.*

She pulled back to look at him. "You got quiet again, Delano. What are you thinking about?"

He looked at her. She was studying him as if he were some puzzle to figure out. That was always dangerous with Emma.

Del knew he couldn't tell her now. Their situation, their life, was tangled up in this mess of an investigation, but he would. He couldn't use the words, but Del would make damned sure she knew how much she meant to him.

"That I'm damned lucky to have made it to your bed, even if I did mess it up."

She frowned. "Why would you say that? I had four

orgasms."

He laughed. Of course, she wouldn't be traditional in any way, even in bed.

"Hmm, well I guess I was decent."

She smiled and slid up on top of him. With ease, she brushed her mouth over his, drawing his bottom lip between her teeth.

When she released his lip, she rose up to straddle him. She was amazing. Not at all modest, and completely comfortable in her own skin.

"You were better than decent."

"That's definitely good. What I meant was that I wanted to take my time, romance you."

Her eyes widened. "What do you call romance?"

"Maybe a little dinner, some flowers."

She snorted. "I think a very sexy man showed up at my door, then he ravished me. That was pretty romantic."

"Yeah?"

"Hmm, yeah," she said as she gyrated her hips. He was already getting hard again. Damn, she was beautiful. The slant of the moonlight from the window illuminated her enough for him to see.

She rose to her knees, and he thought she was going to take him inside of her. Instead, she slipped her way down his body, teasing him in much the same fashion as he had done to her. She nipped at his flesh, teasing his nipples by grazing her teeth over the tips, before she worked her way down. She wrapped her hand around his cock and stroked him, as she licked the crown.

Holy Mother of God. She was going to kill him. Over and over, she teased and tasted him, running the tip of her tongue over his shaft. She looked up at him, and he could tell from her expression, she knew exactly what she was doing to him. That confident look, the woman in charge, almost sent him over the edge, but he didn't want that.

He jackknifed up and rolled them over her mattress. Then, he lifted up, grabbed her by the hips and turned her over.

Lord. She was exquisite from behind. A spine that looked fragile, but he knew it was made of steel. Her ass was heart shaped, perfectly toned. With her in this position, he had the ability to take his time. She was at his mercy now. He kissed down her spine and she moaned; the sound of it danced over his skin and sunk into his soul. She tasted of sweet treats and surrender, and he had never had such an amazing delight. He could not get enough of touching her, this way and that.

He kissed both of her full cheeks, nipping at one of them before he made his way back up. He grabbed her by the hips again, and she rose up, willingly, wantonly, and he enjoyed every minute of it. After donning another condom, Del eased his way into her, slowly, only giving her an inch at a time. He rocked that way for a while, keeping control of the rhythm as her arousal soared. She grew restless, trying to make him go faster, but he was relentless.

"Del," she moaned.

He heard it there...the need, the demand, and he smiled. Damn, she pleased him. She definitely wasn't a shrinking flower.

"What's the matter, baby?" he crooned to her.

She clutched at the sheets, as he held her in place and tortured her. Hell, he was torturing them both. His own control was threadbare, and he knew that it wouldn't be long before he lost it.

He wanted her with him, right there in the end. He pulled out of her, turned her over, and reentered her. This time, she was coming as he thrust inside of her. He slipped his hand up to hold hers, clutching it, their fingers tangled. As her orgasm swept over her, her inner muscles pulled him deeper. She wrapped her legs around him and opened her eyes. In that moment, he was completely captured by what he saw. Complete and absolute acceptance.

"Come, Del, come with me," she whispered.

He couldn't refuse. Not the way she looked at him, the way her voice sounded. He gave himself over to pleasure. His orgasm exploded within him as he thrust into her one more time, her name on his lips as he found his release.

A short time later, with the rain pattering against the windows, she wrapped her arms around him.

"I would definitely call that decent," she said with a chuckle.

He smiled and kissed her neck, secure in the knowledge that for tonight, this was all they both needed.

CHAPTER TWELVE

The call came early the next morning. Del knew the answer before the phone rang, but he still answered.

"Hey, Boss," Adam said. His voice was weary. "We got a positive match. Her parents made a positive ID."

He pulled on his knit jockey boxers and tiptoed out of the room. He glanced back before he closed the door and smiled. She was hugging the pillow and pleasantly snoozing beneath the covers. As gently as he could, he shut the door, hoping he didn't wake her just yet.

"I figured. Call everyone, we'll do a meeting at..." he looked at the time on the kitchen clock. "Let's do it at eight. Gives everyone ninety minutes to get in. Make sure you have Elle's report for us to see. I know she will be there, or I expect she will be, but even so, I would like to see those two reports side by side."

"Okay. I take it I don't need to call Emma."

He opened his mouth to tell Adam to fuck off, when a small hand slipped around his waist and Emma leaned against him. She had dressed, but it didn't mean he couldn't feel her breasts pressed against his back. He had to fight the need to sigh.

"No."

"Hmm, so it was after midnight..."

"Doesn't matter. Money goes to charity."

"Sure, sure, Boss." The tone in Adam's voice told him he wasn't taking him seriously.

"I will write anyone up who profits from gambling. It's

illegal in the state of Hawaii."

"Come on, Del. You know we wouldn't willingly break the law."

Damn, he was definitely going to have to have a talk with his team. "Call everyone. I'll see you then."

"They identified her?" Emma said.

He turned to face her and kissed her nose. "Yeah."

She nodded. "I guess the only comfort in that is she isn't suffering anymore. I can't imagine what that could have been like."

He cupped her face. "Take it from me, don't. Don't *ever* think about that, not while you are working on their case. It can cloud your vision, make you see things the wrong way. The most important thing is finding justice for the victims."

She studied him for a long moment, then her mouth curved slightly. "You're a really good man, Martin Delano."

Del shook his head. "I'm not *that* good. I felt like I took advantage of you last night."

"You did not. If anything, I took advantage of you. You are not always the one in charge, Del. You need to learn to accept that."

"Yeah, then who is?"

She rose to her tiptoes and brushed her mouth over his. The small gesture tugged at his heart.

"Sometimes, you just have to let someone else do the saving."

He felt his mouth curve. "Are you applying for the job?"

She opened her mouth to respond, but there was a knock at the door.

"Who could that be?" she asked. "It's before sunrise."

She walked to the door and he watched her go. It was hard not to. She was wearing an old T-shirt that was three times too big for her. She'd pulled her hair up into a pony tail and it bobbed with each step.

Emma rose up to her tiptoes to look through the peephole. "Good lord, it's that bitchy reporter. And she has her whole bloody crew with her."

"I can hear you through the door, Ms. Taylor. I understand you are working the case, and I want to ask you a few questions."

"Go away. I told you I did not want to talk to you the other day."

"All I'm trying to do is get to the truth."

Del shook his head. Jin Phillips was never going to learn. He understood reporters had a job to do. They were important to help the police in a lot of ways, but there were those like Jin. She didn't care who she hurt as long as it made her a star. That wasn't about the story. It was about herself.

"I don't bloody care what you think you are trying to do. I would just like you to leave."

"I understand that you are on the hunt for the killer. That the TFH is solely dependent on you to catch this man."

He should have seen what was going to happen next, because Emma did have a temper. It was slow to heat, but when it did, people ended up injured. She had given him a broken nose to prove it once.

Emma emitted a sound he had never heard before. It sounded like a battle cry, and her opponent was going to be Jin Phillips and her crew. Before he could stop her, she flipped the locks and flung the door open.

"Emma, no."

But it was too late. The bright light shone into her apartment, and the camera was rolling.

"I understand that in today's twenty-four-hour news cycle, you need to manufacture rubbish on a daily basis, but I will not have someone come to my household like this. This is my private home, and you are trespassing. And even if you are not in my house, you are on private property. I doubt very much if the management of this building would appreciate your behavior."

Jin said nothing for a few seconds, as she looked from Emma to him. "Captain Delano?"

"That's enough," he said, slamming the door.

"That prat. How dare she come to my house and accost me?"

"Emma, do you realize what this means?" he asked.

She nodded. "They need to hire some new security around here."

Del looked to the heavens for help, but found none. He took her by the arms and looked her in the eye. "We are going to be on the morning news, both barely dressed."

She crossed her arms. "It's not my fault. She showed up here at this hour."

"Everyone is going to see that I spent the night here."

"So. The entire office has a bet going on when we would have sex."

He blinked. "You knew about that?"

She nodded. "Your team bets on everything. They have a bet going on about how long it will be before Graeme shoots Elle or beds her. I am leaning toward beds, because there is a thin line between love and hate. They also have a bet on whether or not DGD is into necrophilia, which he is not."

He opened his mouth, then snapped it shut. Damn, he really had missed that they were doing that. "I'm gonna have to talk to them."

"They'll keep doing it."

"And it doesn't bother you?"

"That they bet on my sex life?" She chuckled. "I don't care because I feel like I won the lottery."

For a second, he couldn't think of his next comment. It had been there on the tip of his tongue, but now it had dissolved. Emma was smiling at him as if he were a great big treat she wanted to eat.

"And, I couldn't let her say those things about your

team. They are the real reason you solve so many cases. What she insinuated wasn't true, and you know how I am when people attack my '*ohana*."

She would be ruthless. There was no doubt about it, Jin was probably in for more trouble in her life at the end of the investigation. Emma could be cruel if she detected a threat against those she saw as her family. Maybe it was because Emma had been on her own for so long that now she had people in her life, she was fiercely protective of them.

"I appreciate that, and I am sure the team does too. But there is another issue at hand. We are going to be on the news. And now, she has made you a target."

He saw the moment it hit her. She shook her head. "Oh, no, not me."

"Not you?"

"He goes for single women who are looking for a man. I got one."

She said it like it was the most normal thing, and she smiled at him.

He sighed. "There is that, and then, it will hit the news, and the mayor will want to know why I am sleeping with one of my team."

"First of all, I am not part of your team. I am actually contracted by the state, under the auspices of the governor. You have nothing to do with it."

He blinked. "Is that true?"

She rolled her eyes. "Yes, it's true. You signed the papers. Didn't you pay attention?"

He shrugged, feeling embarrassment creep over him. At the time, he wanted her on his team so badly, he would have signed away his bike to get her on it. Okay, maybe not that, but close.

"Secondly, I don't care who knows we are sleeping together. I don't have hang ups about that."

He blinked again. "You don't have a problem with it?"

She shook her head. "If I had an issue with it, I would

not have slept with you."

He smiled and pulled her into his arms. "You are definitely one of a kind."

She nodded and kissed him. "Of course I am. My mother always said I was."

It was a horrible point in their lives right now, what they were investigating, but just looking at her cheeky little smile made his heart dance.

"What?" she said.

He shook his head and leaned down to kiss her. She responded immediately, slipping her hands up his arms to his shoulders. Opening her mouth, she welcomed him. He wanted more, so much more, but they didn't have time. Regretfully, he pulled back. He kissed her nose.

"Thanks for being you."

She frowned. "Are you feeling okay?"

"I'm feeling fine," he said picking her up. "We need to get into the office."

She laughed, and for a short time at least, he would live in this moment.

* * *

The news broke before they even got into the office. Her phone was buzzing as they walked through the door, and the mayor was already waiting for Del in his office.

Emma saw her brother's face on her phone and frowned.

"Sean, is everything okay?" she asked.

"What the hell was Del doing at your condo this morning?" he asked. He sounded like he was pronouncing every word from behind clenched teeth.

"We just got up."

Del glanced at her, but she waved him on. He continued on to his office. Bloody hell, the man was sexy normally, but when he went into alpha mode after strapping on his gun, it made her want to jump his bones all over again. He had a way of walking into a room that let everyone know he was in charge. It made him irresistible.

"You aren't helping the situation here, Emma," Sean said, bringing her out of her thoughts about Del.

"What does that mean?"

"You are sleeping with Del."

"Yes. But what does that have to do with anything?"

"He's your boss."

"No, he isn't. I work under the auspices of the governor. Why do I have to keep telling people this?"

"I don't think it's right."

His tone told her he thought he had the right to command her what to do. She held her phone away from her ear and looked at it, then brought it back.

"Excuse me?"

"You and Del. It isn't a good idea."

Of all the nerve. The man came and went as he pleased, and lived one of the most unconventional lifestyles. She never questioned him, never looked down on him. Now he was going to tell her she shouldn't be sleeping with Del?

"You know what I think is a bad idea? Calling me up and telling me what I should and shouldn't be doing. Usually, when people do that, I tell them to bugger off."

Then, she clicked the phone off. She was still fuming. After the irritation of this morning, she had calmed down—mainly thanks to Del. From the moment they had met, he seemed to know how to get her to relax. He always knew how to make her laugh. Now, her brother had gotten her ticked off again.

"Oh, he makes me mad."

Cat looked up from her tablet. "Who, the boss?"

"No, well, sometimes, but my brother. I don't know why he thinks he can tell me what to do."

"He's your brother."

When Emma just stared at her, Cat sighed. "I forget, you didn't grow up together. But big brothers feel the need to be protective of their sisters."

"That's stupid."

Cat chuckled. "Many times. One of my older brothers actually brought out his hunting rifle and cleaned it in front of my prom date."

"That's barbaric."

"Yeah, and it didn't scare me a bit, since I convinced Shane Mamoa to do a little bit more than just kissing that night."

She opened her mouth to respond, but she heard the yelling coming from Del's office. The door was closed, so it was hard to tell exactly what was being said. Del was the one doing the yelling.

He came storming out, anger flushing his face.

"Boss?" Cat said, apparently a bit overwhelmed by Del's behavior.

It wasn't normal. He was grumpy, he would get onto his team, but he never yelled like that.

He ignored Cat and looked at Emma. "Please tell this idiot that we have not been sleeping together all this time."

She crossed her arms beneath her breasts. "It isn't any of his business."

He blinked as she looked at the mayor. "It really isn't."

"You are an employee of this city—"

"Again, I have to mention this, but I don't work for the city, or even directly for TFH. I made sure of that when I signed my contract with the state. I work for the governor. Does no one read the contracts they sign around here? Bloody hell."

"I'm not too sure he is going to be that happy about this situation."

The mayor was now really getting on her nerves. Why were people being so judgmental? It wasn't like they were sacrificing puppies and kittens.

"What situation would that be?" she asked.

"You and Captain Delano."

She glanced at Del, who was barely holding onto his temper. If she didn't defuse the situation, Del might just pull off the mayor's arms and beat him over the head with them. Then she looked back at the mayor.

"First, just like you, it isn't his business. But, he knows."

"What?" Del demanded.

"It's not like I called him this morning and told him about sleeping with you. When you first approached me about the job, I felt with our personal lives—being that he is friends with my brother—might be a problem. Also, I knew I had a little crush going, and while I didn't think it would even happen, I wanted to make sure if there were any barriers to that happening, they were out of the way. So, I went to the governor and worked out a deal where I worked for him and not Del. He can ask me to do things, but my rates and my contract are all with the governor."

"Oh," the mayor said. "The report this morning made it sound like you are the only one in the office who can catch the killer."

"If you believe that, you really don't know much."

The mayor blinked. "I beg your pardon?"

"Listen, I have a one sixty IQ, so I understand that without the amazing team Del has put together, I would never be able to do the work I do. I don't detect. I see patterns. It is what they do after I give them the info that makes them so successful. Also, it's kind of rude on your part to think that one person could walk in here and do the job of ten plus people."

He opened his mouth, then shut it.

"Now, what I would like to know is what you are going to do about that catty bitch invading my privacy? She might have very well made me a target today if Del hadn't been there."

"I guess I could assign a protection detail."

She rolled her eyes. "With a brother in the security business and Del hanging around, I really don't think I need that. Just know, next time I won't be so nice to her. Ask Del. I broke his nose the first time I met him."

She turned around, dismissing him, because she really

was too ticked to discuss it further. She wanted to talk about what was important, and some bloody reporter *wasn't*.

She heard Del murmuring to the mayor, and then they walked away. As soon as the mayor was out of earshot, the team started clapping.

"I've been wanting to do that for weeks now," Adam said.

She snorted. "Well, wait until you see what I do to that reporter. She bloody well better stay away from my condo from now on."

On top of that, she didn't like when she lost her temper. It was one of the things her father had taught her to control. Losing her temper made her feel completely disoriented, and she did not like it at all. Which just ticked her off even more.

"You will not bash her with a two-by-four," Del said as he walked up behind her.

"I'll do what is important to protect what is mine."

He smiled at her. "Yeah, she finds out how rich you are, she'll sue."

"Oh. I always forget about that."

"Can we get on with the meeting?" Cat asked.

"Indeed. I haven't had breakfast, and that is never good for anyone," Emma said.

She took her seat beside Graeme, and Del sat beside her.

"Adam, pull up the findings. Elle, let's start with what you found."

"Right," Elle said, standing up. "First, her TOD was just hours before she was found. I guess sometime late yesterday afternoon, maybe around five or six in the evening at the latest. Same types of wounds, burn marks from a car cigarette lighter."

"That means he could have kept her in a garage or near one," Adam said.

"Well, yes, possibly."

"What's that mean?" Graeme asked.

"What she means is there's a way to rig a unit to use outside of the car," Emma said. "If you have the mechanical background, it isn't that hard."

"Yes," Elle said. "And he could have very well used an open flame to heat it. Charity thinks she might be able to come up with a make and model, but so many of them use the same types. It might be difficult. Other than that, she was bound as Grace had been before, raped, brutalized."

"The tattoo?" Del asked.

She nodded. "It took me awhile to figure it out, because unlike Grace, Susan liked a tat. She had one, on her ankle. *Laka*."

A picture came up of the young woman's ankle. It wasn't that easy to see, but Emma made out the word beneath the face that had been inked.

"Has it started fading?" Cat asked.

"Yes, but it hasn't disappeared, which makes me think he had her the entire time from the day she left work," Elle said.

"So, the same killer," Marcus said.

Elle nodded, as Emma took in her appearance. She was pale, the dark circles under her eyes stood out more. While the rest of them probably didn't get much sleep, she knew Elle probably hadn't been home yet. Once they'd finally gotten back to the morgue, there was a good chance she'd been working for hours. Drew kept nodding off in the seat beside her.

"Indeed. No DNA to prove it, but we didn't have anything this time either. She was repeatedly strangled, but this time he did not use his hands. He used a rope."

"Which you think he used the other times, but for the final kill, he used his hands?" Del asked.

"Yes, and reading over the reports that Emma sent, they are almost identical."

"So, do we think this man hates women, most especially Asian women?" Graeme asked.

"I don't think so," Emma said.

Everyone turned to look at her.

"What are you thinking?"

"I think I need to do some more research, because I think this has more to do with goddesses than anything else. If that is the case, it has nothing to do with the ethnicity of the women, but of the goddesses."

"That's actually brilliant," Elle said. "If he killed elsewhere, we need to look to see the correlation."

"It isn't that great. If so, there is no way to zero in on what may or may not be a connection between the women, it is only a guess on who his next victim is."

"Why do you think he killed with a rope this time?" Marcus asked.

Elle shook her head. "It could be he lost control at one point in the torture and actually killed her."

"That would explain why the move up in the date of the murder," Drew chimed in. Everyone looked at him, and his eyes widened. "Sorry."

"No, go on, Drew," Del said.

"If he didn't mean to kill her, that might explain the moved up date. He couldn't hold onto her, because her tat might have disappeared, since we think he knows something about that. That's why there was the rush to get everyone to her last night."

"Brilliant," Emma said. "That could be why. This bastard is probably pissed that the storm hindered his news coverage."

"Until we announce it, no one here knows," Del said. "There's speculation of course, but the press conference isn't until eleven."

Emma noticed a tele was playing the morning news, flashes of her condo, then…the picture of Susan Tanaka with the words Akua Killer splashed over her smiling face.

"Can you turn that up? What is that about?" she asked.

Adam brought it up on the big screen.

"Sources within the HPD tell me that Susan Tanaka is the

latest victim of the Akua Killer. Her body was found at Likeke Falls during the storm last night."

"*Fuck*," Del said. "Adam, call around to your contacts. Find out who the moron was who leaked that. I had that freaking name."

"The Goddess Killer, Boss," Cat said. "I'd like to know who the hell came up with that name."

"Reporters probably," Emma said.

Elle nodded. "They tend to be the people who come up with the gruesome names."

"Well, keep a lid on the fact we have made connections. If the FBI finds out we have more than one string of killings, they will want to step in."

"They usually like to wait until he has at least three, although there is no policy on it. So, maybe that's another reason for three killings. He is hunting for his next woman, or already has her. Then, he will move on."

Del looked at Emma. "What?"

"I said it before. Three seems to be the number."

"I'm going to have to hold a press conference, thanks to that reporter." He looked at her.

"What?"

"I'll have Graeme take you home."

She frowned. "I don't want a keeper."

"Part of it is for my peace of mind. The other is because the press might hound you otherwise. Most of them are afraid of Graeme."

She snorted. "Okay. The one thing you need to worry about is how she found me."

"Why?"

"That condo is in the name of the corporation my father left Sean and me. My name is nowhere on the documents."

"But they could know about you being part of the corporation."

She shook her head. "Yes, but she was damned sure I lived there. We own several homes throughout the islands, and actually around the world. There is no reason she would think I was living there. And while I know people in HPD know I work here, it's not like I am listed anywhere. She zeroed in on me somehow. That theory of a link might just turn out to be reality."

"*Fuck.*"

"Exactly."

* * *

He paced the small space, knowing he made a mistake. He had been too fast with this last one. She had not fought like his last few. When she had realized what was happening, she had just given up. And it had angered him.

Even now he felt the pressure building in his head. Fuck. His skin was crawling with a need. He was in so much trouble, so much trouble. But he could fix it. He knew he could.

He heard her voice on the TV and smiled. He walked over to look. She was the one he wanted, the one who would complete his trinity of Hawaii.

All would be forgiven if he could get her.

CHAPTER THIRTEEN

Emma discovered a reference to a woman found in Greece two years earlier. She didn't get much because the report was incomplete, but the mention of goddesses caught her eye. She marked the spot, sent it to Marcus, since this was his part of the job, along with a translation from Google. Greek was not one of the languages she knew. Little words here and there, but for the most part, she stuck to Asian languages and the English language.

After she sent the email, she started to dig further. Marcus could definitely do it himself, but she wanted to find more right now. More information would lead to more links. Links might just take them to the killer.

She had fought her way through a lot of red tape—meaning firewalls—when her doorbell rang. Damn. If it was that reporter again, she didn't care what Del said. She would break the woman's nose if she didn't leave her alone.

Emma stomped to the door and looked through the peephole. When she saw her brother, she almost wished it was the reporter. With a sigh, she opened the door. He was frowning at her.

"What?"

For a second, Sean's eyes widened at her nasty tone, and he hesitated. It took a lot to surprise her brother, and she took particular pride in the fact that she had. He shook his head and stepped through the door.

"Didn't bring Randy as backup?" she asked, not even trying to hide her cheeky tone. She had work to do and didn't have time to deal with overbearing brothers.

"I can handle you myself."

"Are you sure about that?" she said, shutting the door. Seeing that she knocked him out too the first time she'd met him, he should be wary.

"I thought maybe you might want to explain yourself."

She blinked. This was *not* the brother she knew. This was a stranger who thought he could tell her what to do. He was still frowning at her, and there was a hint of disapproval in his eyes.

"You do realize what you are saying, right?" she asked.

"What does that mean?"

"That *means* that not once since you, Randy, and Jaime moved in together, have I questioned it. *Never.*"

He blinked, mainly because she had raised her voice. She couldn't control her emotions when it came to Del, but this was another level of frustration. She had accepted Sean and his odd living arrangement with no problem, but he questioned her relationship with Del.

"That's different."

A tickle of aggravation clawed at her throat. That was his argument? He was standing there questioning her choices in life, and he thought he could because he *thought* there were different rules for him.

"Exactly how is it different?"

"Well…this is about you."

She shook her head. "Sean, I know you think you have a right to tell me what I should be doing. Just know, you really don't."

He opened his mouth, then snapped it shut. The irritation had drained and was replaced by hurt. She knew he regretted her being kidnapped earlier in the year to get back at him. At the time, the two of them didn't know about each other.

"No. Don't look like that. What happened to me, you can't make up for that. I can't ever go back and have my life the way it was. And, there are times that makes me sad. I would love to have had my mother meet you. She'd have loved you. Dad, well, he had mellowed, and I think he would have been very proud of you. Maybe, you two could have patched things up. All of that is never going to happen. While I regret that you and Dad never made amends, I am who I am today because of the sum of all my years."

He threaded his fingers through hers. "I wish I had been there."

She shook her head. "No. I need you now. Not to tell me what to do, but to be my friend."

"*Dammit.*" He tugged her into his arms and she smiled. The familiar scent of the ocean air that always clung to Sean slipped over her senses. She'd thought she had no one left in the world until he came bursting into her life. Now, no matter what, they had each other.

"It was just hard seeing that. I mean…you're my baby sister."

She leaned back and looked at him. "Get over it."

He chuckled. "Jaime said the same thing."

"That's because she is brilliant."

He looked around. "It looks like a research library exploded in here."

She slipped away from him. "We have to find this bastard, Sean."

"They've tried to keep a lot of it out of the press."

"Yeah, except that bitch this morning. Do you know how she could have found out where I live? We purposely have the corporation's name on it."

His eyes narrowed. "That's a good question."

"Del has Adam questioning people. Not many people knew I was working this case, so he's worried he has a leak. Although, she did see me in the office a few days ago, but I am not a known person. I could have just been his slice on the side."

"Piece on the side, Emma. Not slice. And I doubt very much Del would let his *piece* wander around headquarters."

She shrugged. "Even so, that prat had no idea who I was or what Del is like. I just don't want her causing issues for me to keep working with the team."

"You really like doing this work."

She glanced at him. "Yeah. It gives me purpose. I get paid thousands more in consulting, but this, I feel like I am making a difference."

He nodded. "How about I take you to lunch?"

Her stomach grumbled just then and she smiled. "That sounds brilliant. Let me clean up and we can go."

* * *

As they walked back from Sushi Sasabune, Sean tried his best to convince her to go to Japan with them. She was pleasantly stuffed with sushi, but he was ruining her food high.

"No. I love Japan, but I have too many things on my table right now."

He shook his head. "You have too many things on your *plate* as it is."

She smiled. She still had problems with American idioms, but she was getting a little better at them.

"Right. And don't think I am unaware of what you are trying to do. You want me to walk away from this case. Not going to do it."

He sighed. "I want you safe."

"No, what you want is me away from Del."

Sean slanted her a look and, even with his eyes hidden from her view, she knew he was calculating another response.

They walked down the next block on Queen Street, silently. They'd had fun at lunch and again, he was ruining it. She just didn't understand why.

"It's not like it is that serious with Del. You just need to let things play out."

He glanced at her with a frown. "What are you talking about?"

She hated when they got into these discussions, but she knew he wouldn't let it go. It was one of the reasons he was good in the security business. He set out on a mission and did not give up until it was done.

"Relationships don't always go well for me, Sean."

"I used to say the same thing."

She shook her head. "I just can't see past today. Not anymore."

"Maybe you should. It's been a year since we've known each other. Maybe you need to start looking at where you want to be a year from now."

He didn't understand.

"Emma?"

She stopped and looked at him. "I survived because I lived each day and didn't look for sunlight. I just moved forward and prayed I'd make it to see that. It isn't in me to trust that people will be around."

He wanted to say something else, but he sighed. "Well, I will always be here for you. Just know that."

She smiled. "I like that about you."

"And I am not just trying to get you off the island because of Del. It's because of this case."

It was her turn to sigh. There was definitely enough sincerity in his voice to convince her.

"I am not a target, and I never will be."

"Why?"

"First, I was seen with Del at my condo by just about everyone in freaking Hawaii by now. He only goes after single women it seems. Second, we are adversaries, or I am assuming that is the way he sees us. He needs to go up against someone smart, and I am that person. Although, I don't feel that smart at the moment."

"Why is that?"

She shrugged, embarrassed she had admitted it.

"No, tell me," he urged.

"I can't seem to find this man. He's left a trail, but I can't find him. I should be able to come up with a pattern to give the team, but I can't. It's very frustrating."

"I'm sorry. I know you get a little...involved."

"He's hurting these women. He's not just killing them. He's making their last moments on earth horrible. I have to help them catch the bastard."

He stopped and she turned to face him. "Like you say, Emma. Always go back to the beginning. If you can't find him, it's because you haven't drawn a straight line. Step by step."

She thought about it, letting his words sink in. Then, it hit her. She needed to find something, some kind of report with a name. He wasn't always perfect...he had to practice at some point.

"That is brilliant, Sean," she said, hugging him.

"I take it there will be no more discussions of your relationship with Del."

"No. I know I need to do some more digging. And you need to go calm Randy, because he's probably trying to come up with ways to hurt Del. And then I would have to hurt him. I don't want to see him cry."

Sean laughed and gave her a kiss on the cheek. "Okay. Let's go."

* * *

Del spent the better part of the morning dealing with phone calls. Everyone from the governor to the neighborhood watch folks wanted an answer from him. So, in his mind, it just fit that Sean Kaheaku showed up right about one in the afternoon. He didn't look any happier visiting than Del was about the visit.

"Got a moment?" he asked. From the gleam in his eye, there was no way out of the conversation. Being an older brother himself, Del understood. Had someone been flashed on the local news with any of his sisters, he would want to talk to the man too.

"Yeah, close the door."

He saw the look from Cat when he went to close the blinds.

"Afraid of them seeing something?"

"No, but they are damned nosey, and I feel this should be private."

Sean sat in one of the two seats in front of Del's desk, and waited until he sat down.

"You want to tell me what the fuck you think you're doing with my sister?"

"Not really."

"Try again."

They had both been Special Forces, so any fight would be a draw probably. The difference, Sean had back up from Randy Young, who just happened to be a former SEAL.

"Emma feels we don't have to explain ourselves."

Sean rolled his eyes. It was hard not to see his sister in the gesture. They weren't similar in build, as Sean's mother had been Hawaiian, and Emma's had been Thai. Sean was bigger than life, a good deal over six feet, and well built, thanks to his former jobs of Special Forces and security detail. Emma, well, she was delicately built. The eyes, though, they shared the same green eyes.

"The girl doesn't know what she is talking about." His dismissive tone irritated Del.

"She's not a girl."

Sean's eyes narrowed. "Yeah, I guess you would know that."

He drummed his fingers on his desk. "This is kind of hard to take from you."

"What's that supposed to mean?" Sean demanded.

"That you have one of the most alternative lifestyles that exists."

He frowned. "Still, she's my sister."

"And you want to protect her, I get it."

"That's right, you have sisters."

"Yeah, all three are younger than I am, so I get it. It

doesn't mean I would try to keep them away from a man who loves them."

Damn, he hadn't meant to tell her brother before he told Emma. For a second Sean said nothing. Del took a moment to savor the fact that he had stunned Sean Kaheaku. It wasn't an every day occurrence. Having been trained in the Army, then by MI-6, Sean was usually at the top of his game.

"Loves?"

Del nodded. "Just don't say anything to her. Not sure if she's ready to handle that much change in her life."

"*Fuck*. That is just...*fuck*. Why did you have to do that?"

"Fall in love with her?"

He nodded.

"Kind of hard not to. Been falling for her ever since she smacked me with that two-by-four."

Sean got up and paced the office. "This changes things."

"What, you were going to beat me up?"

He stopped and slanted him a look. "Maybe."

"Emma would be mad."

"That I beat you up?"

"No, when I had to explain why I had to kick *your* ass."

Sean snorted. Del hated to explain himself, but this one time he felt he owed Sean. Not so much because of any debt, but thanks to him, he had Emma in his life.

"Listen, I did not go lightly into this, and I'm not about to ask your permission. That would be a disservice to your sister."

Sean studied him for a moment. "You're afraid of her." he concluded.

"Not of her, but what she might do if I spring a more serious relationship idea on her. Plus, our work right now...it's just a little much. This case has us all on edge."

Sean nodded. "I stopped by to see her earlier."

He looked down at his cell and saw the text. "Ah, yes,

she warned me, but I've been too busy."

"I can imagine."

"And just don't tell her about the love thing. I sense she's not ready."

"She isn't."

Something in Sean's tone caught his interest. "What?"

"She didn't tell me not to tell you, so I feel I have a right. Although, I will deny you heard it from me."

"Oh, good God, quit being afraid of a woman who barely weighs a hundred pounds."

"She told me she wasn't looking for forever."

Del blinked as his heart thudded almost to a stop. "What?"

Sean looked at him. "Damn, you really do love her. I didn't mean like that. You have to understand that it isn't that she doesn't want it. It's almost as if she doesn't think she deserves it."

Del released a breath he didn't know he had been holding. "It's probably because of how her parents died. She told me about it the other night."

Sean's eyes widened. "I've never asked because I thought she would tell me when she was ready. I'm assuming it's as bad as I imagined?"

Del nodded. "Probably worse. So, I understand she's not that trusting. I can prove to her that she can trust me."

Sean studied his face for a long moment then nodded. "Well, I have said my piece. Just don't hurt her."

"Of course I will, Sean. I'm a man. We fuck things up."

Sean chuckled. "There is that. Make sure you keep her safe. I don't like her working on this thing."

"Yeah, well, she claims she isn't a target with a man in her life."

Sean nodded. "She told me the same thing at lunch."

"Oh, good. That woman forgets to eat. I don't know how many times I tell her to eat, she just pushes me aside and says she has work. Worse, when she does eat, it's like feeding a hoard of locusts. That cannot be good for her."

Something he couldn't discern passed over Sean's expression. "Yeah. Randy and I push food on her when we can." He stood. "You know, when you went to pick her up for me, I would have never thought this could happen."

"Well, I guess we didn't know Cupid carried a two-by-four and not a bow and arrows."

Sean chuckled. "There's that."

Still, he stood there staring at Del.

"What?"

"I'm trying to come up with a good excuse for not kicking your ass."

"Emma would not be happy."

"That's true. Randy wanted me to take care of it."

"It? I'm an it?"

Sean nodded.

"Next time you need help, don't call."

Sean laughed out loud at that. "You'll help, Delano. You're a boy scout, and they always play by the rules. Hurt her, we make you disappear."

With that warning, he smiled and left Del alone.

Adam walked into his office, his face grim.

"Don't worry. No pistols at dawn."

Adam shook his head. "We got a couple issues. Seems that after talking to Denise Rutledge—you know the teacher who had been on the mainland—we found out that Grace was actually seeing a mystery man. And, worse, she'd already told Jin Phillips. She's posted it on the news blog."

"*Fuck*. We were keeping that out of the papers for a reason."

"I know. From what Denise said, though, Jin knew about it. She used the term *Sugar Daddy* when talking to her."

"*Double fuck*." He thought about the ramifications. They had kept that close to their vests, but there was always a chance someone not associated with them had info they were divulging to Jin. Of course, the one person who could be feeding her info...

His blood ran cold. "We need to get Jin in here right now. She might have something we don't know."

"Called the office, she was out. Called her personal cell, went straight to voice mail."

He dialed her number, and it also went straight to voice mail. His gut churned. This was not a good thing. The lead detective on the case she was trying to make her own called, and she didn't answer.

"I guess we'll just have to wait. We really need to find out who the fucking leak is."

"You know this is going to cause more problems than just this job, Boss."

"Yeah, they already don't trust me, and if we go on what they will see as a witch hunt, there will be backlash." Del thought over his options. "Ask around, quietly. If they find out, we will deal with it, but right now, I think we need to do everything we can to find out who the hell is giving Jin info."

Adam nodded. "You don't think it could be Kaheaku?"

"No, for a couple of reasons. Emma tells him very few details of the job. He doesn't handle what she is doing well, and I think this one has him more unnerved than any of the others. But, it would have put her at risk. That is something he would not do. Exposing her as part of the research team on this one put her on TV, and put her in the path of a killer. That is something Sean would never do."

"Makes sense. I'm gonna call around, start looking into who has been dating Jin."

"She dates cops?"

He smiled. "I'm assuming. She tried it with me a couple of times in the past. And not so much as dating, but meeting for drinks. She's very good at stroking egos."

"Let me know what you find."

He waved his hand to him as he headed out of his office. Del looked out the windows and fought the need to break something. Right now they were in a holding pattern—waiting. Waiting to hear from Jin...and worse, waiting for the bastard to steal another woman.

Del was an impatient man.

* * *

As Jin waited in the dark parking garage, second thoughts started to crowd her mind. She had done some insane things to get her name out there, but none of them had been as chancy as this one. Still, she was looking to get the desk job that would be opening on the weeknight news cast here. Getting a scoop about how both women had been seeing a mystery man—that would help. It would inch her ahead of that bitch Maggie, because Jin couldn't—and wouldn't—do what *she* was doing to get ahead. Sleeping with Frank Han, the station manager, was over the line for Jin.

She knew the moment she posted about the mystery man that someone would contact her. If this man was dating these women, someone saw them somewhere, even if it was just a drive-thru window. Also, she had wanted to jab at the informant who had told her about it in the first place. She wanted more contact with whoever had the info. If she could get the person on camera, even if he or she was hidden, it would guarantee her the weeknight anchor job.

With a sigh, she looked at her watch. The person was already thirty minutes late. She would wait a little longer, and then she would leave. She knew for a fact that Adam Lee had been trying to contact her. And, truthfully, she would much rather be trying to pump the sexy Hawaiian for more information about the case than standing in the very back of a dark and dirty parking garage. That one weekend two years ago had been the best two days of her life—well almost. Then, he had assumed she'd worked him for a story and he'd walked away. It had hurt, but she had moved on.

It still didn't explain why she felt the same pain each

and every time she saw him.

Minutes ticked by and just as she was about to leave, she heard someone behind her. She turned, but never saw who it was. Someone grabbed her, and she felt a sharp prick in the side of her neck.

Then, her world faded away.

CHAPTER FOURTEEN

Emma had gathered more info than she could ever possibly figure out in her lifetime when there was a sharp knock at the door. She looked at the clock and realized it was six in the evening. The whole afternoon had blown by, and she hadn't noticed. She opened the door and Del smiled.

"What are you doing here?" she asked.

His smile faded. "That's sort of what people who are dating do."

"It is?"

He cocked his head to the side. "I would rather not have this discussion out in the hallway."

She stepped back to let him enter. He removed his shoes, then walked into her living room. "Been busy, I see."

Emma nodded. "I don't feel like I have accomplished much. My head is getting fuzzy. It's just...I know there is something there and I can't seem to grab hold of it."

He said nothing for a few moments as he looked over her work. She watched him, his hands in the pockets of his jeans, studying her work. Many people dismissed her at times. They would happily take her work, use it, but most of them took no time to look at it. They wanted to utilize her brain, but they could care less about learning what she was doing or how she was doing it. Del was different. Still, he was acting kind of odd even for him.

"So, you want to tell me what this is about?" she asked.

He turned to face her. "What?"

"Why are you here?"

"Oh, well, we are dating."

"Sort of."

"No *sort of* about it. We *are* dating, or did I confuse what went on here?"

There was something in his tone, something she wasn't understanding.

"Are you trying to ask me if I am sleeping with someone else?"

His expression grew colder. "I didn't think there was a question about that."

All of a sudden, it clicked. She wasn't good with subtle undertones any more than she was with sarcasm. He apparently needed some kind of reassurance that she wasn't sleeping around.

"Well, there isn't. Why would I want anyone else? I can barely keep up with you now."

His mouth twitched. "Is that a fact?"

The way his eyes warmed made her heart beat faster, her palms sweat. How could he do this to her? Just a little look, a change in the tone of his voice, and she was melting.

Then, he did nothing. Just stood there and stared at her. She didn't know what he wanted or what to do. Men she had relationships with...well, she hadn't had relationships with them. She'd had sex and that was it. For her, these kinds of interactions with other people were difficult. She didn't understand some of the cues, and she definitely never understood what they wanted from her.

"Listen, while I like you, and sex is fantastic, I need to work."

He nodded. "Why don't you pack a bag?"

She blinked, confused by the question. "What for?"

"To stay at my house."

He said it as if it was fact. "No."

Now it was his turn to blink. "What?"

"I need to work and right now, I can't acclimate to a new place."

He frowned. "I don't think you understand."

"No, *you* don't understand."

"What's wrong with my house?"

Great, now he sounded as if his feelings were hurt. She shoved her hands through her hair and tried to keep calm. Sean had told her that people did not understand her need for the status quo. Right now, she could not fathom moving everything over to the cute little house Del had in Hawaii Kai. She liked it, had stayed there months ago for protection, but at the moment, the idea had her skin crawling. Most people would label her difficult, and she didn't care. There were things she could handle and right now, this was not one of them.

"I wouldn't mind going over when we are done with this, but I need to have everything where it is."

He sighed and looked around her flat. Comprehension filled his gaze, and he nodded. "Normalcy. I get it. Well, then I need some clothes."

"Alright," she said looking back at her notes. She saw a name that she had seen before. *Stanton.* Where had she seen that before? It was on some report, she was sure of it. The bugger had been arrested somewhere else there had been a goddess killer.

"Just alright?"

She looked up and shrugged. "I figure you're going to want to sleep with me, so yeah, you need clothes for work."

His lips twitched again.

"What did I say now?" she said, narrowing her eyes at him.

"Nothing. Just...you."

"Great. And people say that I am not good at communicating."

"I'm Italian. Italian men don't feel the need to communicate unless we are yelling."

"Great. And just for the record, I don't like yelling. At all."

"Noted."

But he still just stood there. He apparently wanted to talk, but she really didn't know what about.

She stepped closer and her head spun. Damn, she needed to eat. "Have you eaten lately?"

"No, I haven't. How about a stop at the Side Street Inn, then we can run out to my place and grab some things?"

She wanted to research more, but the truth was, she had missed him today. Also, a break would be good. It had helped earlier when she went out to eat with Sean. Stepping back always seemed to refresh her ability to think better.

"Sounds good. Got your bike?"

He nodded.

"Yay. I love riding at night."

He stopped her before she could bounce away into the bedroom. He kissed her, sweetly, deeply. It turned her knees to Jell-O and her mind to mush.

"What was that for?"

"For being you."

She shook her head and went into her bedroom. The man was messing with her mind and making her act as if she had an *average* IQ. As she dug through her drawers looking for a pair of long pants, she knew she had to keep her mind on work. If she was right, he might be bringing clothes over for more than one night. The overly large dresser definitely had room for his clothes. She didn't have many clothes. Board shorts and T-shirts just didn't take up that much room.

She looked up at herself in the mirror...stunned. She was standing there thinking about giving Del his very own drawer. A year ago, she hadn't even met the man.

Just this morning, she was talking about how she couldn't trust anyone. She had told Sean she wasn't looking at an extended relationship. Okay, she had used other words, but she had meant that. She couldn't. She had survived day by day for so long, she couldn't look past that.

Emma waited for fear to hit her, or maybe panic. She did not do well with abrupt changes, but now that she thought back on the last six months, she realized she had been moving to this point all along. In her reflection, her lips curved. This felt right. She liked the idea of having her clothes next to his and that they were spending all this time together.

"Hey, hurry up in there," he shouted from the other room.

Hmm, they would just have to do something about his manners.

* * *

Del stepped out of the shower and grabbed a towel. They'd had dinner, rode out to his place for his stuff, and returned. Emma was practically humming with the need to work. It was his damned fault he found it so sexy.

Great, Delano, you've lost your damned mind.

He used to take out women who cared more about their makeup than their IQ. Now, he found hearing her talk to herself as sexy as a woman who spent thousands on lingerie. Sexier actually. Hell, he was pretty sure she didn't even give a second thought to lingerie. Now, thinking about the way she would look while so focused on work turned him on more than any small scrap of lace.

His mother always said a woman with a brain would be his undoing, and she didn't know how right she was. Emma's brain, the way she thought, the things she could accomplish with that intelligence was appealing to him. Hell, he wanted to brag about her all the time to people he knew.

Worse, she was a woman who was complicated. Until now, complicated women. And Emma didn't come with regular complications. Her brain and her quirks made her even more of a challenge. He had been a man who shied away from entanglements—especially with difficult women. While he was in the military, Del hadn't wanted to get married. Special Forces made it challenging, and he hadn't met a woman worth it. Until Emma.

Damn, he had told her brother he was in love with her, but Del really hadn't realized just how deeply it went. As it turns out, gone under for the third time deep.

What happened to the man who liked easy women, the kind who understood the game, and wanted nothing more than some fun? He got hit upside the head with a two-by-four six months ago and he hadn't recovered.

He finished drying off, grabbed a pair of his boxers, and stepped into them. It was getting late, and while he knew she wanted to stay up and work, Emma needed sleep. She wasn't thinking straight, which always led to a meltdown of some sort.

He stepped into the bedroom, grabbed a condom off the bedside table, then approached the doorway. She was standing in view, a pencil in her mouth as she stared at one of her whiteboards. She was wearing a pair of old flannel boxers and a tank top that had seen better days. It was probably the most unappealing piece of clothing he had ever seen a woman wear, but it was the sexiest thing to him at the moment. Bottom line, it had everything to do with the woman who wore it.

Del could wait until she finally noticed him, but he knew that would probably be around sunrise. She was overly focused on work, and it wasn't good for her. He knew from what she had said at dinner that she was getting stuck. And when Emma got stuck, she had issues.

Walking up behind her, he slipped his hands around her waist.

"Oh, hey."

He kissed her neck and she hummed. Damned, she always smelled so good. Exotic, and tonight there was the aroma of cool, Hawaiian night air clinging to her.

"You taste good, Emma."

"Yeah," she said, distracted still by her board. If he didn't know her as well as he did, he would be irritated. With Emma, a man had to learn a way to capture her attention. Right now, her focus was a man who needed to be stopped. And they did need to do that. But, she needed a break and he didn't see anything wrong with both of them enjoying it.

He licked her neck up to the earlobe, which he took into his mouth. Another hum.

She shook her head, even as she shifted from foot-to-foot. He knew she was getting aroused, but she was, as always, single-minded. "Del, I'm trying to work."

He kissed her neck again, scraping his teeth over her pulse point causing it to scramble. Satisfaction wove through him. "You need a break."

"I can't stop now. My brain won't shut down."

He chuckled. "I have a remedy for that."

He turned her around so that she faced him and drew her closer. Dipping his head, he nibbled on her bottom lip before slanting his mouth over hers. He stole inside for a taste and she moaned. The vibrations of it danced over his tongue, then filtered through his body.

He heard something ping against the table, and he realized she had tossed her pencil so she could slide her arms around his neck. He picked her up and she wrapped her legs around his waist. He walked them to a big oversized chair and collapsed. There was no way he would make it to the bedroom. Del grabbed the bottom of her tank top, tugged it over her head, and threw it on the floor. She laughed, one of the most carefree sounds he had ever heard.

She looked down at him with those damned mermaid eyes of hers, and he leaned forward. Without breaking eye contact, he pressed his mouth against her nipple, and drew it in. She leaned her head back and moaned again. The tips of her hair tickled his legs as he moved from one breast to the other, giving it the same treatment.

When it was almost too much to ignore, he pulled her up off him, so he could strip her shorts off. He settled her back down on his lap. She slipped her hand beneath the waistband of his boxers and grabbed hold of his cock. He handed her a condom he'd stashed into the waistband of his boxers, she ripped it open and rolled it on him. As she lifted up, she caught his gaze. Inch by inch, she slipped down on his erection. She moaned when she finally had him inside of her all the way.

"So good," she said, her voice a deep whisper of need and satisfaction that fed his own arousal.

Slowly, she started moving. She was wet, slick with her desire for him. He accepted her pace, moving with her and allowing her to set the rhythm of their lovemaking. Again and again, she moved over him. Each time she rose up, then descended down on his cock, he thought he would lose it. But she held back. Every move pushed them both closer to the edge, but she didn't let them go over. Instead, she built the anticipation. Soon, though, it was too much for her. She increased her rhythm as her moans increased.

"Oh, Del, yes, there, Del," she screamed. He watched as her orgasm slammed into her. She leaned her head back, arching her back so that her breasts were in perfect placement. He took one in his mouth and she shuddered. Another wave tore through her at that moment, drawing him inside her further. His own release followed as he gave himself over to the pleasure. It ripped a shout from his throat as he thrust up into her one more time and let his release wash over him.

She collapsed on top of him, snuggling against him. The scent of their lovemaking hung heavy in the air around them. He drew in a deep breath and sighed. They sat like that for a long time before he lifted her and carried her into the bedroom.

"I have work to do."

He chuckled. "It'll wait. Let's get some rest."

He laid her on the bed, went to the bathroom to discard the condom, and returned to find her sleeping already. He slipped into bed beside her, and smiled when she rolled right to him and snuggled against him. Her breath was against his neck, and one of her hands rested on his chest right over his heart.

With a sigh he settled back, his body satiated, his mind ready to shut down, if only for a few hours.

The woman was going to be a lot of work, but she would definitely be worth it.

* * *

Jin woke up with a scream. She looked from side to side and tried to sit up. She couldn't. Her hands were strapped down, as were her legs. Worse, she was naked. Fear wound through her. What the hell had happened? She'd been to meet her source, then nothing.

What the hell had he given her? Her mouth was dry, as if she had been trying to eat cotton. Even now that she was awake, her thoughts seemed to not make sense. She studied her surroundings. It was dark, so dark, and she heard the sounds of night beyond the walls. She wasn't in a house, but in something else. Before she could think of a way out of there, she heard the lock at the door.

Closing her eyes, she feigned sleep. Strong, masculine steps sounded on the floor. It was a wooden floor, but not strong wood. It sounded more like plywood. He stopped, fiddled with something on the table beside her. He turned to her and in the next instant she felt his breath against the flesh on her right arm. It took every effort she had not to freak out. The only way to get out of there was to pretend to be sleeping so that maybe he would leave.

He apparently wasn't stupid.

"Tsk, tsk, Ms. Phillips. I am not quite ready for you."

Then Jin felt a prick in her arm, the rush of something hitting her bloodstream, and she started to fade again.

* * *

The next morning, Emma was drinking coffee and

looking over things on her tablet when the same name she had previously seen appeared in a report from Italy. Damn her for not knowing Italian. She was pretty sure Sean knew it though, or maybe it was Randy. One of them knew it. She would definitely have to call them and go over. She really hated romance languages. Too weird to her ear, and that irritated her even more. She wanted to learn to speak them, but had some kind of barrier.

"What has your beautiful mind ticking this morning?" Del asked as he walked into the kitchen.

He leaned over to give her a kiss. It was all very…normal. And weird. She hadn't really lived with another person for years. The short time she had spent with Sean didn't count. At that moment, she realized she really liked having him there. Not just for the sex, but also because she just liked him. He didn't make her feel as if she were weird, and he seemed to like having her around also.

She watched him go to the coffeepot and pour himself a cup of Kona.

"I found this report in Italy with a man's name I've seen before, but I can't read the report. It's in Italian."

He glanced over his shoulder. "Can't you read Italian?"

She shook her head. "My forte is more the Asian languages. Romance languages make my head hurt."

"Let me see it."

"You can read Italian?"

He nodded. "Not that well, but I can read it. My forte, as you call it, is more the curse words, because my Nonna yelled them at us."

She handed him her tablet, and he sat down at the table. With the first blush of sun brightening up the room, it brought out the golden highlights in his hair. For a man, he had the longest lashes. The sweep of lashes against his golden skin seemed to mesmerize her. If his face wasn't so masculine, it would make him look like a woman. But there was no doubting he was a man.

He murmured the Italian words, and she almost sighed out loud. Bloody hell, she knew why they called them the romance languages now. Hearing the words fall from his tongue, all that Italian beauty to back it up, she was ready to jump his bones right there.

He looked up.

"What?"

She shrugged. "You're really pretty."

He didn't say anything for a long moment, before returning his attention to the report. Then, ever so slowly, his cheeks turned ruddy.

"As I live and breathe, Martin Delano are you blushing?"

"I am not blushing. Men don't blush."

Delight filled her, and she couldn't help but smile at him. "Drew blushes all the time. Any time Cat looks at him, he stutters and blushes."

"He's also barely twenty."

"He's actually almost twenty-eight, but you still can't change the fact that you blushed," she said laughing.

"I am going to ignore all of this. And tell you that a man named Stanton was detained. It seemed that a French woman, who had been on a holiday in Rome, claimed that he drugged her and raped her. There was no evidence of rape. The man claimed they'd had rough sex."

"Yes." She popped up out of her chair.

"What?"

"He was mentioned as a person of interest in Korea I think. Or Greece. Yeah, it was Greece." She found the piece of paper and showed it to him.

"We need to find out if he is here, and if he was in the other places. This guy might just be the one."

He looked over the paper. "It's thin, but it's more than we had. Let's head into the office. I want you and Marcus working on it together. He's been going through all males in the last couple of months who arrived in Hawaii. As you said, he had to have money, so he's looking for high priced rentals off the regular path."

"Okay. I'll go in with you."

He paused. "Are you sure you want to advertise that to everyone?"

"What?"

"That I came from your condo."

"Everyone knows you're at my flat."

"Still..."

She rolled her eyes. "Seriously, all of Hawaii saw it on the news. And the bet is done, so who cares?"

He shook his head. "You never fail to surprise me."

"Good. I would hate to be boring."

* * *

It took them less than twenty minutes to make it to the office. There was one thing to be said about a woman who could care less about clothing and makeup; she could be out the door at a moment's notice.

They went in the back way. Reporters were still being a nuisance out front. As they stepped into the office, Del's phone went off.

Adam saw him and clicked off his own phone. When Del saw his friend's grim expression, his blood chilled.

"Hey, Boss, I was just calling. Seems we have another missing woman."

"Got a name?"

He nodded, something close to desperation clouding his gaze. "Jin Phillips."

CHAPTER FIFTEEN

If the press had been bad before, they became relentless when Jin disappeared. In the hours that followed, the team went into overdrive. Del spent a huge chunk of his time and energy fending off both the mayor and governor. They had wanted to call in the FBI, and while he didn't mind their help, he knew that they would want to take over, not just help. Add in that there was definitely a chance there was a leak in the HPD, they really couldn't trust anyone but themselves.

They assembled around lunchtime in the squad room. Del wanted to get everyone on the same page, and make sure no one missed anything one of the other team members had discovered.

"What do we have?"

Adam shook his head. "Nothing, Boss. She went to meet a source, then…nothing."

"Cell phone?"

Marcus shook his head. "Nothing. Just like before. Probably removed the battery."

"So, no one knows who the source was, or are they keeping that from us?"

Adam shook his head. "I think they would tell us if they could. The other reporters did not like her, and the anchorwoman on the weeknights, lord, she was nasty about Jin. But, the crewmembers really like her. While the people in front of the camera might hold back, the others would not. They seemed seriously upset over this."

Emma came out of his office then, her hurried steps

propelling her so fast, she tripped over her own feet. He caught her just as she went flying. Her laptop landed on the tabletop.

"Whoa, what's up?"

"I think I found him."

Everyone turned to her.

"Him—as in the suspect?"

"Yes. Thanks to the information Marcus gave me, I worked it out."

She stepped in front of Adam and punched in the info. A photograph appeared. It was a newspaper in Japan. The man was white, blond-headed, a square jaw—he looked like a freaking movie star from the 1940s. He was dressed in a tux, and it looked like he was at some kind of public event.

"Everyone, meet Richard Stanton. He's a land developer who now calls California home."

"California?" Del asked.

She nodded. "Well, he has his residency there, but he rents his home in Napa for several thousand a week. He hasn't really returned to the mainland for quite some time now. Actually, as far as I can tell, when he arrived here, it had been over six years since he had stepped foot on American soil."

"Is he a resident of California, in the legal sense?" Adam asked.

She nodded. "And from the records, he has paid his taxes on time. He has no issues with the law—at least in the US."

"Him being here means nothing," Graeme said. "What other connections are there?"

"First, let's talk about the locations." She tapped a few more keys on her laptop. A world map appeared on the screen. "Mr. Stanton has been a busy man. He's developed shopping malls and condos around the world. He started in the US, but moved on to other countries. He first hit Britain four years ago. At the moment, I don't know of any cases connected to him there, but he moved on to Italy, and we have that arrest."

The arrest report came up.

"Sexual assault?" Adam said.

She nodded. "Del translated it this morning. Charges dropped because he claimed it was consensual. Next, he moved to Greece. There were three."

She brought up the pics of the three women. "All abducted, raped, then strangled. They were left in places with a significance to the goddesses. No DNA was found."

"That was three years ago."

"And they did not connect them until the third one; by that time, he was gone. That is when Stanton went on to Finland. There were three murders there. Again, it took them awhile to connect them. Then, Korea, which you all know about, and finally Japan."

"Why do you think we zeroed in on it so fast?" Adam asked

She shrugged. "He spaced the murders much further apart then. Plus, think of the nature of Hawaii. While these other countries aren't huge, Hawaii is just a small town where everyone seems to know everyone else. As they like to say, there is probably fewer than six degrees of separation between everyone on this island. Killing women here gets front page news. I'm not sure if he expected it, or it completely threw him off. He does seem to be thriving on the celebrity that he is getting here."

Cat nodded. "That makes sense with what you said, and what Elle and you were talking about the other day. Elle has a little background with serial killers, and the obsession is now a full-blown addiction."

"What do you mean, Elle has experience with serial killers?" Graeme asked.

Cat frowned at him. "Ask her. I'm sure she'll tell you."

"So, getting back on track, we have a rich man who has been in every one of the locations of the attacks. We have nothing else to connect him other than a rape accusation that was thrown out?" Marcus said. "Not enough for a search warrant."

Emma smiled. "No. But he is going to be at a charity event tonight. Amazingly enough, it is for women in need. The bastard probably gets a kick out of it. I found all kinds of things referencing him giving large contributions to charities that helped women."

"And that is going to make it even harder to pin it on him," Marcus said with disgust.

She nodded. "Exactly, and he counts on that. But, I'm going tonight, so we can get a better handle on the situation."

A rush of fear swept through him, and a roaring sounded in his ears. Did she just say she was going to be in the same room as the suspect? Everyone kept talking, and Emma was giving logistics; Del just couldn't make out the words. He was still trying to get his mind wrapped around the fact that Emma wanted to work surveillance on a man who got his kicks out of hurting women.

"You are *not* going to go," he practically growled.

The pronouncement stopped her in her tracks. "Excuse me?"

"You will not dangle yourself out there as some kind of treat to this man."

She looked at him as if he had lost his damn mind. Which he almost had at the moment. The idea of her being in danger made him think horrible thoughts.

"I don't know what you are talking about," she said, confusion filling her voice and her expression.

"You're just as stupid as your brother. And look what happened in *that* operation."

When a terrorist had targeted Sean months earlier, her brother thought using himself as bait had been the best idea. He had almost been killed in the process. Del was not about to have that happen here.

"First, I keep telling everyone, the man isn't going to be

interested in me. He knows I am involved. He is looking for single women. Stanton might talk to me, but that's about it. He wants to use me."

"What about Jin Phillips?"

"I don't know about her personal life, but she wasn't actually out on the dating scene when she was taken," Adam said. "All of her dating revolved around work from what I can tell."

There was something in his tone that told Del that Adam knew a little more about Jin's dating life than he let on. He'd have to corner his second-in-command soon.

"Her obsession probably fed his own," Elle said from the doorway. Everyone turned to her. "She put herself in the spotlight as his ally, and he probably couldn't allow her to continue on her own. He had to possess her."

"That makes a lot of sense," Adam said.

"Wouldn't he want her out there telling people about him, though?" Cat asked.

"Maybe. If the theory of the Trinity, of there always being three, tells us that he probably has one more kill here. What better coup than to grab a woman in the spotlight? It will make world headlines if he succeeds. He craves it like an addict craves the drug."

"So far, he always has gotten away with it," Cat said.

"Yes, but he would not have stepped this up in this manner if he wasn't after notoriety. He wants to get noticed, not caught. Many of them do in a way, but I think this bastard doesn't. I think this is all about gaining air time. Who are they going to pay attention to? A regular single woman, or a single woman who had been following him?" She looked at Del. "He's after making you look like a failure.

"I got that. I don't think it is something we need to worry about. We just need to focus on catching him."

"I need to get a dress," Emma announced as she bounded back to his office where she'd left her things. He followed her.

"You are still not going tonight."

"I can go because KT Corporation will be there. We bought two plates, so I will go. And you. Get a tux."

"This is *not* a good idea."

"What other ideas do we have? He has Jin, and we only have a short period of time to save her. It might not even be him, but we need to eliminate him as a suspect. We need to move forward and this is the first lead we have."

He realized his team was very interested in the conversation. He closed his office door and faced Emma.

"The same woman you called a bitch yesterday."

"Not even she deserves this…and the longer she is with him, the worse it will be."

He sighed knowing in the end, she would win. Del understood the danger, and everything she said was true. They were looking at a ticking clock, and he could not even imagine what Jin was going through. Still, he felt he should try one last time.

"I could call your brother and tell him."

"And then I would have to smack you with a two-by-four again." She set her messenger bag down and stepped closer. She slid her hands up his arms. "Listen, I know that you will protect me. I will be safe with you there. He isn't going to grab me. We might be able to rattle him. Then your team can step in and take the bastard down."

"You do have kind of a mercenary way of looking at things."

She shrugged. "I believe in Karma, and this wanker deserves the worst payback. I want to see you make him cry."

He chuckled and bent his head to brush his mouth over hers. "I like that about you."

* * *

"We should feel wrong for watching this," Elle said.

"Naw, it's his fault for not drawing the blinds," Adam said as he crossed his arms.

"Yeah. And how can we *not* look? It's so damned

sweet," Cat said. "Who would have thought the boss would fall for someone so fast? If anyone, I thought you would, Adam."

The two had known each other since he was in junior high and she was in the fifth grade. He had dated her cousin in high school.

"And why would you say that?"

"Marie said you were sweet."

He remembered the heartbreak he had felt at the time, as if his world was ending. "So sweet that she dumped me."

"Marie has issues."

"I guess we're working the party tonight," Marcus said.

"Yeah, and I want you to see if you can double check these things for the boss. We need to make sure that others weren't connected to the murders."

Marcus nodded. "I also want to check out the guy with him in the picture. He's in a few of them."

Cat stepped closer. "His name is Frederick Morgan from what the caption says. He is in a lot of them, isn't he?"

Marcus nodded. "If anyone knows insider information, it's that guy. Also, let's hunt up the owner of the property. My guess is Stanton didn't buy the property. He rents it."

"And if he does, the owner can give us permission to search."

"Depending on their lease, but yeah," Marcus said.

"I really hate weddings," Graeme said out of the blue.

Everyone paused and looked at the Scotsman. Adam glanced around at the team, then back at Graeme. "Is that a fact? And what does that have to do with this?"

"Look at him. That man is going to get married, mark my words. And we'll have to go."

"What's wrong with weddings?" Elle asked.

"You have to get dressed up, yes? I hate ties."

"Dude," Adam said, "You're in Hawaii. No one gets *that* dressed up, and when the boss gets married, I doubt it will be too fancy."

"I think the fact that you're assuming there will be a wedding is a little premature. Remember, her brother isn't married," Cat said. "Maybe they are more about live and let live. I get that vibe from her."

"That's because Sean lives with a man *and* a woman. They can't marry one and exclude the other," Adam said. "And, if you think Martin Delano, only son and eldest child of the Delano family, isn't going to insist on a marriage, you don't know our boss."

"I was at one last month. One of the interns got married. I would have killed to have worn a simple dress and been barefoot at my wedding," Elle said. Everyone turned to face her. "What?"

"You're married?" Graeme asked, a thread of anger shimmering in his voice.

"No. Was. Divorced now."

Graeme opened his mouth to say something that would probably result in a fight; thankfully, Del's office door opened up. He and Emma came to a stop and looked at them.

"What's going on here?" Del asked suspiciously.

"Looks like Graeme and Elle are about to have another fight. I gotta call Jaime, get some help. See you later," Emma said, brushing her mouth over his jaw and heading off. Del caught her by the arm.

He looked at Adam. "Got a moment? I have to call the mayor and give him an update."

Adam nodded and escorted her out the back door.

"So, who won the bet?" She asked with a smile.

Adam chuckled. "Doesn't matter, money went to the Humane Society."

She slanted him a look.

"Okay, if the money was to be won, it would have been me."

Emma smiled. "I had a feeling. You really *do* know your timing, Lt. Lee."

***

Emma was putting on a jade green cocktail dress when Jaime walked into her bedroom. "I think that's the one that will do it."

She had been lucky enough that her brother's lover understood her issues with shopping and had brought four dresses in her size. Along with the dresses, she'd brought a box from Liliha Bakery and bags of girl things.

"I don't really care. Just one of them will work. I have to look like I belong."

It was the fourth and final dress. If this didn't work, Emma was worried that Jaime might overrule her and tell her she had to go out to a store. That worried her more than tracking a killer.

Jaime said nothing as she helped zip up the back of the dress. "Now turn."

She did and blinked. The vision in the full-sized mirror was someone else; it had to be. Jaime had been right. The dress was perfect. The color matched her eyes and brought out the golden undertone to her skin. The cowl bodice made her look as if she actually had a chest. Her waist looked unbearably small, and accentuated the slight curve of her hips. The soft satin draped her body perfectly, and ended in a pool around her feet.

"Oh, wow."

Jaime smiled. "That man isn't going to know what hit him."

She rolled her eyes. "I keep telling everyone that the killer isn't interested in me."

"I'm not talking about *that* wanker. I'm talking about Del."

Emma shrugged. "I think he prefers me with no clothes."

Jaime laughed. "Oh, you do make me happy, Emma. No one else would say that."

"Please, if you think about it, Randy and Sean are the same way about you."

She nodded. "Yes, but every now and then, it is nice to give them a pretty package to unwrap."

"That sounds wrong."

"What do you mean?"

She watched as Jaime pulled out newly bought packages. "I don't know. You know, all the people like to say he should like me the way I am."

"Oh, love, he does like you very much the way you are. But, dressing up every now and then is good too."

Emma looked at all the containers she had on the counter. She had never owned that much makeup in her life.

"Out of the dress and put on a robe. Then we need to get down to putting on the makeup."

"I don't do makeup."

"Tonight you do."

Emma frowned.

"Don't look like that. This is all part of the job. You will always stand out because of who you are, but part of watching this bastard is getting close enough to observe. From what you told me, unless Marcus can come up with something on him to get that search warrant, or gets the owner of the property to agree, you are left with getting the guy to slip up. Or, you need to buy time. Looking pretty and gaining his attention does just that. He knows you are involved with the investigation, so he will be watching. Distract him while you work on obtaining what you need to catch the bastard."

"It sounds like a long shot when you say it like that," Emma said as she stepped out of the dress then grabbed her green robe and put it on.

Jaime shrugged as she opened up some very dark eye makeup. "It is, but it doesn't mean that you all can't make it work for you. Now, wash your face with that stuff and let's get to work."

Emma reached for the container, then paused. She looked at Jaime's reflection in the mirror as she was setting out the makeup.

"Thanks."

Jaime looked up, and smiled. "You are very welcome. It's fun to have a sister to do things with."

A *sister*. Tears burned the backs of her eyes. A year ago, she had been alone. Now, not only did she have her brother, she had Randy and she had a sister. They were a family. Warmth filled her chest as she sniffed and blinked away the tears.

"Emma, are you okay?"

She nodded and smiled. "Yeah. And you're right. It's really nice to have a sister."

* * *

Del was having a difficult time trying to concentrate on the mission. He should be focused on the monster they were there to capture. He had been trained to work under all kinds of circumstances. The problem was, as he walked into the hotel, he could only think about one person. Emma.

She was a beautiful woman, in mind and spirit, but tonight was the first night he'd ever seen her in makeup. He didn't care one way or the other, but it had left his nerves frazzled. Worse, the woman had no idea the effect she was having on him.

Worse, he was having to control his reaction. With the entire team listening, he had to be careful. It was bad enough that they were treating Emma and Del as their own personal soap opera to watch. Having it on a recording would be worse.

"Do you know anyone here?" she asked.

"Um, probably not. Although the mayor might be here. Seems like something he would support."

She nodded. The little sparkle of something shimmered in her hair. He had never seen her with her hair curled and up in such an intricate design. It looked like one little tug and the multitude of curls would come tumbling down around her shoulders.

"What?" she asked.

"Sorry, still trying to get used to you looking like that."

She shook her head. "Well, don't. It's not going to happen again anytime soon."

"Hmm."

She gave him a sharp glance. "What does that mean?"

"Nothing."

"I can't believe you're getting all bothered by a little makeup and a dress. I would have never said Jaime would be right, but there you have it."

"Right about what?"

"She said you would get distracted by me in a dress. I told her you would rather see me naked."

He snorted. "True. But then, wondering what kind of lingerie you have on under the dress, that would be interesting."

"I'm not wearing any lingerie."

He froze for a second, unsure if he'd heard what he thought he'd heard. Slowly, he turned to face her.

"What?"

She leaned closer, a little smile curving her lips. "My panty lines kept showing, so I decided not to wear any. The bodice makes it easy to go braless too."

Heat seared through his blood as it headed from his brain to his cock. Dammit, how was he supposed to think like this? There was no doubt about it, he had done something horrible in his life. It was the only explanation he had for it. He tried to swallow and found his mouth too dry to accommodate. He grabbed her by the hand and pulled her out onto the patio. He found a secluded spot.

"What's the matter?"

"Nothing...just had to do this."

He cupped her face and bent his head to brush his mouth over hers.

"You are acting very weird."

He smiled at her. "You think? I think I'm being terrifying."

She frowned and opened her mouth. He pressed his fingers against her mouth.

"Don't. We don't have the time, but just know this—you have made me fall head over heels for you."

For a second, she looked stunned. He drank in the confused look, then his heart sang when her lips curved. That look on her face made him feel like he owned the world. Who would have thought making Emma smile was all he needed to get through the day? But right now, the entire ballroom full of people had faded away, and it was just the two of them. He wanted to tell her, wanted to let her know exactly how he felt. That his little comment did not do his feelings justice.

"Indeed?"

He nodded. "You and I are going to have a serious talk."

"Now?"

He shook his head. "No. When we get done with this. All of this."

The expression in her gaze told him that she knew what he was talking about.

He led her back into the room. "I need to get us some drinks. I'll be right back."

"Wait," she said.

"What?"

"Just that?"

He stepped closer and leaned down so only she could hear his voice. "Well, the thought of pulling up that dress and taking you on the balcony had entered my mind, but since we're on a job tonight, I thought I would refrain."

She shivered as he pulled back from her. "I'll be right back."

She nodded and he walked away. They needed to get this case closed because they definitely had a lot to discuss.

"Uh, Boss, I've been told by Adam to remind you that we are all listening," Marcus said chuckling.

Fuck. He had just reminded himself about that, then

completely forgot the moment he got close to her. He seemed to have been losing his head over her from the moment he'd met her.

"I would suggest that you all forget about it. And, if there are any bets about us per that conversation, just know whoever initiates them will end up working weekends for the foreseeable future."

* * *

Emma tapped her foot to the music as she watched Del make his way through the crowd. There was something so alpha about the way he cleared a path. He said nothing. People just moved out of his way. She chuckled to herself. It was quite impressive, seeing that the room was filled with leaders from all the Hawaiian Islands. Even those people in charge were intimidated by Del.

She heard a sound beside her and realized she had lost track of her surroundings. It was a common thing when she was around Del—not to mention stupid.

Turning, she found a well-dressed man with a strong jaw, a wealth of blond hair, and an expensive smile within a few feet of her.

Richard Stanton was standing beside her.

"I've been wanting to meet you all night, Ms. Taylor."

CHAPTER SIXTEEN

The air around Emma seemed to still, as if all of it had been sucked out of the room, as she looked at Stanton's smiling face. Her blood chilled to ice, as she tried to come up with something to say. Her brain took a few seconds. Fight or flight? Which way would she normally respond? If she didn't know what she knew about him, would she be afraid?

Hell yes. Just looking at the expectant exuberance in his expression had her wanting to take a step back. She often got that response from people at the conventions and conferences she had been going to over the last few months. It made her want to go find a hole to hide in.

"Excuse me, do we know each other?"

He shook his head. "No, but I was reading one of your articles in Southeast Asian Business Monthly, and was intrigued by your thoughts on green energy and how it should be implemented in Southeast Asia."

She blinked, feeling a little flustered. He had read her article? "I think I explained it well in the article."

He took a step closer, and Emma had to fight the urge to step back. A man like him would be aroused by any fear she showed. Instead, she straightened her backbone and kept eye contact.

"Yes, but as a businessman who builds in the area, I was intrigued by your thoughts on how it would be more profitable."

"Indeed?"

"Yes," he said, his eyes lighting up.

Most people would not be put off directly by the man. He was attractive, and he definitely knew how to wear a tux. It had to have been tailored especially for him—and from the finest fabrics. However, when one looked into his gaze, there was something else present. Many others would dismiss it, but those people who paid attention would notice the way his pulse hammered in his chest. And his eyes were another tipoff. The quote *they were the window to the soul* was not far off. His unhealthy gleam should make anyone uncomfortable. Once again, with his money and looks, people would dismiss it and only look at the surface. The expensive clothing, the styled hair, and the perfect teeth would dazzle them. They would never see the sociopath beneath the surface.

"For you to be successful in that part of the world, you need to make sure that you protect the environment. It is very important to the locals, and it adds to the overall design in the end. What kinds of things do you build?"

He hesitated. Did he expect her to know who he was? Was it his own self-importance, or the fact that he thought she should have zeroed in on him as the killer already? Either way, she felt a little jolt of triumph. Wanker needed to learn that he wasn't God's gift to women. Of course, having to kidnap them pretty much proved that—but still.

"I build condos and resorts."

"Oh, then, it is vitally important to you to make sure you take care of the environment. As someone who grew up in Southeast Asia, I can tell you, they believe in protecting nature. Also, you want to appeal to westerners. The movement to support green business is growing. You add that into your marketing, and you will definitely end up winning in the end."

He opened his mouth to argue when she felt a warm hand slide around her waist.

"Darling, who do we have here?" Del said.

She looked at him. *Darling?* It wasn't a word she would ever peg Del using.

"I am not sure. He never introduced himself."

They both turned to Stanton.

"I'm so sorry. My name is Richard Stanton. I was just talking to Ms. Taylor about one of her articles."

"Oh, how nice." Del's tone told her that he thought it was anything but nice. In fact, it sounded like he wanted to beat the bloody hell out of the man.

"When I saw her across the room, I knew she looked familiar."

That caught her off guard. "Really? I don't think my picture was in the article."

"Oh, but I remembered you from the conference here. There was a picture of you and Dr. Harris at a conference here at UH."

Damn, she had forgotten about that. "Oh, yes. Odd, but I didn't think that was a very good picture."

"I think it was amazing, and I do have to say you also look beautiful tonight."

Del's fingers twitched on her waist. She knew that he wanted nothing more than to wrap them around Stanton's neck.

"Thank you."

"I would be very interested in a consult with you about green building."

"I am not that much of an expert on it. There are many more experts who might serve you better."

He nodded as he completely focused on her. She could see that a woman looking for attention, one who wanted to escape her loneliness, might find it appealing. For her, it made her skin crawl. When she lived on the street, she had learned to be wary of that kind of intense study.

"True, but you are right here and I am here working at the moment."

"I wouldn't mind discussing it with you, but I wouldn't

feel right if you considered it a consult."

He didn't look happy with that. She didn't understand it, but maybe it was all about getting his way.

"I would like to talk to you privately."

Again, Del's fingers twitched.

"Oh, that would be fine. I just meant I could not have you pay me for it."

His features eased and his smile became more genuine. Or, at least as genuine as a sociopath's could be.

There was an announcement that she couldn't quite hear, and Stanton said, "The auction is starting. I would love to catch up with you later if you have the time."

She smiled and nodded, not saying yes or no. The sooner he was gone, the better.

"Good evening," he said, then walked away.

She let go of a breath she hadn't realized she had been holding. Her nerves were still jangled, even with Del by her side.

"Bloody hell, that is one cheeky bastard. Walking up to me like that?"

Del grunted. "The fucker didn't even ask my name."

She glanced at him. "Because he didn't care. It was about making contact with me. Do you think he knows I am working on the case?"

"Hell, everyone in Hawaii knows you are working on the case. Remember, you were caught on camera, barely dressed."

"Oh, yeah." She looked back to where Stanton was. He sat at his table. "I don't get it."

"He went on an Internet search for you and found that article."

"I've had a lot more articles written about my strategy planning in games. They are easier to find because gamers obsess. Of course, he had to find one that worked for his business. I definitely would know he wasn't a gamer."

"What do you mean a lot more articles?"

She glanced at him and shrugged. "About six or seven

in the last few months. What do you think he did that for?" Referring to Stanton again.

"Maybe trying to throw us off guard?"

"He didn't even bat an eye when you showed up."

"He looked like he wanted to fight me for the honor of touching you."

She rolled her eyes. "He did not."

"He did. He wanted you all to himself."

She sniffed at that. "One thing is evident, he knows who I am."

She continued to watch the man. A younger man, a little shorter and not as attractive slid into the seat next to him.

"I wonder who that is…"

Del narrowed his gaze. "I think that might be his assistant. Some of the information Marcus found out about him indicated he traveled with one."

"Oh, yes, I remember him in some of the pictures."

She watched the interaction, and it was…weird. They looked like they were having an argument, but keeping it in low tones, so that no one would overhear them. Suddenly, the assistant snapped his gaze in her direction. She did not look away. It would do no good.

"I think we need to check out the assistant too," she said, as she waited for the man to turn back to Stanton.

"I definitely agree."

* * *

A couple hours later, Del led Emma out of the massive ballroom. He wanted to get out of there and far away from Stanton. The rational side of him knew that she was safe, but getting her further away from the bastard would help his irrational side. Cheeky bastard, indeed. To walk up to her was a bold move.

Stanton was a man who wasn't worrying about attracting attention, and that worried him. Men like that did stupid things, because they thought they were invincible. Stupid things like kidnap a woman dating the man in charge of the investigation—especially if she was involved with the investigation.

"Delano," the mayor said.

Dammit. They had almost made it out the door before he had to talk to him. He had avoided the mayor most of the night. The need to scream almost strangled him. The photographers were there, definitely, and an election was coming up. Del knew the mayor wanted to bend his ear, and make it look like he was hard on crime.

"Mayor."

"Oh, and Ms. Taylor, so nice to see you again."

Emma said nothing, but he knew she did not like the mayor.

"I didn't know the department had tickets to this."

"We don't, sir. The corporation Emma and her brother own do."

Something changed in his demeanor. "Oh, I see. Well, it is nice to see you both supporting such a worthy cause. Hope you had a pleasant time."

"The food was horrible," Emma said. "It was for a good cause, though."

The mayor apparently didn't know what to say to that. Mentioning her corporation must have made him dumb. Knowing that he offended Emma, and she apparently could afford a thousand dollar a plate function was probably freaking him out.

"Of course. These things always seem to have the worst kind of food, and, like you said, a worthy cause."

She nodded, then looked around. That was a tell for Emma. When she got bored, there was a good chance she would offend people. She hated things like this, and he knew the number of people in the room was starting to get on her nerves.

"It was nice to see you this evening, Mayor Smith."

They were turning to leave when Stanton and his assistant ran them down.

"Ms. Taylor, please tell me you didn't forgot about

setting up a meeting."

She blinked. Damn, the man had some balls. Walking right up to her in front of him and asking to see her. Granted, he had draped it in a business meeting, but Del knew better. He knew that Stanton was after something else entirely.

"A meeting?" Emma asked. She had added enough boredom in her voice to tell the man that he wasn't that important. The woman really did know how to work a suspect.

Del coughed to cover his laugh.

"Strictly business, I assure you. As I said, I was looking over your thoughts on the development business in Southeast Asia, and how it is important to work within the environment. I have been implementing green energy ideas with all my newest designs, and would like to bounce some ideas off you."

"Oh, well, then, that I can understand."

"Tomorrow?"

She hesitated, apparently taken aback by his forward manner. "Ten? I don't have a personal office, but I will be working tomorrow at a consulting job, and they give me office space."

She was doing what? She hadn't told him she was going into work somewhere else tomorrow. When Emma rattled off the address, he realized that she had just invited Stanton to TFH headquarters.

"Until tomorrow, my dear."

As they watched the two men walk away, Emma shook her head. "That is one odd duck, that's for sure. And that assistant is weird too. Did you see the way he stood back?"

Del nodded. "So, you will talk to him at headquarters?"

She smiled and patted him on the chest. "I have learned a thing or two in the last few months. We need to get an office ready."

He nodded as they stepped out of the hotel and walked to his truck. The hotel had allowed him to park in VIP up front because of his position. He helped her in the truck, then jogged around to his side. Knowing the team was still listening, he talked to them over his earwig.

"Guys, we are headed in so we can discuss this. We need to be ready tomorrow morning."

* * *

They walked in to whistles from the male team members. Emma frowned, confused.

"What?"

"Love, you are dressed up."

She looked at him, then at the guys. She shook her head. "Men are so simple."

"You do look lovely, Emma," Elle said.

"You didn't need to be here, Elle," Del said.

"I wanted to be on call just in case. I didn't know what would happen, or if we would need a rescue."

"I wish we could have taken him to a back room and beat it out of him, but I didn't think there was a chance we would catch him tonight."

"Either way, I wanted to be here."

"So, I need an office tomorrow," Emma stated, trying to move things along.

Adam nodded, but didn't look her in the eye. "We could use one of the interview rooms."

"No. I don't think that is a good idea. If we do that, he'll immediately be on guard," she said.

"Let's just use that extra office Emma uses," Charity said walking into the room. She held out her hands for their earwigs. "It will be easy enough to set up the monitoring in there. Should take me less than half an hour."

Emma nodded. "And, more than likely, he will be there with that creepy assistant."

"Did you find anything else on him, Adam?" Del asked.

Emma realized that Adam still wasn't looking at her. He punched a few keys on the computer, and the giant screen in the middle lit up.

"A little. Morgan graduated from Vanderbilt, so he's American. Not English. Came from a pretty affluent background. He was hired by Stanton six years ago."

She nodded as she studied the pictures. He hadn't changed much in the last six years. "They looked like they went everywhere together. And he was none too happy about me being there, I will tell you that. He did not want his boss setting up that meeting either."

"Yes. It was almost...not jealousy, but something else," Del said. "Weird does not even begin to describe those two."

"Well, they have been joined at the hip for years." Adam punched a few keys. "There have been rumors about their relationship, but I don't think they are sexually involved."

"If there is someone who will know about things, it's Morgan," Del said. "We definitely need to look at him as an accomplice."

"He might suspect and not know," Elle said.

"What the bloody hell does that mean?" McGregor asked.

"It means, reading over this information Adam found on him, he would not question. He came from an affluent background, but other than a trust to send him to school, his family had no money left when he went to college. His father died when he was in high school," she explained. "The family didn't realize that the money was gone until after his father was dead.

"And?" Del asked.

"He might want to live the life he previously had so badly that he would just ignore those feelings that told him Stanton is a sociopath. I am not saying that means he should not be investigated, but it might help you to know that. He might have just wanted to pretend nothing was wrong."

"We can use it against him," Del said nodding.

Emma shifted her weight again. How did women wear heels all the time? One night in them and she was ready to take them off, find the designer, and beat the person to death with the stupid little tiny heel.

"Is there anything else?"

"No."

Adam refused to look at her still. She opened her mouth to ask him why, but Del stepped in. "I say we call it a night."

"I'll be here in the morning around seven," Charity said. "I'll make sure it is all in working order before the bastard shows up."

* * *

As they walked into her flat some time later, she sighed in relief, flinging off her shoes.

"They might be pretty, but they hurt like the devil. How do women walk around in them all the time?"

Del shrugged as he toed off his shoes. "Rosaleigh avoids them, but she doesn't like to dress up. Marlena will wear them when she has to. Abs lives in them. But then, she's the crazy one."

She laughed. "I thought you were."

He shook his head and slipped his arms around her waist, pulling her closer. Damn, it felt good to finally have her to himself. The tension in his back eased as they stood there. It seemed that the long day had worn on forever. And the fact that he felt they were treading water in the investigation did not help. He had never been fond of Jin Phillips, but he hated that she'd gotten tangled up in this mess. Granted, part of it was due to the fact of her reporting, but it didn't make what was happening to her right.

"Did I say something to offend Adam?" Emma asked.

He thought back over the night and shook his head. "No. Why?"

"He wouldn't look me in the eye."

He had to fight the smile. Apparently, she had

forgotten the entire team was listening on their evening. "It isn't something you said. It's what he heard."

"That makes absolutely no sense at all."

He sighed. "Love, they heard us on the balcony. As in what I wanted to do with you."

She blinked. "Oh."

"Yeah, oh."

"But they all made bets on us going to bed."

"Adam has always seen you as sort of a little sister. Making a bet on something like that is okay. Hearing it is different."

She thought about it for a second or two then nodded. "Okay, I can understand that. I am pretty sure that Randy and Sean would probably try to hurt you if they heard what you said to me. Which, if you ask me, is very hypocritical."

"Is that a fact?" he asked, as he kissed her neck. She smelled divine. He knew that Jaime must have sprayed her with stuff, but it mixed with Emma's natural scent, and it was driving him insane.

"I told you about the kitchen incident."

He chuckled. "Ah, yes."

She bent her head to give him more access to her neck. He raised his hand to her hair and slipped his fingers through it. Small pins fell from it as her curls tumbled around her shoulders.

"Oh, that feels wonderful. They were giving me the worst headache."

She was smiling at him, with all those curls lose, and he couldn't help himself. He cupped her face.

"I love you, Emma."

She blinked, then tears filled her eyes.

"Oh, don't cry."

"I'm sorry. Since my parents died, there has only been one other person who told me that. No man has ever said that to me in the romantic sense."

It hurt his heart to hear. This woman was so sweet, so

fragile, but people didn't see it. They didn't look past her quirkiness and her big brain to see that she needed love just as much as everyone else.

He leaned in close enough to kiss her, but she set her hands on his wrists. He opened his eyes.

"I'm not good with things like this. With emotions. I know I care for you, Del. It hurts so much to know how much I do. But I am not sure just what I have to offer you. I don't do well at long relationships."

He knew what it cost her to say that. She needed to learn to trust him, to learn that he would always be there. The only way to prove it was to do just that.

He leaned closer and watched as her eyes fluttered closed. He kissed her, sweet, long, and wet. Pulling back, he set his forehead against hers.

Then, he bent down and picked her up.

"What are you doing?" she asked with a watery laugh.

"I'm going to show you just how much I love you."

She smiled, and in that moment, right there, he knew there would never be another woman for him.

He set her on her feet, then turned her around. After unzipping the dress, she let it fall to the ground in a pool of green satin at her feet. She hadn't lied to him. She wasn't wearing a stitch of clothing beneath the dress. She turned around to face him. Her curls dripped over her skin, and she looked like Aphrodite to him. No shame, completely comfortable in her own skin.

He picked her up then, laying her on the bed. He took his time, using his hands, his mouth, and his tongue to love her. There was no doubt in his mind of what he felt, what he wanted from her. And now, he wanted her to understand.

Kissing her flesh, reveling in the taste of it, the feel of it against his tongue, he sighed in appreciation. Nothing would ever fill him with such satisfaction as making love to Emma. He took her over into pleasure twice with just his hands and mouth.

When he finally entered her, it wasn't a joining for sexual needs. He felt connected to her as he had never been connected to another human. He was on his knees and she was on his lap. As his orgasm approached, he knew he wanted her there, right there with him.

"Emma," he said. "Look at me, love."

She did as he asked, and he felt his heart take a tumble once more.

"Come with me. Together."

And in that instant, he held her gaze and watched as her orgasm rushed though her body. Her eyes went blurry with desire once more, before they slid closed and she moaned his name.

It was enough to send him over the edge. He thrust into her one more time, then he gave in to his own pleasure. Together, they fell into blissful surrender, their bodies, their hearts, and their souls joined as one.

CHAPTER SEVENTEEN

The next morning, Emma sat on her lanai drinking her first cup of coffee with Del. It was peaceful, unlike it had been before. She'd had some peace at times. Sean had given her that, the security she needed, the family connection. But this was different. Sitting there, smelling the first whiff of her Kona, and watching the reflection of the sun as it shimmered over the waves—all while sharing it with Del—it filled her with such happiness.

Of course, the man who was making it so special wasn't really paying attention to her, she thought with a smile. Instead, he was going through the texts he'd gotten in the last few minutes. She didn't blame him. Hopefully, they would get some kind of information today that would end everything. And maybe, they would be in time for Jin.

He looked up from his phone. "Charity already has the room set up."

She nodded. "Yeah, I figured she would. She's a little like me. When she has a job to do, she can't sleep."

Del leaned forward and rested his elbows on his thighs. Inwardly, she sighed. He was about to give her another lecture. She would much rather he try to talk her into bed. Although, honestly, it wouldn't take much. She would also love to hear he loved her again. That would do the trick. As he droned on, she thought about that moment he'd said it. It must have been at least the tenth time she'd thought about the memory, and how different making love had been the night before.

"Hey, are you paying attention?"

She blinked. "Sorry."

Del's sigh was loud and filled with irritation. "You need to be very careful, Emma."

"I will be."

"This man has fixated on you."

"Not to get me. Not that. He wants to dance around in front of me then disappear. He wants to best me. And in turn, best the team. We won't let that happen."

He took her free hand. "I'm serious. Just make sure you do what I say. I don't know what I would do if anything happened to you."

She smiled as she set her coffee cup down on the small table beside her chair. Leaning forward, she took his other hand.

"I will listen, don't worry."

He studied her for a second, then he leaned forward and brushed his mouth over hers.

"I would much rather spend the day here."

She smiled. "So would I. Apparently, though, we have a killer to catch."

He studied her again, like he had the last few days. Something in his gaze told her he had something on his mind, but he just said, "We will talk, really soon."

"We have been talking."

He rolled his eyes. "About other things. It's not the right time."

She wanted to ask him what, but his phone chimed that he had another text. He gave her a quick kiss and picked it up.

"That's Adam. He's going to talk to the owner of the property. Evidently, he knows him."

She smiled. "It's Honolulu. Everyone knows everyone else."

He laughed and kissed her again. "Let's get going."

* * *

Adam looked up from his desk when Del and Emma

walked into the squad room. Del knew from his second-in-command's expression that he had something.

"What do you have?"

"I talked to Henry Faang. He owns the property, and has offered to let us search it. I explained how important it is to make sure Stanton doesn't know."

"And he agreed?"

He nodded, a smile curving his lips. "The man didn't know what the hell was going on, but he doesn't really like Stanton, or his assistant. He said he got a real uncomfortable vibe off the two of them."

"Then why did he rent to them?" Emma asked.

"They wanted an eight-month lease, but would pay for a year in advance. Seems Stanton told Henry he was working on a project here. You know, those high rises that there have been all kinds of protests about on Kauai?"

"Oh, yeah. It looks like the developer is going to lose those. There's some kind of state law about it or something."

"Yes. Also, he said he talked to Stanton just a few days ago, and he told Henry he would be leaving soon."

"Of course he is. He's got his third victim," Emma said. She looked at the board. "But...that is a thought. Maybe the loss of the project sped up his plan. Could be that is why there is a rush."

Adam nodded. "That might be true. I thought Graeme and I could go out there."

"You need a woman to go with you. Take Cat," Del said.

"I can go," Elle said walking into the squad room. "If you find her, you'll need a doctor."

"Good idea." Del glanced at the clock, and noticed it was inching toward their meeting time. "Best if you go now while the assistant and Stanton are here. It will make it easier."

"Right, Boss. Make sure to ping me if he doesn't show. I don't want to put Henry in any kind of danger."

He nodded. "Will do."

"McGregor, let's go."

The Scot came out of the office and looked at Elle. "You're coming?"

"You might need a doctor." Then she brushed by him.

Del knew what this meant for her, what memories it might bring back up, but she was going to do it for Jin, and to catch Stanton. No one else on the team knew of her past, so he decided to intervene.

"Elle? A word?" She nodded, and they walked over to the other side of the room. "Are you sure?"

Without taking her gaze from his, she said, "If we find her alive, she will need someone who understands. Adam and McGregor have their strengths, but this is not one of them. I can handle it."

He nodded.

"We can have EMTs on call," McGregor said, as Elle walked toward the exit behind Adam.

She turned to respond, but Del had heard enough.

"Quit bitching and go."

McGregor nodded and followed them out.

"No one else knows?" Emma said.

He looked at her. "About Elle? You know?"

She nodded. "I had everyone on the team checked out. Well, I didn't. Sean insisted on it."

He thought about her brother and that he'd probably looked over his career in the military. If there was someone who could hack into the military database, it was Sean. The man had years under his belt working for MI-6. And if he couldn't, one of his lovers or Emma could do it for him.

"Ass."

"Hey, you would do the same thing if your sister was going to be working in this job."

He opened his mouth to say no, then snapped it shut. "Okay, point taken. Although, your brother can probably hack into more places than I can."

She chuckled. "First, it was all over the London tabloids when it happened. I know that is probably one of the reasons she left. Secondly, you can't hack into anything. Just ask me, and I'll do it for you. Sean is good, but I am much better."

"I did not hear you say that."

"Do I need to repeat it?"

He looked at her. "No, love, I was just saying..." he saw Charity rounding the corner. "We'll talk about what you should tell your boss later."

"You're not my boss."

Charity smiled. "Hey, you two. I want to go over what I set up in the room. We only have a few minutes before they arrive."

Emma straightened her shoulders. "Let's do this."

* * *

An hour later, Emma felt as if she had worn a massive hole in the floor. Patience was not her strong suit. Not when she wanted to complete a project. And if ever a project needed to be completed, this was the one. She might not have proof right now, but she felt it in her bones that Stanton was the murderer.

Del's phone chimed, and he looked down. When he looked up, the expression on his face sent ice slicing down her spine. She had never seen that particular look from Del before. Determination stamped his features and his eyes had grown cold.

"They're here."

She nodded and tried to keep her nerves steady. Her stomach turned over and she pressed her hand against it.

Del glanced at her hand, then back up at her.

"Are you okay?" Del asked. "Just say the word and we abort."

"No. We have to do this. If anything, we need to keep them here so that Adam can search the house."

"You tell me, we stop."

She smiled. "Don't worry. I'll let you know if I need

you to come in and beat him up."

At that moment, Stanton appeared in the hallway. Marcus was accompanying him, as was that assistant of his. Morgan followed a couple paces behind Stanton. The expression on his face told Emma he was not very happy about being there.

Marcus held the door open for them. Stanton smiled at her, but there was nothing pleasant in it. It didn't reach his eyes, and there was a predatory feel about it.

"Ms. Taylor, I had no idea you worked with the police."

She smiled. "Sorry, I thought everyone knew. This island is so small, we are always in everyone else's business."

"No worries."

"I just work on a contract basis when they have complex cases or issues. They really can't afford me full time, and I don't like to be tied down. My office is right down here."

He followed her down the hall, then turned to his assistant.

"I'm sure they can find some place for you to wait."

Morgan did not look any happier with this situation, but he nodded.

She waited until Stanton stepped into her office, then she turned and closed the door in Morgan's face. Stanton settled in his chair as Emma sat down behind her desk.

"A bit on the Spartan side," he said, looking around the room with disgust.

"I don't do much work here. Team meetings, and sometimes I meet with clients, but not that often. I only permit face-to-face meetings with people I find to be important."

"And you say you work on contract with the police?"

"As I said, they really can't afford me, but I do like the work. It fills the time and keeps me from having to pay parking tickets."

"That is understandable. You must make a large amount from gaming organizations."

"It definitely pays the bills. So, what did you want to discuss?"

* * *

"I really don't know what you're looking for, Adam," Henry said as they walked through the house.

Adam nodded. He knew Henry from his days at UH. He had been a big supporter of Warrior football. He was barely over five feet tall, and dressed as Adam always found him. Shorts, Hawaiian shirt and *slippahs*.

"Just let us look around," he said. "If we need your help, we'll ask."

"No problem. I didn't like Stanton at all. And that stupid assistant of his. He was an odd one."

"Mr. Faang," Elle said with a smile.

"Call me Henry, dear."

She nodded. "Henry, thank you so much for doing this for us."

"No problem. I've known Adam for years, and when the police need help, I always help."

Adam didn't correct Henry's idea that they were cops. They were, but different. He also didn't have time for it.

"Have you been out here much since they rented? Does anything look out of place?" Elle asked.

"Not really. It was rented as is."

Adam walked into the master bedroom and looked around. It looked completely normal, if a little too tidy for two men who lived together. Immaculate condition, not a speck of dirt or dust. It was weird.

"This place gives me the creeps," McGregor said as he stepped into the bedroom.

"I know what you mean. I have a cousin who has OCD, and it isn't this clean in his house."

Adam stepped into the bathroom and looked through the drawers. Nothing. He noticed a window over the tub. In the middle of the yard stood a steel shed. It looked brand new. No rust, no paint worn off. It couldn't be more than six months old.

"Henry," he called out. "What's in that shed?"

Henry poked his head through the doorway. "Shed? There isn't a shed on the property."

"Then what's that?" he asked, pointing to the window.

Henry shuffled over to Adam and stood beside him. "That was not here when I rented it, and it wasn't approved."

They walked back out into the living room. There was a sliding glass door that led out to the lanai then to the yard.

"Henry, I need you to stay in the house while we check it out."

Elle opened her mouth, but Adam caught her eye. He did not want Henry to see anything, just in case they found Jin's body. The woman had been through enough. Elle must have picked up on his reasons and nodded.

"Just an FYI, gentlemen, there are some keys hanging by the back door that leads to the lanai," Elle said. "They might be to the lock on the shed."

Adam smiled. "Thanks."

He grabbed the keys as they walked out the big sliding glass door.

"This bloke is definitely a freak."

Adam nodded as they approached the shed. He slipped the key into the padlock and felt the snick. Slowly, he undid the lock and slipped it out of the holes. They both pulled out their guns. He looked at Graeme, who nodded. He opened the door, standing to the side, as it swung open. There were bars in there, a cage of some sort. It was dark, and he couldn't see very well, but he saw a gurney in the middle of the cage with a body on it.

"Bloody hell," Graeme whispered, shock dripping from his words. Weapons lined the walls...things no ordinary person should own. Many of them looked to have been handmade, and definitely fashioned for torture. Adam saw the lock on the cage and looked around. There, on the wall beside the door, was a key. He grabbed it and prayed it would open the lock. He sent a prayer to the heavens.

"Get Elle."

McGregor hurried off to do his bidding. Adam had the lock undone by the time Elle came rushing in, her bag with her. He walked into the cage, his revulsion growing by the moment.

Elle said nothing as she approached him and the body. There were tables of tools, some for tattoos, and some he was sure were used in torture. Lined up in precise order were ropes of various sizes. Blood stained all of them.

He watched as Elle felt for a pulse, holding his breath as he waited. A sigh escaped from her lips as she looked up at him. Tears shimmered in her eyes, but there was also hope.

"I have a pulse. It's weak, but she's alive."

He pulled out his phone and started punching numbers. He hurried out of the shed, but Elle stopped him.

"Wait, Adam, get a sheet or blanket or something. Then get McGregor. I need help turning her over, and I want to start getting her warm. She might be suffering from shock."

He did just as she asked. McGregor was still in the living room with Henry.

"She's alive. Elle needs your help."

McGregor nodded, and for once, just did as ordered. Henry looked ready to follow him, but Adam shook his head.

"No. Please stay out here. She...just stay out here. You don't need to see that."

Horror filled Henry's expression, and he nodded as he made the sign of the cross. Adam knew all of them were definitely going to be sending a lot of prayers up for this one.

* * *

Del sat in the room with Charity and Marcus watching

the meeting. He ground his teeth together as he tried to hold onto his temper. It wasn't easy with the way Stanton was acting.

"What I would love to do is fly you to Thailand and let you talk to my developers there," Stanton said, his voice dripping with sugary sweetness.

The longer he watched Emma talk to Stanton, the more ways he came up with killing the ass. He was practically begging her to run away with him to a foreign country. While sitting in his fucking office. *Bastard.*

"That sounds fabulous, but at the moment, I am lined up with work for the next six months."

"Oh? I am sure I can double anything that you're paid here."

Del growled. He couldn't help it.

There was a knock at the door, and he could see Cat's face in the little window.

"Watch him," he said to Marcus.

"Do I have to growl at him like you do?" he asked.

Charity chuckled but said nothing. Del tossed him a nasty look, then stepped out in the hallway. The moment he saw Cat's expression, he knew she had good news.

"They found her, Boss," Cat said, relief easy to hear in her voice.

"Alive?"

She nodded. "Really bad off from what Adam said, but she's alive. They're transporting her to Tripler as we speak."

"She was found on the grounds?"

"In a shed with a makeshift cage inside. There was a ton of horrible things in there. Adam said tools, and the damned tattoo needles."

"Jesus."

Cat nodded. "It means we can arrest him, right?"

"Yes. First, I want to talk to that assistant. Where is he?"

"He's waiting in the conference room."

He nodded and strode out the door. When he burst into the room, Morgan looked frightened. "I-is there something wrong?"

"Yes. We found a woman who has been missing for days on the grounds of your employer's house."

His face paled, and his eyes rolled back as if he were about to pass out. "I know nothing about that."

"You know about the shed?"

He nodded. "But I was not allowed to have anything to do with it. Like, normally."

"Normally."

He swallowed. "Yes. Mr. Stanton likes his privacy. He claims he paints out there. He always has a private place kept under lock and key no matter where we are living. I am not permitted."

Del grabbed the bastard by the collar and pulled him up off the ground. "You didn't know what was going on? I find that hard to believe."

"I s-swear. I didn't know. I never know," he said as he started to cry.

"You didn't want to know. It doesn't mean I can't count you as an accessory."

"N-no. I didn't know, but I can help. I can help you. If Mr. Stanton did this..." He swallowed again, and Del started to worry that he would throw up on him. "I know everywhere he has lived for six years. I kept an account of all of his business dealings."

"And you'll hand all this over?"

He nodded. "Everything."

Del dropped him and looked at Cat. "Get Marcus, and you two go over everything with him. Don't leave anything out."

Morgan nodded. "I have my laptop with me and the flash drive."

Del walked out of the room and down the hallway. He drew in a deep breath, then opened the door to Emma's office. Stanton was giving him that same smirk, and he wanted, more than anything, to smack it off his face. Instead, he stepped in, and smiled.

"Richard Stanton, you're under arrest for the abduction and rape of Jin Phillips."

CHAPTER EIGHTEEN

Long after the medical transport had taken away Jin, Elle, Adam and McGregor were still going through Stanton's belongings. Henry continued standing outside, ready to offer them any assistance. Adam's heart went out to the old guy. He'd aged at least a dozen years in the hour they had been searching the house.

"I don't *even* want to know what went on in that shed," McGregor said.

Adam watched CID folks comb the area. Drew had joined them earlier, while Marcus and Del had stayed behind to interrogate Stanton.

"You haven't heard from Elle, have you?" McGregor asked.

He shook his head. "She said she would contact us as soon as Jin's condition was assessed."

Adam still could not get that image out of his head. Her body was bruised, a new tattoo on her back...open sores. Along with the bruising around her neck. It was a sight he would never forget, and he knew he was partially to blame for it. He should have known she would become a target, but seeing her was too hard...too much. He couldn't deal with her being near, so he had used the orders from Del to keep his distance from her.

And she had paid for it.

"I know you knew her better than the rest of us."

"I know her."

"What?"

"I *know* her. She isn't dead. She survived. And, she didn't deserve this. No one is bad enough in this world to deserve this."

McGregor nodded as they both watched Drew step out of the shed. The usually smiling tech had a grim expression on his face. The horror would be imprinted on his memory forever.

"That one is never going to forget this."

"Hell," Adam said, thinking of the reaction of the seasoned CID personnel. "None of us will."

* * *

"Do you want to explain why you built a shed on the property you leased?" Marcus asked Stanton.

Del stood in the corner, allowing Marcus to take the lead. With his years of experience with DC Metro PD, Marcus knew just how to run an interrogation. Del had learned a lot since taking the job, and one thing he'd learned was that Adam and Marcus were the best at getting the truth out of people. Well, without beating the crap out of them.

Stanton said nothing as he ran his finger down the lapel of his tailored suit. He looked bored. He hadn't said a word since they'd processed him, not even asking for a lawyer. It didn't mean he wasn't guilty, only that he was screwing with them.

"They are processing the shed right now," Del said.

Something flashed in Stanton's eyes. Del looked at Marcus, who nodded. He had seen it too.

Marcus sat back, relaxing his pose. "Yes, they are going through all of your special tools, you know? Bagging and tagging them. Hell, some of them are here in the building, being handled by the staff. They get to touch them, but you'll never see them again. Well, except at trial. They will bring them in, but you will just get to look at them and not touch them."

Stanton shifted in his chair and frowned. Still, he said nothing.

"You did a good job of keeping your bodily fluids off the women. You cleaned them well. But, do you think in the last few months that you have been playing around in that death chamber that you didn't leave something, somewhere? That we won't find your semen?"

He looked at Del, then Marcus, as a sick smile curved his lips. "I can guarantee you won't."

Marcus' eyes narrowed, and he opened his mouth, but Stanton stopped him.

"This has been very entertaining, but I think I would like to call my lawyer."

A good five seconds ticked by before Marcus rose from his chair and walked out of the room.

"We'll get a phone to you as soon as we can, Stanton," Del said as he walked out into the hallway.

He found Marcus pacing back and forth. "That bastard was just fucking with us."

"Yeah, he was. What are you doing?"

"Trying to walk off my anger."

Cat came around the corner and came to an abrupt stop. "Uh, what's up?"

"He asked for a lawyer."

She nodded. "Everything on the assistant checks out. He was not in Japan during that last attack. He was off the island for a family emergency. His mother died."

She handed him a piece of paper. Del scanned it, the proof she had spoken about.

"It's still hard to believe that little bastard didn't know what was going on."

"There is a good chance he just didn't want to know. He knew it was bad, but kept his eyes closed to what was going on," Marcus said.

Cat nodded. "Just talked to Adam. The shed was insulated."

"He soundproofed his torture chamber, the sick fuck,"

Marcus muttered.

"It does check out though. I'd like to put Morgan up in a safe house, but it was denied," Del said. The mayor had cited budget concerns, but congratulated him on catching the killer, because that made a difference.

"We can't keep him here," Cat said.

Del rubbed the back of his neck. "And he can't go back to the house."

"He said he would be happy to get a room in Waikiki," Cat said. "We can send a black and white with him, say it is for his benefit."

"Yeah, that might work." He looked at Marcus. "Since we have all the info he has for right now, tell him we will escort him to Waikiki. He can pick the hotel. You take him, but get a black and white to keep watch on him. I want people inside the hotel in the hallway where he is staying. I still don't trust him, but we can't keep him here."

Marcus nodded. "Heard from Emma?"

Emma had left two hours earlier, irritated with everything. She hated this part of the job, and rarely stuck around unless he insisted.

"A text saying that the news had gotten wind of it. Which reminds me, take him out the back way. She said that Morgan's name wasn't mentioned, but you never know. They will dig it up soon enough. Also, get Stanton a phone and let him call a lawyer. Then, get someone to watch him."

Marcus nodded as he and Cat went off to do Del's bidding. He headed back to his office. He had to call the mayor and governor.

Something was bothering him about the entire situation. Something was...off. The comment about not finding his semen? Was Stanton overly confident? Before Del could work it out, his phone rang. Damn, the governor.

He shoved his thoughts aside and took the call.

* * *

Graeme arrived to find Elle standing beside Jin's bed. They were in a private room, a guard at the door, but he hadn't expected to find Elle still there.

She was dressed in scrubs, mainly because her clothes had been bloodied at the scene. When she looked up at him, he felt a sharp kick to the gut. Her eyes were swollen, as if she'd had a long bout of crying. It was hard to remember that she had been barking orders at the EMTs like a bloody drill sergeant just a few hours earlier.

"You didn't need to stay," Graeme said, trying to keep his voice low.

"Yes, I did. And it will be better if I'm here. She needs a woman. Cat is busy with more important things. Charity will process the evidence with Drew. The staff can't sit in here waiting on her. She needs someone here and she has no family."

He nodded and took a seat. He studied Jin, taking in the way her face was swollen from the beatings she had taken. Yellow and purple bruises marred her neck. If Graeme did not know who she was, he would have never picked this person as the woman he knew as Jin Phillips. She was almost unrecognizable.

"Did you find any more evidence?"

Graeme shifted his attention to the doctor. He didn't like the woman much, but he had to give her credit. She had kept her nerves steady, and she was still sitting here hours later. He had no issues with her work ethic, and his reasons for not liking her were personal.

"Too much. Morgan turned over a lot of it. He had files, records of where they had been. He had a listing of every house they rented. Addresses, rental agreements, contacts. They will be running down all the information."

In that next instant, Jin came awake with a gasp. Elle was on her feet and by her bed instantly. The wild-eyed look from the young woman told Graeme that she thought she was still in the house.

"Jin, it's okay, shhh," Elle said, her voice softer than he

had ever heard it. "You're okay. You're safe."

When Jin saw Elle, she started crying. "What? Where?"

Then she couldn't continue as she broke down. The sobs filled the room, and suddenly, he wanted to be anywhere but there. The pain he heard in them, even with the thread of relief, hurt to hear.

"It's okay, love, you are going to be all right."

"You don't understand. You have no idea." The strangled confession was filled with shame.

"Jin, look at me." Elle took her hand and looked her in the eye. "Look at me."

She waited for the woman to look at her. "I *know*."

Elle whispered the words, and he was barely able to hear them over the beeping machines. Those two words seemed to defeat Jin, and she started crying again.

"Jin, we have the man in custody. We just need you to tell us who did this."

At that point, Jin noticed him and turned white. It was as if she had never seen him before. They had talked more than once, but the sheer panic in her expression told him that her mind wasn't ready to accept that.

Elle turned toward him, and then turned back around. "That's McGregor, he's TFH."

"I don't..." Jin looked away. He heard the shame in her voice and the fear. It made him want to find Stanton and beat the bastard to death. It was better than he deserved.

While still holding Jin's hand, she turned to McGregor. Her eyes were pleading as she asked, "Could you give us a minute?"

He nodded. He stepped out into the hallway to wait. He had some bloody horrible things in his life. He'd served in special forces for the Royal Marines. Humans could do some awful things to each other especially during war. But the idea that someone chose to do something like that, to torture women was almost too horrible to comprehend. And he knew that the bastard had enjoyed it.

He scrubbed his hand over his face and thought back

to the conversation Elle and Jin had had just moments earlier. What the bloody hell was Elle talking about when she said *I know?*

Before he could answer his internal questions, a female doctor came down the hall. "She awake?"

He nodded. She knocked, then went in when Elle said to enter.

Elle opened the door a moment later, her face pale, and her eyes wide with fear. "We need to call Del. Now."

* * *

Cat came in, her face grim. "We have a problem, Boss."

"What now?"

"It seems that Stanton wasn't here the day that Jin was taken."

"What?"

"He was at a meeting on Kauai about the land development. It was their last bid to get the approval from the council. He couldn't have taken her."

Fuck. This was not possible. It was his house, his room, his money. The woman was there. How the hell had that happened?

"Are we sure? Did you talk to people there?"

Cat nodded. "They all said he was there. What are you thinking?"

"I think that we have something wrong. The way he acted when we said we would find semen...he was sure he couldn't be caught that way."

"He said that?"

"Not in those words, but he was pretty sure we would find no trace of him."

"I don't know what to tell you. He could be just screwing with you."

As he turned the idea over in his mind, his phone rang. It was McGregor.

"What?"

"It's Elle. Please tell me you have Stanton *and* his

assistant there. *Please*."

"Why?"

"Jin woke up. She woke up and said both. They were *both* in on it."

Marcus came down the hall, his face grim. Del's stomach tightened at the expression, and he knew it couldn't be good news.

"Morgan is missing. He gave the detail the slip."

Fuck. Could anything else go wrong? "Tell McGregor to stay there. You need to make sure no one gets in to see her, except staff. Do you understand?'

She didn't hesitate. "Yes."

He hung up without another word. His phone buzzed. *Emma*.

"Hey, is the interrogation over?" she asked as she munched on something.

"No. Where are you?"

"At home."

His heart started beating again. "Stay there and don't leave."

"Why?" Suddenly, he heard a crash over the phone.

"Bloody hell," Emma yelled.

He was already running to the door. "Emma, what was that? What happened?"

"It's Morgan, he broke in here. You bastard—"

He heard a slap, as if flesh had hit flesh. Then, something fell crashed against the ground, then the line went dead.

CHAPTER NINETEEN

Emma saw stars as she tried to stand up. Pain radiated from her cheek. She grabbed hold of the kitchen counter, trying to gain her balance. The room spun around her as she blinked, trying to slow it down. The bastard slapped hard.

"You ruined everything, you bitch," Morgan screamed, his voice vibrating with disgust and anger. He was a mess. His hair was a tangled heap, his clothes looked like he had slept five days in them, and rage poured off of him in waves.

Before she could right herself, Morgan backhanded her again. He used enough force to send her stumbling back again. She tasted blood, this time.

"I had everything planned, everything perfect."

He definitely did not sound as if he were thinking straight. Of course he wasn't, she thought. He'd broken into her apartment and slapped her upside the head.

"I didn't do anything. You're a murdering bastard. You were bound to get caught."

His eyes widened and his face turned red. He fisted his hands and held them up in the air.

"*We. We* were bound to get caught."

She blinked, as everything seemed to fall into place. We. He said *we*. That meant they were both involved. Now it made sense. With two perpetrators, they had an easier time of handling the women and dumping the bodies. She had often wondered just how someone could pose a body without someone finding them doing it. With two people, one of them could look out and make sure they were not caught.

"Ah, I see you have worked it out. You are the first to do so. No one ever thought I was involved. It was easier that way, you know. Stanton has a thing for hurting women. He doesn't like them very much."

"And you stood by and watched. That makes you worse."

He shook his head, his eyes glassy with sick amusement. Her stomach roiled. The bastard was reliving his actions right then. Right at this minute, he was thinking about what he did to the women.

"No. I participated. I didn't do any of the torturing though. My act was much more humane."

She realized all of a sudden what he meant. "You're the one who raped them."

Oh, God, she was going to be sick to her stomach. This man was truly a monster. He saw what he did to the women as better than torturing them.

"Yes," he said as he approached her.

She stepped back, trying to put as much space between them as possible. He wasn't going to let her make it to the front door. She was still a little fuzzy, thanks to the couple of slaps, so she wasn't sure she could even walk straight at the moment.

"Everything was going fine until that woman exposed you as one of the investigators."

"I'm *not* one of the investigators."

He didn't pay any attention. He just kept rambling on.

"Of course, you are one of our smartest opponents. By the time they linked the killings in other countries, if they even did, we were long gone. Everything would have been fine if Stanton had not fixated on you. The moment he saw you, he could not stop thinking about you. He wanted to rub it in your face. Did you know, he wanted to be a member of Mensa, but they denied him?"

Emma said nothing. She was trying to think of something, anything that would get her out of there. Or at least draw out the time. Del would be there any minute. She just had to hold on until he arrived. At the moment, she wondered just where the hell the building security was? There was a good chance that Morgan had done something to them.

"He always thought he was so smart. He wanted people to understand that, and I think there was a part of him that thought if he could get away scot-free with you helping the police, it proved he was the smartest one around."

"What was the meaning of the tattoos?"

For a moment, she didn't think he would answer her. But he shrugged. "I told him that was a mistake, but he couldn't let it go. That's what you zeroed in on, wasn't it?"

She nodded then immediately regretted it. Pain exploded in her head.

"I told him that would happen, but he would not listen."

"What did it all mean?"

"You haven't figured it out?" She said nothing. "Stanton had issues with women, that is easy to see. But he had more issues with his mother than Norman Bates. She was devout. She punished him for a being a man and told him that it was his fault for everything damned thing in the world. Men, you see, were the root of all evil."

"Ah," she said. In her head, she was trying to figure out a way to get to the door but she didn't think it was going to happen. She would have to inch close enough to kick him. A roundhouse kick might work, but her head is still spinning.

"He became fixated on mythology then…I guess his way to rebel. Fucked up family if you ask me. He saw himself as the only one who could save their souls."

"And you stayed with him? He sounds completely nutters."

He smiled and evil lit his eyes. "He was, but I reaped the benefits. There he was, running around taking all the risks, playing God, killing his trinity, while I did nothing but took what I wanted."

Lord, the man was vile. There wasn't a place deep enough in hell for him. But, she knew she had to keep him occupied. Del knew what was going on and he would be there soon.

"So, what happened? You let Stanton reel them in? It was his job to get the women to come to you two?"

He nodded. "Sad, lonely, needy women don't see the monster beneath that expensive surface. They only see the man he presents to the world. But, the one in there lurking, it's worse than anyone could even imagine."

She snorted. "I understand the situation now."

"What do you mean?"

"You can't get women on your own. You're not that attractive, you're not rich, and women want nothing to do with you. So, he abducts them, and that is the only way you can get a decent shag."

"Shut up," he screamed

"What?" she asked with a sneer, hoping she would drive him mad enough to lose what was left of his control. "Were you a virgin when you were hired? You stayed on all these years, because you know deep down, you could never get a woman to look at you, let alone fuck you?"

The scream that released from his mouth sounded like a wounded animal. It still vibrated through the air as he jumped at her. She saw the opportunity, raised her foot, and kicked him right in the balls.

"Fucking bitch," he said, grabbing for her.

She ran away, but still could not get to the door. If she headed that way, he would have her easily. Still clutching his nuts, he pulled out a rope and started to approach her. His eyes blazed with murder. She kicked him twice, just like Sean had taught her, but the third time, he caught her foot and pushed her down. She popped back up, adrenaline snapping through her, giving her the ability to fight back.

She balled up her fist and punched him. But he caught her hand. With a gasp, she tried to pull her hand away, but he dug his fingers into her flesh. As she tried harder to pull away, he drew her closer. They stumbled out onto the lanai. She had worked her way around so that his back was to the edge. She struggled, trying to get away from him, but he yanked her closer. Her weight and his unsteadiness got the better of him. They both lost their balance and then, they were falling over the railing.

* * *

Jumping over Emma's damaged door, Del burst into the apartment just in time to see Emma and Morgan fall over the edge. In that one second, his world almost ended. He ran across the apartment. When he looked over, he found Emma holding onto a small railing.

She was alive.

He released a breath he did not know he had been holding and reached down to her. Relief coursed through him making him feel slightly dizzy.

"Give me your other hand."

Emma grunted and raised her hand toward him. She was bloody, her face beat all to hell, but he ignored that. He concentrated on grabbing her other hand. He caught it, but he didn't have a good hold on her. On top of it, he could feel that she was losing her grip on his hand. Panic had him shouting at her.

"You hold on, Goddammit. If you let go, I swear to God, I will come down there and strangle you, Emma. Do you hear me? I will make you regret letting go."

Just then, her fingers tightened on his, as he leaned further over. Marcus came running in behind him, and grabbed him by the waistband.

"Pull her, Boss, just pull her up."

He used every ounce of his strength to tug her up and over the edge of the balcony. He knew she probably scrapped her legs on the concrete, but at the moment, he didn't give a damn. He set her on her feet. Cupping her face, he kissed her gently, his heart still beating out of control against his chest, and his head spinning from the fear that was still pounding through him. When he pulled back, he smiled at her.

She smacked him on the back of the head. He blinked.

"You're going to strangle me? Seriously, Del, why I love you is beyond all reason. You are a freak."

He was so stunned by her comment that it took him a moment to recover. A bubble of laughter escaped as he pulled her closer. "Well, that makes two of us, love. I guess we're stuck together."

He heard feet pounding with the arrival of Marcus, this time with Cat and a few EMTs. They approached him, and he thought he heard Cat sigh.

"Good to see you're still alive, Emma," she said, her voice a little shaky.

Emma smiled, then winced. "That wanker split my lip."

"Del, the EMTs need to check her out," Cat said.

He nodded and picked Emma up to carry her to the couch. He settled her there, and stood back as they examined her.

The first thing the EMT did was check her eyes. He glanced at Del. "I think we need to take her to the hospital. She has a slight concussion from the looks of it."

"I don't like hospitals," Emma said, and he heard the panic in her voice. She had issues with hospitals but she needed to go.

"I'll go with you. They will let me ride in the ambulance, and I am sure they will give you excellent drugs when we get there. Everything will be fine. You'll see."

If he repeated it to himself enough times, he might really believe it.

* * *

It took over an hour to get her settled in her room at Tripler. She wasn't happy about being there, but the doctor had insisted. Del knew he had work to do…that he should be doing, but he had left Adam in charge and had gone with her to the hospital.

Thankfully, he used his badge for the privilege of being in her room. He was damned if anyone was going to push him out.

"My mouth tastes purple," she said.

When they'd gotten to the ER, the doctor said she wasn't concussed, but he thought she should stay for observation. The pain had been immense, and she had a gash on her head they had to stitch up. She'd also strained her wrist when she caught hold of the railing as she went over with Morgan. So, they had wrapped it, and put her arm in a sling to stabilize it.

"You'll feel better soon."

"I feel well now. Very well. Like floating off the bed well. It's just that my mouth tastes like purple. It was an observance, not a complaint."

He smiled at her. Emma on painkillers was a new experience.

"Are you sure I look okay?"

This was new too. Emma rarely worried about her appearance, but she had a gash on her forehead and bruising on her face. Her lip was swelled up from the smacks the bastard had given. Morgan should be happy he was now burning in hell. If not, Del would have made sure he begged to go to hell by the time he was finished with him.

He looked at her battered face and smiled. "You're beautiful."

That seemed to ease her worries for the moment.

"Hey," she said scooting over and patting the bed. "There's enough room on here for you."

"I think you need to rest."

She pouted, and Emma never pouted. She demanded, complained, and knocked him upside the head. She *never* pouted. "I need some spooning."

He opened his mouth to respond, but Sean's loud voice echoed down the hall outside her door. Fantastic.

"I'm looking for my sister, and I want to see her now," Sean shouted loud enough for people on the mainland to hear.

"Uh oh, Sean's here," Emma said. "Why's he being so loud?"

"I think he's worried about you."

She rolled her eyes. He wanted to laugh, but it just wasn't in him at the moment. Now that he had gotten her there, and she was safe, he started thinking about what could have happened. He almost lost her, and he didn't know what he would have done if he had. There was a good chance that he would have found the bastard and shot his corpse.

The door burst open. Sean stood there, his face a mask of anger, his eyes blazing. He looked like some kind of avenging angel.

"Sean, hey," Emma said.

His eyes widened and his skin paled. "Oh. My. God. You look *horrible*."

Emma looked at Del with a narrowed gaze. "You said I looked beautiful."

"You *are* beautiful," he said.

"You've been beat all to hell, Emma," Sean said, still talking much too loud for a hospital.

Tears welled up in Emma's eyes. "You lied to me. You said I was beautiful."

He really did not know what to do. His youngest sister was like this, crying at the drop of a hat, but Emma, she was strong. She didn't cry. She fought tears, and denied them when they were falling.

Del tossed Sean a nasty look. "She *is* beautiful."

Randy and Jaime had finally caught up with Sean. He

didn't even want to know what they did about getting into Tripler, which wasn't exactly easy to do. But, knowing the trio, they had their ways. And they probably had a few alternative identities to help.

"Love, I think you need to tell her she's beautiful," Jaime said, humor lacing her words.

"It does not matter because I am ugly," she shouted between sobs.

Sean's face softened when he realized he had upset his sister. "I'm sorry. You are very beautiful."

"You're just saying that because you are worried I won't stop crying."

His lips twitched. "No, really. I mean it."

She sniffed. "You do?"

"Yes."

She smiled and brushed her tears away.

"Are you doing okay?" Randy asked.

She nodded as she reached out for Del's hand. "Del's here."

Sean looked at Del and nodded. "How about we all stay here for a little bit? It will make me feel better."

"That's good, as long as Del can stay."

"Don't you need to get back to the office?" Randy asked.

He shook his head. "Adam can handle it."

As they were settling in their seats, Elle poked her head in. "Oh, wow, you have a full house."

"Ellllllllle."

The doctor chuckled and stepped in. "I see you've had pain killers."

"Lots and lots of them."

"You had one dose," Del told her.

"Del, I hate to bug you, but may I have a word?" Elle asked.

He nodded and leaned over to give Emma a kiss on her forehead. "Behave."

"Where are you going?"

"Remember Elle? She's here and needs to talk to me. Sean will come here and hold your hand until I get back."

"Do you promise?"

He heard the fear in her voice, knew that it was more than the incident tonight. Except for Sean and Del, she had always been left on her own, isolated. He hated it and knew they had a long way to go to settle her mind in that regard, but he could make sure that, at least at this moment, she understood.

Del looked her in the eyes. "I will always come back for you, love. Just like when I first met you. Just like tonight. Without you, I'm nothing."

He thought he heard a sigh of appreciation behind him, and it was definitely female.

Her smile turned into a grin. She was a mess, with the bruising and the swollen lip, but she was beautiful, and she was his.

"Okay."

He kissed her forehead again and followed Elle out of the room. He knew this would not be pleasant.

"How's Jin?" he asked.

"Shaky, but she's resting right now. They've given her a sedative. I've fended off the news people, as Tripler is good about that, but I think we need to offer her some protection. This is different from other cases where we can keep the rape victim's name out of the papers. Everyone knows it's her."

He nodded. "And we might need her to testify."

She sighed and rubbed her temple. "I hope she can do it. It's early, but she freaked out when she saw McGregor…and she knows him. He told me she's tried to interview him a number of times."

"She has no family, right?"

Elle nodded. "Mother and father are deceased, no siblings or extended family."

"I really appreciate you looking after her."

She shook her head. "It's for the best. I've put in a call

to the support group I work with. I still think it is too early to expect anything from her, but laying the foundation from the beginning will help."

He nodded.

"I take it Emma is okay? McGregor related what happened."

"He's still here?"

"No, he left a little while ago."

Del nodded. "And yes, she's fine. A little bump on the head, a gash, a swollen lip. Of course, she almost fell to her death, but hey, all in a day's work."

"Don't do that, Del. Don't get mad at her."

"I'm not. I'm mad at myself."

She shook her head. "Don't. It ruined my marriage and left me a broken shell. She beat the hell out of him before he fell over, from what I understand. She's strong, and part of the reason she is that way is because of you."

Del smiled. "How did you get to be so smart?"

"I survived hell, then dealt with a man who blamed me for it. Don't do it to her *or* yourself. Be happy. Life is too bloody short for guilt."

He nodded, then gave her a kiss on the cheek. "Thanks."

* * *

Emma still felt as if she were floating above the bed.

"When they let you out, you can come stay with us," Sean said.

He wasn't asking, he was telling her. And he was ruining her nice little buzz the meds had given her. *Wanker.*

"No."

"You can't stay in your condo right now. It's a crime scene," Randy said.

Jaime remained silent, which meant she was going to make Emma tell them no again.

"No. I am not staying with you."

"But—" Sean started, but he didn't get to finish.

"She'll be staying with me."

All of them turned around and looked at Del. She smiled, then winced. Bloody hell, the drugs were definitely starting to wear off.

"You didn't do a very good job of taking care of her this time around," Sean said.

"Are you accusing me of putting her in danger?"

Their voices were growing louder and starting to hurt her head. She knew it would only be a matter of time before an orderly showed up to say something to them all.

"Shut up, both of you."

They turned to her. "I am staying with Del. He can take care of me."

"*I* can take care of you," Sean almost shouted.

"No offense, Sean, but I would rather stay with Del."

He frowned, but she didn't miss a little hurt flash in his gaze. She held up her hand and waved him back over. He walked over.

"Del will take care of me because he loves me. I want to be with him. I love you, but ya know, not that way." Her voice came out in a stage whisper.

Okay, the drugs were still not worn off all the way.

"I guess I can let you go."

"I'm twenty-seven, Sean, I can go where I want. If you want to give me issues, you can bugger off."

He smiled and leaned down to kiss her nose. "I love you, kid."

"I love you too. Now go home. In a day or two, when they are still not allowing me to drive, I will need someone to rescue me and take me for sushi. I elect you."

"It's a date."

Jaime and Randy turned to leave. Sean stopped in front of Del.

"Take care of her."

"With my life."

He nodded and they finally left them alone.

"Bloody hell. I thought they would never leave," she

said.

He chuckled. "They were worried about you."

"I have you to take care of me. That's all that matters."

He nodded, sitting down beside her, taking her hand again. He kissed her bruised knuckles.

"You really put up a fight, didn't you?"

"Sean taught me well," she said, feeling herself start to drift.

Before she fell asleep, she felt his mouth on her hand again, a simple kiss. Content, she let herself relax and dream.

CHAPTER TWENTY

Del frowned as they walked up the steps to TFH. He didn't want to stop on the way home from the hospital, but Emma had insisted. She wanted to see everyone and thank them. He had wanted to get her home so she could rest. Of course, she won the argument.

If she had looked bad the day before, she looked ten times worse today. The bruises had blossomed on her face, but at least Sean refrained from saying anything. Sean, Jaime, and Randy had shown up that morning and helped him check Emma out of the hospital. Del agreed to bring her to their house in a couple of days to keep Sean from following them back to Del's house. His plan had been to keep her in bed to rest once they got there.

Emma had other plans.

She was still a little wobbly when they reached the door.

"I told you we should go straight home."

She shook her head. "We have to stop by my flat anyway. I need to get some clothes."

"Jaime did that for you already. She stopped by my house and left them in a bag."

"Oh," she said. "That was sweet of her."

He nodded. It had been, especially since she had her hands full with two very irritated men, who wanted to take Emma home and watch over her themselves. *Forever.*

There had been discussions of taking her to Japan too. Jaime had calmed their tempers and had been instrumental in making sure that Sean did not claim Del's couch.

Del held the door open for her, since she had her arm in a sling still. He still didn't like the way she looked.

The entire team was standing in the squad room, and began to clap when they walked in. Emma turned around as if to see who they were clapping for.

"They are clapping for you, love. You caught the killer."

She shook her head, and he nodded.

"No. I caught the rapist. You all caught the killer."

Adam chuckled. "She has you there, Boss."

Adam stepped forward to give her a kiss on the cheek and a gentle hug.

"It is so good to see you looking okay."

"My heart about stopped when I showed up there and had to help Del," Marcus said. "I thought I was going to lose you both over that lanai."

"And you did help us catch the killer," Cat said.

Emma shook her head. "We all did. It was a team effort."

"And, we got you a treat we know you love," McGregor said, picking up a box from Liliha Bakery. "A wee treat for a mighty, wee lass."

She laughed, and it was music to his ears. She had been somber for most of the day, thinking things over. She blamed herself for not picking up that there had been two perpetrators. He knew it was part of the job, and that she was going to go over it again and again. They all were.

"Thank you."

Charity walked in then. "I heard there were coco puffs."

"There are indeed," Emma said.

"You don't look too bad," she said.

"Thank you. My brother said I looked horrible."

Charity shook her head. "Brothers are the worst."

"You sit. I'll get some paper towels," Del told her.

She smiled at him and then sat in the chair as he went into the break room. He turned and found Adam standing there.

"So, when's the date?"

"What date?"

"I took a phone call from your mother. Seems that she couldn't get hold of you today, and called here looking for you."

Damn.

"And?"

"She said, tell him I have his grandmother's ring, and will send it to him as soon as he wants."

He shook his head. Geraldine Delano did not know how to keep her mouth shut. He'd called her this morning while Emma was taking a nap. His mother was on Eastern Time, so she was up before the crack of dawn Hawaiian time. She had promised to get his grandmother's ring out of the safety deposit box and get it to him. He thought it might take her several days, not several hours.

"Listen. Don't say anything yet. I haven't had a chance to ask. What with the whole serial killer trying to kill her thing."

"So, did she say yes?" Marcus asked when he came in.

"What the hell, Adam, did you tell everyone?" He looked at them both. "And there better not be a bet on whether or not she will say yes."

They both suddenly found the ceiling interesting.

"Hey. I mean it."

"Okay, sure, Boss," Adam said. Del didn't feel that reassured.

He sighed and walked out into the squad room. "Oh, one thing."

He turned to face Adam. "They moved Stanton over to HPD, then they will transfer him to Halawa."

Del nodded.

"They have him on suicide watch," Marcus said. "That

is one crazy fucker. You should have heard all the stuff he was spouting off about the goddesses and how they must be destroyed."

"And Morgan wasn't much better from what Emma told us. The idea that those two found each other out of all the millions of people in the world turns your blood cold."

"Yeah, it does, but thank God we stopped him before he got out of Hawaii," Adam said.

"Did you see Jin before you left the hospital?" Marcus asked.

"No. Elle was returning as we left. Said they are keeping her there, mainly for her mental situation, but also because she was severely dehydrated. She's going to stay with her and help her get counseling."

But they all knew that the emotional scars wouldn't completely heal because of the memories. They would all be there for as long as she lived.

"Where are those paper towels?" Emma called out.

"Look, she's already ordering him around," Marcus said with a chuckle.

As Del walked out into the squad room, he stopped. They were all sitting around the table, chatting and laughing, and they looked like...a family. They were in a way, and from all the good wishes—not to mention the constant text messages in the hospital—he knew they accepted her as one of their own.

And now he had to step up his game before one of those idiots told her about the ring.

* * *

In the early evening, Emma and Del sat on his small lanai, which looked out over the Hawaii Kai canal. She liked where his house was situated. It was close enough to the beach that she could feel the ocean breeze, but it was quiet, as if it were in another world.

"I like it here," she said.

He glanced at her. "I think you took too many pain pills."

She rolled her eyes. Emma was still embarrassed by her behavior the night before. She had never had pain pills or even liquor.

"I did not. And I like it here. I liked it when I stayed here before."

He took a long draw off his beer.

"Then why did you move to Waikiki?"

She had to fight a smile. He might think of himself as an outsider, but he already thought like a *Kama'āina*. Hawaii Kai was less than forty minutes from Waikiki on a good traffic day. Only a local would refer to living in Waikiki as if she had moved to another state.

She shrugged. "Sean found the condo. I looked here, but there was nothing that would work."

He slanted her a look. "I thought you didn't like me then, but you wanted to live in my neighborhood?"

"I liked you, but you didn't like me."

He smiled. "You did hit me with a two-by-four."

She asked, "Why do you keep bringing that up?"

He gave her what Jaime called puppy dog eyes. "It really hurt."

"Yeah, right."

"It did. I still have issues with the injury."

"Really?"

"Yeah. Been knocked senseless ever since then. First the board, then that amazing mind, and, finally, your sweet heart."

She blinked, as tears filled her eyes. "Oh, why do you say things like that to me, Del?"

"Because I love you. And, you love me. You yelled it at me last night."

She blinked. "I did?"

He nodded. "Yes, you said you didn't know why you loved me."

"Well, that's rubbish."

His smile faded. "What the hell does that mean? Everyone heard you yell it at me."

"What I meant was that I know exactly why I love you."

His expression eased. "Yeah? Why?"

"You're tough, smart, kind, and you think I'm beautiful, even when my face is a mess. On top of all that, you make my brain melt when you kiss me."

His lips curved as he leaned closer to her. "That sounds good."

He brushed his mouth over hers, slipping his free hand up to cup her face. He pulled back a few inches. "Marry me, Emma."

"Oh…marriage?" Panic filled her at first. Marriage meant forever, until the end of time. She didn't do forever with anyone.

"Yeah." He studied her for a long moment. "And that is not what I thought you would say."

"It's that…marriage. I never thought I would marry."

"Well, think about it." He popped up out of his chair and started to pace. "Damn, woman, I get all romantic, blah blah, and you do this."

She bit her lower lip and tried not to laugh.

"What? Don't you dare laugh at me."

Then, she let the giggles spill out of her. Only a man who understood her and loved her would still be around. She'd hit him with a two-by-four, walked out on the job, and drove him crazy on a daily basis.

"Yes."

"Yes, what?" he asked, his voice distracted.

"Yes, I'll marry you."

He stopped and looked at her. "You will?"

She nodded. He set his beer on the table, then scooped her out of the chair.

This time, he kissed her loudly. "Ow."

"Oh, sorry," he said, his voice filled with regret as he kissed her gently.

When he pulled back, she said, "But nothing big. Justice of the Peace."

"No. We have to at least have a ceremony. My mother will want to be here."

Oh, lord, the mother. A whole other reason to panic.

He laughed. "I don't think I have ever seen that particular look on your face before."

"It's just, I never had a real relationship before, and I definitely didn't meet a mother."

He cupped her face. "She will love you."

"How can you say that?"

"Because, I love you, and you are going to give her grandbabies."

She felt slightly dizzy. "Babies. I hadn't thought about that, either."

"Whoa, there, Emma. You look like you're going to pass out."

"I am not so sure about this baby thing."

He frowned. "You don't want kids?"

How did she explain this? "I'm like my mother. A lot like her. My issues come from hereditary genes."

Understanding filled his expression. "First of all, I do not think there is anything wrong with you."

She took a step back from him, the air seemingly evaporating in her lungs.

"I have meltdowns if things get too overwhelming." Like right freaking now. She was about to have a meltdown. Her first thought was to run. This was dangerous, this could hurt. He could turn away from her when he realized that she would produce children that had her personality.

He nodded and slipped his hands around her waist and held her tight.

"First, I don't find that too challenging. I once had a girlfriend who had to have her sheets match her underwear."

She opened her mouth, then snapped it shut. "You did not."

"I did. She wasn't that smart, but she did have about

ten sets of sheets."

A giggle tickled her throat, but she fought it. This was too serious to joke about.

"Face it, Del, living with me forever, or a whole bunch of little Emmas, is going to be difficult."

"My father always said to marry a difficult woman."

"Now I know you're lying."

"He did. He said that women who always agreed with you and were easy to please were boring."

"Still..."

"Besides, my genes are far more superior since I am Italian. You're kind of a mutt, and probably not as strong in the hereditary line."

She blinked again. "Excuse me?"

"You know, survival of the fittest, and all that crap."

"All that crap?"

"Yeah. What do you have in there? Some Thai, English...what was your father? Doesn't really matter, because I'm just about one hundred percent Italian, so there is a good chance those kids will take after me. Add Sean into the mix and you definitely have inferior genes."

Irritation and amusement threaded through her. "That is a bunch of rubbish."

He grinned. "Yep, it is. Because the truth is, I don't care if we have five little Emmas running around our house spouting theories, or telling me why American football is just stupid. Or five very handsome Martins showing you why you are wrong. All that matters is that we are together."

Her vision wavered, and she knew she had tears in her eyes again. "Yeah?"

He nodded and kissed her. "They will be beautiful and brilliant, just like their mother. And they will all know how to beat the hell out of anyone, as long as they have a two-by-four."

She laughed. "That's true."

"Emma, marry me."

Joy exploded within her as she rose up on her tiptoes to brush her mouth over his.

"Yes, let's get married."

And there, with the sun setting over the Pacific, she kissed him, knowing that she had finally found her home.

COMING DECEMBER 2015
THE NEXT EXCITING INSTALLMENT OF TASK FORCE HAWAII

As a cold case heats up, two former adversaries discover there is a thin line between love and hate.

TASK FORCE HAWAII, BOOK TWO

Seven years ago, Dr. Elle Middleton's world crashed and burned. She has rebuilt her life and found comfort in her work as the medical examiner for TFH. When a new case leads to a cold case, she is beyond excited for the challenge, until she finds out the one man she wants to avoid is her partner on the case.

Graeme McGregor isn't any happier with the assignment. The doctor gets under his skin in more ways than one. He's avoided her and his attraction by keeping his distance from her, but working with her has made it impossible to resist taking a little taste.

One kiss leads to another…then to a full blown affair. But even as they draw closer to each other, secrets from that long ago murder rise to the surface. The killer's determination to stay free leads to a dangerous confrontation that puts both of their lives in peril and could leave TFH in shambles.

GET THE BOOK THAT INTRODUCED YOU TO DEL AND EMMA!

A LITTLE HARMLESS RUMOR

Loving someone doesn't mean you can save him from himself.

Rumors are swirling about the fall of Sean Kaheaku, but he's ignoring them. Six months earlier, he had his entire world turned upside down and he still doesn't know what to do about it. He retreated to his home in Hawaii to recover and reassess what he wants to do now that he's been burned as a security agent.

Now lovers, Randy and Jamie arrive in Honolulu to find the lover they once knew is now even more secretive and belligerent. He refuses their help, but they are both too stubborn to leave—especially since they sense something dangerous is stalking Sean.

As the three lovers spend more time together, old feelings float to the surface and the twosome becomes a threesome. Nights are even hotter than the Hawaiian sun, and all three lovers find the connection exciting and overwhelming. But, the trouble is still out there and arrives intent on destroying Sean and everything he loves—including Randy and Jaime.

»WARNING: This book contains three spies who like to play games in and out of the bedroom, hot m/m loving, more m/m/f loving, dangerous games, lies, a few misdemeanors, and love scenes so hot, even most Addicts will be shocked. There is also a group of Alpha males with badges who will have their own series, a heroine who knows how to handle her two men, and two men who know exactly what she likes. As usual, ice and towels should be handy to help you through the book.

PLEASE ENJOY THE FIRST CHAPTER FROM A LITTLE HARMLESS RUMOR, NOW IN PRINT AND DIGITAL!

Sean came awake in a rush with the knowledge of two things: he drank too much the night before, and he was not alone. The first one had to do with the bottle of bourbon he'd crawled into the previous night. The latter came from years of experience.

He slipped his hand beneath the pillow to get his gun and found it missing. Unfuckingbelievable. Since his trip to Thailand six months earlier, everything in his life had gone to shit. That's what he got for being greedy. One bad job with a high price tag, and he couldn't seem to shake the clusterfuck his life had become.

"You don't need to worry about that," said a familiar female voice behind him. Her English accent had faded, but he knew the tone. She was pissed.

Damn, his luck was getting shittier and shittier.

He turned over and tried to keep from groaning in pain—and failed miserably. His head spun and his stomach threatened to revolt. Every inch of his body ached as if someone had beaten the living shit out of him. He had only himself to blame for his present situation.

He blinked at the vision standing in his room. Jaime Andrews dressed as if she were *Kama'aina*. But then, that was something she had always been good at. She could fit in any situation. The blue t-shirt made her Pacific blue eyes stand out even more. She had tied the shirt in a knot beneath her breasts, allowing for a view of her smooth rich brown flesh. She still had the belly ring she had gotten when they had done a job in Venezuela. Her hair was up, off her neck, and he liked it that way. It always gave him better access.

"Oh, you are a right mess, Sean," Jaime said.

"What the hell are you here for, and why did you break

into my house?"

"I wanted to knock on the door like a regular person. Randy decided we needed to break in."

She motioned with her head across the room and, sure enough, Randy was there. Of course Randy was there. It was the way his luck had been going lately, not to mention, Randy and Jaime had been joined at the hip for over a year now.

Shit. He couldn't catch a fucking break. The two people who meant more to him than anyone else—until that trip to Thailand where there to see him look like an ass. His world had been turned upside down, and he hadn't wanted to pull his former lovers into the mess his life had become.

He didn't want to face them, to let them see where he had ended up.

Sean tried to sit up and found his stomach roiling. A soft trade wind blew through the opened window, bringing with it the smell of plumeria. It was a scent that never failed to remind him of Hawaii and give him comfort. Now, the usually pleasant fragrance made his mouth water and his belly tremble. Fuck, he'd had too much to drink. He sort of remembered the night before. It came to him in flashes. Someone had been there giving him shit about drinking too much. Del—that's who it had been. He'd appeared at Rough 'n Ready and dragged him out of the club. The memory of Del's voice as he yelled at him on the drive home pounded through Sean's head. Then, Sean remembered a very pregnant Ali was there, helping him into bed and telling him he would feel like rubbish in the morning.

"Whoa, I would not move too fast if I were you," Randy said. He was dressed in cargo pants, a tight blue t-shirt, and his feet were bare. At least Randy could remember the rules of his house, even if they weren't sleeping together anymore. He'd been in the sun recently. The tips of Randy's hair always had turned to gold silk when he'd spent time on a beach. And, as usual, Randy looked fucking good enough to eat. Sean knew just how tasty that treat was.

That thought had him scowling. He'd moved on. He didn't need either one of them. He was independent and didn't need the pain.

"I think I know what I can handle."

Randy rolled his eyes and walked over to the open doors that led out to the lanai. Sean could hear the lapping of waves against the shore. Normally it soothed him, but today, it made him want to throw up. Everything did.

Jaime sat down on the bed. "What the bloody hell are you doing?"

He saw the concern in her eyes and heard it in her voice. Years ago he would have been thankful for it. Hell, he would have begged for it. These days, he needed to keep her far away.

"I think I'm sitting in my bed asking questions that are not getting answered."

"Oh, well, someone isn't in a good mood. Not our fault that you got pissed last night," Jaime said.

"I didn't know you were living on Oahu now," Randy said, breaking into the conversation.

Sean didn't think he needed to answer that question. With as much dignity that he could muster, he scooted over to the edge of the mattress and stood up. He wobbled a bit, but recovered before he could embarrass himself.

"Oy, where are you going?" Jaime asked.

He slanted her a dirty look and decided to hit her right where it would hurt. "Be careful, Ms. Alexander, your roots are showing."

With that, he walked into his bathroom and shut the door. Closing his eyes, he drew in deep breaths.

When he opened them, he saw his reflection in the mirror. His eye was blackened. His torso was yellow and purple. *Shit*, what the hell had he done last night?

With a shake of his head, he decided he'd call Del later to find out what happened. Sean knew it wasn't going to be a story he would enjoy, and there was a good chance he would owe his old friend more favors.

* * * *

"He doesn't look *that* bad," Randy said.

Jaime looked over her shoulder at him, then back out at the waves rolling in from the Pacific. The sound of the surf coming in was the only thing keeping her calm. Her nerves had been on edge since both she and Randy had realized Sean was missing from their lives. Of course, as soon as they arrived, Randy was rationalizing the situation. Men, they always stuck up for each other.

"He looks like shit warmed over."

There was a pause, as if Randy was trying to figure out what to say next. "He's looked worse."

Irritation fluttered through her. How could he not understand? "Maybe after a job. Not when he's been lying around like some kind of slacker. Just what the hell is that about anyway? He has never been a man who liked to waste time."

"Well, it's not a bad place to do his laying about. I wonder where he got the money for this?"

Jaime looked around the grounds below and knew something was really wrong. This was a house that would be featured on Hawaii Five-O where a socialite might have been killed. The furnishings had been masterfully chosen, and not by Sean. He'd like finer things, but he had no sense of style. The colors, the styles, they all looked as if someone had spent time and money to perfect the look. That definitely wasn't Sean. And, she knew one thing for sure; this had taken money. Sean had always had money, but he hadn't had *this* kind of money. The house was four million—at least. The way real estate prices had been ballooning on Oahu in the last couple of years, it was probably going for a lot more. That kind of money did not just plop down in your lap.

She knew the last few years, Sean had been playing fast and loose with his jobs. Getting involved with Lassiter was one of the worst decisions Sean had ever made after they split up. Randy and Jaime had walked away from taking jobs with Lassiter, partially for personal reasons, but also because Lassiter had made some dubious connections lately. Sean had kept working for him. It was his involvement with the bastard that had been Sean's downfall—or so they heard. Both Randy and Jaime had done jobs with Sean that were sketchy, mainly because they had wanted to protect him. Knowing he had gone on a job by himself, then disappeared off the edge of the earth had worried her. Subsequently...as the months had rolled by, and they didn't hear anything about him...both she and Randy had started to worry. They couldn't really put the call out for him because it might cause him issues, so they had sifted through the evidence. It had been long and painstaking, but they had finally found out what the hell happened.

Burned. As in, no connections, no protection...ruined in their business. He was considered a security risk, thanks to Lassiter—another man who had let her down more than once.

The race to find him overtook their every thought. She knew that Sean would be an ass and say he didn't need them, but he did. Burned in their world was ten times worse than being dead. At least dead you knew the pain was over.

"Babe?" Randy asked. He was worried about her. She had been a bitch on a mission from the moment they had found out.

"He's not working, we both know that."

Sean was always resourceful, but the massive mansion on Oahu was beyond his means. Not to mention the Jag and the pimped out Escalade in the driveway. There was something very wrong going on with Sean, and it wasn't all about his burning.

Randy stepped up behind her, slipped his arms around her waist and pulled her back against him. She took comfort in the warmth he offered her. He was a calming influence.

"He's okay. We'll figure out what's going on."

She sighed and let the worries she had been holding in for more hours than she wanted to think about release. It wasn't easy. It never was when it came to Sean. He was the one person who could hurt both of them without even thinking. He never understood why the two of them kept coming back.

Wanker.

"We should have gotten here sooner."

It was Randy's turn to sigh. She had repeated that phrase over and over for the past week. "Babe, you know we couldn't. We didn't know about his burning until last week."

"We should have known."

The world of security experts—especially on their level—was a small one. Everyone knew each other and, on some days, your enemy could be your best friend. The fact that she and Randy had not heard anything was, to say the least, odd. Lassiter had not told them, but then, Jaime and he were barely speaking.

"It's weird that we had not heard anything. If he's been burned for six months, someone would have said something. Hell, Lassiter should have told us."

Just another transgression to lay at the feet of Royce. The man had been nothing but trouble from start to finish, and now he had hidden Sean's status from them. She had an idea why, but she couldn't tell Randy. Not yet.

"You heard what Ross told us," she said. "He's been hanging out here in Oahu. Lord only knows why, because he always said it was too busy for him. He preferred the Big Island."

"Let's face it. There is no Rough 'n Ready there. Of course, after his behavior from last night, he might not have a membership anymore."

Club owner Micah Ross had been furious last night, but she got the feeling he was more worried about Sean than mad at him. It was definitely the reason he poured out all the info he had on him when they had shown up. If an acquaintance Sean didn't know that well knew of his issues, it was definitely getting bad.

Randy shook his head. "There is something bothering him. You know he likes to brood."

"Yes, but he has never been a drunk."

And she knew why, they both did. Control was something that was so important to Sean, and drinking to excess was something he never did. Not in all the years she had known him had she ever seen him pissed, but apparently, he had been spending most of his nights that way.

"Hey," Randy said, resting his chin on her shoulder. "We'll help him sort it all out. I promise."

She closed her eyes. Tears threatened, but she would not show it. She would not lose it. She had her dignity left—and that was something she planned on holding onto.

"I don't know what the two of you are cooking up, but I don't need your fucking help."

Randy moved away from her to look at him. Jaime opened her eyes and turned to face Sean. He didn't look any better…and he looked so damned beautiful. From the moment she'd met him all those years ago, she had never been able to take her eyes off him. He was one of those men who just seemed to capture the attention of everyone in the room.

He'd changed clothes, pulling on a pair of loose white pants and a shirt to match. At least now she couldn't see the purple bruising that had covered his chest. Even if she didn't know what he did for a living, she would recognize the lethal grace in his movements. And sweet. He was so damned sweet, but people didn't see it in him. They only saw the player. She knew the man who could make her laugh, and who would happily feed her chocolates in bed.

It didn't excuse him for being an ass, however. She decided to lay it out on the line so Sean knew exactly where they stood.

"Let's just say that we are here for answers and we aren't leaving until we get them."

GET THE NINTH BOOK IN THE WILDLY POPULAR SANTINI SERIES: A SANTINI TAKES THE FALL!

A man avoiding his destiny.

Anthony Santini is happy with life. The former Marine is now working a dream job for NCIS in a dream location: Hawaii. He's watched his cousins and now his siblings fall into the Santini Curse and that is not for him. Not yet. He's happy to play the field and enjoy life. It still doesn't stop his cousin's wife from trying to fix him up.

A woman avoiding love.

Lalani Hawkins has had enough heartache to last a lifetime. The professional dancer isn't looking for love and she definitely doesn't need a man like Santini in her life. After the worst blind date in history, she thinks she'll never see him again.

For two people who want to avoid each other, Lalani and Anthony can't seem to achieve that. Each time they meet, Lalani falls a little more under the Santini spell, and for Anthony, he is drawn to the vivacious dancer. But when Anthony senses her hesitation to commit, he starts to formulate a plan. Because when a Santini man decides he's found his mate, there is no stopping him.

PLEASE ENJOY THIS EXCERPT!

She sighed. "I avoid relationships with men like you."

"Men like me?"

"Yeah. You like to tell people how to behave, control the situation."

"I get it. You're a *brat*, and you're one without daddy issues. I wouldn't be interested if you were looking for a guy who reminded you of your father."

"Is that a fact?"

He nodded. "I grew up with one and really don't want to play that role."

She felt her lips twitch. "Okay. And thank you for at least being honest."

"That's me. Honest Anthony."

"I had a really good time today."

He chuckled. "Don't sound so surprised."

She stopped when she reached her door. "No, really. It's more that I haven't had a real date in forever, and it was nice just to relax."

"Oh, you were relaxed? My hands were sweating the whole time."

She looked at that seductive smile; the way he leaned against the wall, and knew this man did not have sweaty hands.

"Wanna come in for a drink?"

He shook his head, never taking his gaze from hers.

"Why not?"

"I told you the truth earlier, Lalani. You test my control, and neither of us are ready to make that next step yet."

He leaned forward and cupped her face. Slowly, he kissed her. This was not the same over the top passionate kiss from the other day. He nibbled at her lips, teasing her bottom lip before fully pressing his mouth against hers. Still, he took his time, before she felt the glide of his tongue against the seam of her lips. She opened willingly, wanting nothing more that to taste him. He was just the same as she remembered. Desire lanced through her veins, her blood pounding a primitive beat in her veins.

Needing more contact, she stepped closer, pressing her body into his as she slipped her hands around his waist. He shuddered and lifted his other hand to cup her face completely. It wasn't enough. She wanted to feel his flesh against hers, to taste every inch of him…but he stepped back. They were both breathing heavily.

"I told you we needed time."

Lalani had never been good at being denied pleasure, and she lashed out.

"Is this some kind of control thing with you?"

The moment she said it, she wished she hadn't. She opened her mouth to apologize, but he stopped her by reaching up and rubbing his thumb against her lips.

"Not at all. I just want to make sure we both want it for the right reasons. And, as I told you, I don't want some quick fuck. I want a long time with you in that bed, because I aim to take every second to enjoy."

She drew in a shuddering breath, then released it. "Well, when you put it like that."

He smiled and leaned in to brush his mouth

against hers. He pulled back then. "I'll wait until you're inside."

She nodded, her body still yearning for another taste. She unlocked her door and turned back around.

"Are you sure?"

He chuckled, and it sounded like it hurt. "No, not at all, but I think it's for the best. I'll call you tomorrow."

"Drive safely."

He nodded and waited. With a sigh, she shut the door.

"You need to turn the deadbolt."

Rolling her eyes, she did as he ordered, and waited to see if he said anything else. He didn't, and she knew he had left.

She walked through her apartment, her body still humming with need, her head spinning from that kiss. She should be happy he stopped the progression, but she wanted it to continue. As a dancer, she had always been able to give into her passions. Being denied the pleasure of Anthony Santini for the night was irritating.

She wandered over to her lanai and slid open the door. She stepped out and looked down to see if she could see him. There he was, walking down the street in that confident stride he always had. She liked a man who knew who he was, didn't mind letting everyone else know it either. And, the man could definitely kiss. He had barely touched her, and she was ready to run down and beg him for another kiss. When he reached his truck, he turned and looked back up in her direction. Even from a distance, she could tell he was smiling as he waved up at her.

Damn the man. He was going to turn her world

upside down. Already had. At that moment though, Lalani didn't care. She sat down on one of her chairs and watched the sun as it glistened over the water. She'd had a perfect day and a pretty great date. A girl couldn't ask for more than that.

ABOUT MELISSA SCHROEDER

From an early age, USA Today Bestselling author Melissa Schroeder loved to read. First, it was the books her mother read to her including her two favorites, Winnie the Pooh and the Beatrix Potter books. She cut her preteen teeth on Trixie Belden and read and reviewed To Kill a Mockingbird in middle school. It wasn't until she was in college that she tried to write her first stories, which were full of angst and pain, and really not that fun to read or write. After trying several different genres, she found romance in a Linda Howard book.

Since the publication of her first book in 2004, Melissa has had close to sixty romances published. She writes in genres from historical suspense to modern day erotic romance to futuristics and paranormals. Included in those releases is the bestselling Harmless series. In 2011, Melissa branched out into self-publishing with A Little Harmless Submission and the popular military spinoff, Infatuation: A Little Harmless Military Romance. Along the way she has garnered an Epic nomination, a multitude of reviewer's recommended reads, over five Capa nods from TRS, fifteen nominations for AAD Bookies and regularly tops the bestseller lists on Amazon and Barnes & Noble. She made the USA Today Bestseller list for the first time with her anthology The Santinis.

Since she was a military brat, she vowed never to marry military. Alas, fate always has her way with mortals. Her husband retired from the AF after 20 years, and together they have their own military brats. She now resides in Virginia.

YOU CAN KEEP UP WITH MEL ALL OVER THE WEB:

www.MelissaSchroeder.net

Twitter.com/Melschroeder

Facebook.com/MelissaSchroederFanpage

Facebook.com/TheSantinis

Facebook.com/TaskForceHawaii

www.facebook.com/groups/harmlesslovers- Mel's Harmless Addicts Fangroup

www.pinterest.com/melissaschro

Join Mel's Newsletter to keep up with releases, sales, and appearances. http://eepurl.com/N2iob

OTHER BOOKS BY MELISSA SCHROEDER

HARMLESS

A Little Harmless Sex
A Little Harmless Pleasure
A Little Harmless Obsession
A Little Harmless Lie
A Little Harmless Addiction
A Little Harmless Submission
A Little Harmless Fascination
A Little Harmless Fantasy
A Little Harmless Ride
A Little Harmless Secret
A Little Harmless Rumor

THE HARMLESS PRELUDES

Prelude to a Fantasy
Prelude to a Secret
Prelude to a Rumor, Part One
Prelude to a Rumor, Part Two

THE HARMLESS SHORTS

Max and Anna

A LITTLE HARMLESS MILITARY ROMANCE

Infatuation
Possession
Seduction

MELISSA SCHROEDER

TASK FORCE HAWAII

Seductive Reasoning

THE SANTINIS

Leonardo
Marco
Gianni
Vicente
A Santini Christmas
A Santini in Love
Falling for a Santini
One Night with a Santini
A Santini Takes the Fall

SEMPER FI MARINES

Tease Me
Tempt Me
Touch Me

ONCE UPON AN ACCIDENT

An Accidental Countess
Lessons in Seduction
The Spy Who Loved Her

THE CURSED CLAN

Callum
Angus
Logan

BY BLOOD

SEDUCTIVE REASONING

Desire by Blood
Seduction by Blood

TEXAS TEMPTATIONS

Conquering India
Delilah's Downfall

HAWAIIAN HOLIDAYS

Mele Kalikimaka, Baby
Sex on the Beach
Getting Lei'd

BOUNTY HUNTER'S, INC

For Love or Honor
Sinner's Delight

THE SWEET SHOPPE

Cowboy Up
Tempting Prudence

CONNECTED BOOKS

The Hired Hand
Hands on Training

A Calculated Seduction
Going for Eight

SINGLE TITLES

Grace Under Pressure
Telepathic Cravings

MELISSA SCHROEDER

Her Mother's Killer
The Last Detail
Operation Love
Chasing Luck
The Seduction of Widow McEwan

COMING SOON

Hostile Desires
A Santini's Heart

SEDUCTIVE REASONING

Printed in Great Britain
by Amazon.co.uk, Ltd.,
Marston Gate.